Chain Reactions

By
Lynn Ames

CHAIN REACTIONS
© 2019 BY LYNN AMES

ISBN: 978-1-936429-16-5

OTHER AVAILABLE FORMATS

eBOOK EDITION
ISBN: 978-1-936429-17-2

PUBLISHED BY
PHOENIX RISING PRESS
PHOENIX, ARIZONA
www.phoenixrisingpress.com

CREDITS
EXECUTIVE EDITOR: ANN ROBERTS
AUTHOR PHOTO: JUDY FRANCESCONI
COVER DESIGN: TREEHOUSE STUDIO

Dedication

To my beautiful wife, Cheryl, who inspires me every day. You are the best teammate and most supportive writer's wife ever. Thanks for making it possible for me to do what I do, and thanks for dropping that book on my desk. I think there might be a story here too.

Other Books by Lynn Ames

Stand-Alone Romances
Bright Lights of Summer
All That Lies Within
Eyes on the Stars
Heartsong
One ~ Love

Romantic Comedies
Great Bones

The Kate and Jay Series
The Price of Fame
The Cost of Commitment
The Value of Valor
Final Cut

The Mission: Classified Series
Beyond Instinct
Above Reproach

Anthology Collections
Outsiders

Specialty Books - Humor
Digging for Home

Lynn Ames books are available in multiple formats through www.lynnames.com, from your favorite local bookstore, or through other online venues.

CHAPTER ONE

The doctor's office smelled of disinfectant and latex, and the protective paper covering the examination table crinkled under her bare legs. Nora Lindstrom tugged at the cloth gown that kept slipping off her shoulder and drew in a wheezing breath. The rattle in her chest echoed in the stillness of the space.

Why doctors' offices made appointments for patients was beyond her, since they never seemed to keep to the schedule. Nora had half a mind to leave, although in truth she had nowhere else she needed to be these days.

"You used to be more understanding, old girl," she mumbled. "Old age has made you impatient and priggish."

The door opened and a short, handsome, neatly bearded man in a lab coat walked in. Nora smiled at her old friend.

"Sorry to have kept you waiting, Dr. Lindstrom. Seems everyone picked today to come down with the flu."

"How long have we known each other, Daniel? To you, I'm not Dr. Lindstrom, I'm just Nora. And I was going to scold you for making me late for my disco dance lesson, but I've decided to forgive you."

"Disco went out in the '80s, Nora. Hip-hop is all the rage now."

"Then you saved me from an indignity, and I should thank you. Hip-hop? I tried to do that once. Broke the darned hip and needed a month in a skilled nursing facility."

He smiled warmly as he approached with a stethoscope.

"Seriously, how kids call that stuff music is beyond me. Then again, I stopped listening to music when the Beatles broke up."

"I'm glad to see you haven't lost your sense of humor."

"It's practically all I have left."

"I doubt that." He warmed the instrument in his hand. "Let me take a listen to your chest."

"Careful, it might blow out your eardrum."

He listened as she breathed in and out on cue. When he was done, he sat on a wheeled stool to face her.

"You have your serious face on, Daniel."

He frowned. "I'm afraid this *is* serious."

"I know what you're going to say." She held up a shaky hand to forestall his next words. "It's okay. I'm one hundred years old, and I'm not afraid of death. I've had a good, long life. Heck, I've outlived everyone I know. 'Bout time I went to join them."

"You are a marvel. You teach me more about life every time I see you."

"Which is far too often lately, if you ask me," she said. "No offense."

"None taken."

She felt the cough bubble up in her chest before it exploded forth, shaking her frail form. When she pulled her hand away from her mouth, it was liberally coated with blood.

"Let me get that," he said. His kind eyes reflected concern and sadness as he gently cleaned her hands and around her mouth.

"Thank you." The words came out as a rasp as she struggled to catch her breath.

"Have you given more thought to what we talked about last week? You need both a health care proxy and a durable power of attorney in place."

Nora shook her head. "I told you before. I trust you to make the decisions for me."

"And I told you before, no can do. You must have someone you can trust to make life decisions on your behalf?"

She cast her eyes downward. It had been thirty-five years since that last heated discussion with her brother and his son and daughter-in-law. Thirty-five years since she kissed ten-year-old Diana on the forehead as her daddy pried her little fingers off Nora's pant leg.

"I'll always be with you in your heart, Diana. Carry me there," she had whispered.

"You can't go. I won't let you," Diana pleaded. "You're my best friend."

"I love you, Diana. Always remember that."

Nora couldn't bear to look back at the girl's tear-stained face. That was the last time she'd seen her great-niece. More precisely, it was the last time Diana had seen *her*, Nora corrected herself. After all, she'd continued to keep a watchful eye on Diana from a distance. How would Diana react now if Nora or her lawyer reached out and told her Nora was dying and needed her?

Diana Lindstrom plugged her right ear with a finger and pressed the cell phone tighter against her left ear. "This is Diana Lindstrom. Who did you say you were?"

"This is Charles Fitzgerald. I'm the attorney for your great-aunt, Nora Lindstrom."

Diana was certain she'd heard him wrong. "Excuse me? Wait. Hang on a second and let me get somewhere quieter." She motioned to her lab assistant that she was leaving and headed down the hall to her office.

Once there, she shrugged out of her lab coat, lowered herself into the desk chair, and put the phone back to her ear. "Now, that's better. I'm sorry to keep you waiting. The centrifuges in the lab are so loud I can't hear myself think."

"That's not a problem, Dr. Lindstrom. I'm sorry to have disturbed your work day."

"Tell me again who you are?"

"My name is Charles Fitzgerald. I'm the senior partner with the law firm Fitzgerald, Osborn, and Chase. We represent your great-aunt, Nora Lindstrom."

Diana's eyes narrowed. "I don't know who you really are, or what scam you're trying to pull, but my Aunt Nora's been dead for at least twenty years."

"I'm afraid you've been misinformed, Dr. Lindstrom. I can assure you Nora is not deceased. In fact, she's the one who asked me to contact you."

Could it be? Diana wondered. No. Surely her parents and grandfather wouldn't have been so cruel as to lie about something as serious as the death of her beloved great-aunt.

"Nora recently celebrated her hundredth birthday," he continued. "I have to tell you, she's amazing. She still lives by herself, has all of her mental faculties, and completes the *New York Times* crossword puzzle every day."

"If that were true, and I'm not saying it is," Diana said, unwilling to abandon her skepticism quite so easily, "why would Aunt Nora wait until now to reach out to me?"

"As I am bound by attorney-client privilege, that's a question you'll have to ask her. If you're so inclined, and I sincerely hope you are, I have contact details for you."

A breath caught in her throat and her heart hammered painfully in her chest. How many times had she wished and longed to talk with Aunt Nora?

"Aunt Nora wants me to...?" She couldn't even finish the question. She pressed the palm of her hand to her chest to stanch the pain blossoming there as she recalled her father's sneer when he told her the night before grad school graduation that Nora was dead and she should stop expecting her to show up. It was too horrible to think about that right now. Instead, her mind immediately gravitated to all the many instances as a small child she'd begged her parents to explain Aunt Nora's disappearance from family gatherings, from family photos, from reminiscences and conversations at reunions...

"Your Aunt Nora is off doing top-secret work out of the country. We're not allowed to contact her."

"Your Aunt Nora no longer wants to be part of this family."

"Your Aunt Nora is working for the government and travels constantly. She's made it clear she has no room in her life for the likes of us. She's too focused on her career."

The diversity and breadth of explanations, excuses, and prevarications from her parents and grandfather made her head spin. While she was never sure what to believe, the one thing she knew for certain was that her favorite person in the world, the woman she most admired, had abandoned her childhood self without a backward glance.

"...as I was saying..."

Diana struggled to focus again.

10

"Whether you make the phone call or not, whether you opt to see Nora or not, whether you accept the duties and responsibilities as Nora's healthcare proxy and power of attorney or not—"

"Wait. Aunt Nora's designated me as her power of attorney? Me?"

"As I said, that's primarily the reason I'm contacting you today. Yes, Nora finally has been persuaded to get her affairs in order."

"Why? Is she sick?"

"I am not at liberty to discuss her medical condition. But I will say that if I were you, I wouldn't take long to act."

Diana tried to digest that bit of information. Aunt Nora was taking the extraordinary step to break her silence. She was filling out end-of-life contingency paperwork, and she obviously was alone. "Where is she?"

"Resting at home."

"Where would that be?" Part of her brain urged her not to get sucked in. What if nothing about this turned out to be true? *What if all of it's true?* her heart whispered.

"If you'll provide me with an e-mail address, I'll provide you with all the details."

She recited her e-mail address and Mr. Fitzgerald read it back to her.

"Dr. Lindstrom?"

"Yes?"

"On a personal note, I've known your great-aunt for many, many years. She's one-of-a-kind. As Nora's friend, I would advise you to make haste. Whatever you might be thinking or feeling, she needs you now. Trust that you have always, always been in her heart."

Diana heard the raw emotion in his voice. Clearly, Aunt Nora was far more to him than simply a client. She choked out, "Send me the information, please. I'll take it from there."

Nora's gnarled fingers fluttered through her hair and then down along the front of her blouse, smoothing the material. Perhaps she should check herself in the mirror one more time.

Settle down, old girl. You're jumpy as a cat.

The doorbell rang and she blinked. Was Diana here already? "It's open," she called out, hoping the strength of her voice carried through the sturdy wooden door.

Several seconds later, a fair-haired, long-legged, younger version of herself appeared around the doorway. In fact, she could've been her daughter or granddaughter, right down to the blue-green hazel eyes she remembered—eyes that gazed at her now, filled with uncertainty and wariness.

"Hello," Nora managed. She realized she was staring. "I'm sorry, where are my manners? Diana, I don't imagine you remember me all that well, and I certainly wasn't old and decrepit when last you saw me. I'm your great-aunt, Nora. I'd get up, but…" She indicated her frail form propped up on the loveseat, and her motorized wheelchair parked just off to the side.

"You leave your door unlocked? In this day and age?" Diana hadn't moved beyond the threshold.

"At my age, what in the world would anyone want with me? Besides, this is Cape Cod. There hasn't been a crime more serious than jay walking since I retired here nearly twenty years ago."

She thought she saw a ghost of a smile. Maybe she was getting somewhere. "Please, come in. If it makes you feel better, lock the door behind you."

Finally, Diana stepped fully inside the cottage. "Can I ask you a question?" Still, she maintained a distance and remained standing.

"You can ask me anything in the world. I promise you I'll do my best to answer honestly. Would you like to come and sit down?"

"Not just yet, thank you." Diana's lips formed a thin line and she furrowed her brow.

Nora recognized the expression as one Diana wore as a child when she puzzled through a difficult problem.

"Why…" Diana began. She closed her eyes for a moment and cleared her throat. "Why did you leave me? And why didn't you ever come back?"

Even though she had expected the question, it was a punch in the gut that knocked the wind out of her. She leaned forward, struggling for air as a coughing jag overtook her.

"Oh, my God," Diana exclaimed. "You're coughing up blood."

The voice was close and Nora felt a hand gently rubbing her back. The cushion next to her shifted, and she smelled a perfume

12

that wasn't her own. Finally, after what seemed like hours, she sucked in a breath with a shuddering gasp.

Diana drew her in and cradled her against a shoulder. "Are you all right? Never mind, that's a stupid question. Is there anything I can get you? A glass of water?"

She continued to wheeze, the sound a staccato rhythm in near-perfect synchronization with the ticking of the large antique grandfather clock in the corner. After several attempts at speech, she was able to whisper hoarsely, "I'm fine, dear. Just give me a minute."

One minute turned into five, and, when her breathing finally returned to normal, she sat up straighter. She was surprised to see Diana had tears in her eyes.

"It's all right." She patted Diana's cheek. "And I want you to know that I wasn't trying to sidestep your question or curry sympathy either."

"I would never think that. Gosh, what kind of person do you think I am?"

"I need you to know that walking away from you—never seeing you again—broke my heart."

"Then why did you?"

She pursed her lips. This was the crux of the matter. Telling her great-niece the ugly truth likely would forever change the way she viewed her parents and grandfather. But Nora promised honesty, and her word was her bond.

"I had no choice," she said quietly. "Your grandfather—my brother, Bill—and your parents forbade me to see you anymore."

"They…" Diana recoiled. "Why? Why would they do that?"

How much should she say? This was uncharted territory. "You'd have to ask them that."

"I haven't spoken to Mom and Dad in years."

She said it matter-of-factly, but the pain behind the comment didn't escape Nora's notice. "I didn't know. I'm sorry for that."

"Yeah, well, I'm not," Diana said bitterly.

"What happened, if I might be so bold as to inquire?"

"I was a disappointment to them."

She wasn't sure what she'd expected, but that wasn't it. "You were a disappointment to them?" She tutted in disgust. "You've built a brilliant career, published important papers, taught and trained bright minds at one of the most prestigious universities in the country—"

Diana stiffened. "How do you know all that?"

"I—I…" Well, she'd put her foot in it now. "Just because I wasn't permitted to interact with you directly doesn't mean I didn't keep my eye on you from a distance."

"You've been spying on me all this time?"

"When you say it like that, it sounds so untoward." She reached out and took Diana's hands. "As I told you, it was never my desire to be separated from you. I loved you then, and I never stopped. I am so proud of you, Diana."

Diana swallowed hard and withdrew from Nora's touch. "Well, you might change your mind when you hear the full story."

"There isn't anything you can say that will make me love you any less."

"How about that I'm a lesbian?"

Nora nodded slowly. The admission didn't come as a shock to her. "Is that why you don't talk to your folks anymore?"

Diana laughed mirthlessly. "More like the reason they don't talk to me. I'm an embarrassment to their sensibilities, something intolerable and abhorrent."

Nora sighed and closed her eyes. She'd hoped that somehow Robert and Edwina had broadened their minds over the years. When she opened her eyes, Diana was staring at a spot on the floor, discomfort and defeat evident in her posture. Well, that wouldn't do at all.

"I'm sorry for you. I'm sorry your grandfather taught his son to be as small and narrow minded as he was." She frowned. "Your father always was a daddy's boy. The sun rose and set on Bill for him. All the time I knew him, Robert tried everything to win Bill's approval. I could've saved him a lot of time and heartache; Bill never cared about anybody but himself. I never understood how he got to be that way. Our parents didn't raise us like that."

Diana met her gaze. "You don't seem the least bit fazed by my sexuality."

She shrugged. "Why would I be?"

"Why…?" Diana blinked. "Your generation…"

"Look. I've lived a long time. Long enough to see too many wars, too much hatred, and never enough love." She paused. "Are you happy?"

"Am I…?"

"Do you have a girlfriend?"

Diana blanched.

"Well, do you?"

"No. I was in a long-term relationship for twelve years, and then Bethany decided she should've played around more before settling down. Our life was too staid. I was too boring."

Nora raised an eyebrow. "Too boring, eh? Well, her loss. She probably wasn't good enough for you, anyway." Another cough rumbled up in her chest and she grabbed for the box of tissues on the end table.

Again, Diana rubbed circles on her back as she fought her way through the spasms. When the episode was over, Nora fell back against the seat cushions. Her breathing was shallow and her chest felt as though someone were sitting on it.

After several moments, Diana asked, "What does the doctor say?"

She shook her head.

"How long?"

"It's an inexact science, but not long now."

Diana got up, grabbed her glass from the end table, and disappeared into the kitchen. She returned with water and helped Nora hold it while she drank.

"What's the diagnosis?"

"Advanced small cell lung cancer."

Diana nodded as tears once again filled her eyes. "Is that why you had your lawyer call me?"

She struggled, and failed, to sit up straighter. She hated that these coughing jags robbed her of her energy.

"I should go," Diana said. "You need to get some rest."

She closed her eyes momentarily as she tried to gather her strength. There was so much she wanted to say, so much she wanted to hear. "This damned disease takes a lot out of me. The doctor says it might also have something to do with my age. Seems some people consider one hundred old." She winked.

Diana offered a sad smile. "You need to lie down. Can I help you into your bedroom?"

As independent as she was, she recognized she was too weak and exhausted to get herself into the wheelchair and from that onto the bed. "That would be most helpful."

When Diana had her situated in bed, with pillows propped behind her and a glass of water on the night table, Nora asked the question that weighed heavily on her. "Will you be coming back?"

"I booked a bed and breakfast in Provincetown. I'll be back first thing in the morning. Will you be all right until then?"

"You could've stayed with me. I have a guest bedroom."

"I didn't want to impose."

She felt herself starting to drift. What Diana meant, she was sure, was that she wasn't certain she wanted Nora back in her life at this late stage.

"We're family," she murmured. "There's no such thing as an imposition." Warm lips brushed against her forehead.

"Sleep well, Aunt Nora."

"I love you, Diana. Always have. Always will." She heard the quiet click of the front door closing.

CHAPTER TWO

Diana stood with her hands inside the pouch of her hoodie. Her bare feet sunk into the sand, soaking up the remaining warmth from the day's heat. The wind flowed through her hair, brushing it off her face. She watched as the sun set, the orange glow on the horizon disappearing from sight, leaving behind faint pastel streaks across the darkening sky. Her thoughts scattered like the swirling wind, impressions overlapping like the grains of sand slipping between her toes.

She hadn't been the cool, calm, consummate professor of neuroscience and neurobiology today. No, she'd been that devastated little girl, looking for answers, longing for love and acceptance.

The woman she remembered as larger-than-life, vibrant, effervescent, young, and endlessly fascinating, was dying. Her frail, fragile, faded, elderly great-aunt barely resembled the dashing figure Diana recalled with ease.

How could it be that the reunion she had dreamed of for so long would serve as Aunt Nora's last act? It hardly seemed fair. Diana stopped short. "Last week, you weren't even sure you wanted to see Aunt Nora or talk to her. Now you're mourning her loss before she's even gone. Make up your mind, D."

She reviewed what Aunt Nora shared about her parents and Grandpa Bill. Those facts didn't jive with the narrative she'd been fed as a steady diet in her formative years. Whom should she believe? Which source was more trustworthy? A scientist would evaluate the available data and reach an objective conclusion. Her father told her Aunt Nora worked for the government on top secret projects and traveled frequently. Her mother insisted Aunt Nora shunned the family and didn't have either the time or the desire to remain in touch.

What was it her grandfather had said about his older sister? She'd been twelve when Grandpa Bill died suddenly of a heart attack. She remembered she didn't enjoy spending time with him. He was a stern, joyless man—such a sharp contrast to Aunt Nora's gentle, teasing, loving demeanor. In truth, she resented that Grandpa Bill wasn't Aunt Nora.

Her eyes popped open wide as an image crystalized. She'd had a bad day, and her parents had insisted they were too busy to pick her up from school. In the past when this happened, Aunt Nora would drive her home, they would talk about whatever piece of science Diana was studying, and Aunt Nora would devise an experiment they would conduct together to solidify the lesson in Diana's mind.

In this particular instance, several months after Aunt Nora's abrupt departure, Grandpa Bill was coming for her and Diana was in no mood to filter her feelings.

"Where's Aunt Nora?"
"Not here."
"Why not?"
"Because."
"That's not a reason."
"Don't sass me, young lady."
"When will she be back?"
"She's never coming back."

It was after uttering those words that Grandpa Bill spat on the ground and muttered something under his breath, too low for her to hear. The two of them never spoke of Aunt Nora again.

Diana wondered if Aunt Nora knew her brother was dead. She made a mental note to ask her in the morning.

A large wave broke close to the shore and she jumped back in order to avoid getting splashed. She rolled her pant legs up one more turn and walked a little farther down the beach, reaching into the recesses of her mind for glimpses of moments she'd done her best to leave in the past.

Inevitably, her thoughts turned to late spring, 1998. She was about to receive her doctoral degree in neurobiology and behavior from Columbia University. Her parents had driven into the city from their home in Greenwich, Connecticut, to take her for a celebratory dinner in the Crystal Room at the fabled Tavern on the Green restaurant in Central Park.

"Your father and I are so proud of you," her mother gushed.

"Thank you." She dug into the petit filet mignon with gusto.

"That's right, pumpkin. We still can't figure out where you got the math and science gene from. It sure wasn't either of us." Robert Lindstrom buried a piece of lobster tail in melted butter.

Diana bit her lip, something she often did when weighing whether or not to risk a confrontation with her parents. For once, they'd been having such a nice time. Still, she was only going to get her Ph.D. once. Maybe, just maybe...

"I know where I get it from," Diana ventured.

"What?"

"My aptitude for science. Do you remember all those neat experiments Aunt Nora used to do with me when I was little? She was a genius!"

Her father's back stiffened at the mention of his aunt, but Diana was determined to push on anyway. "Do you know where she is and how I could get in touch with her? I bet she'd come to graduation if I invited her."

She peeked up just in time to see a look pass between her parents. After several awkward moments, during which the only sound at the table was the clanking of silverware against the plates, her father said, "Aunt Nora is dead, so you can stop this fantasy that someday she'll just show up on your doorstep."

The words cut through her like an arctic blast and she shivered. "Aunt Nora died? When? Why didn't you tell me?"

Her mother shrugged. Her father said, "Her name hasn't come up in years. We didn't think there was any need to talk about it."

She dropped her fork and knife on the plate, the clatter loud enough to draw the attention and disapprobation of nearby diners. "Aunt Nora is the reason I became interested in science in the first place. She's the reason I'm about to graduate with high honors. I always was driven by how proud she'd be of me if she knew."

"We're the ones who paid for your education, young lady." Her father pointed his fork at Diana. "Not Aunt Nora. Us."

"I got a scholarship. A full ride, or have you forgotten that?"

Her mother broke in. "Don't you dare—"

"I can't believe you kept this from me. I can't believe it."

She pushed her chair back and ran from the restaurant. She kept running until she couldn't see through the tears. Then she flopped down on a park bench and put her head in her hands. All her dreams of walking across the stage on graduation day, looking out into the audience and seeing Aunt Nora beaming proudly at her...

Diana wiped the moisture from her cheeks. It was true that Aunt Nora hadn't seen her walk across that stage, but clearly she had kept track—she'd said as much.

Diana bent down, picked up a stone worn smooth by the ebb and flow of the ocean, and skimmed it through the waves. She had no doubt it was Aunt Nora who'd been telling the truth. Why had everyone else lied to her?

Tomorrow. She would start to get answers tomorrow.

✧✦

Brooke Sheldon stopped running, held up a hand, and bent over to catch her breath. "No más, Daniel. You win."

"Say that again, this time a little louder? I'm not sure I heard you correctly." Dr. Daniel Goodwin jogged in place next to his best friend.

"Don't push it."

"You're getting soft in your old age."

"Old age?" She gave him a playful shove. "Fifty is the new twenty, or haven't you gotten the memo?"

"I must've missed that one."

"Well, it's true." She inhaled the salty ocean air. "Do you have time for a cup of coffee?"

He checked his watch. "I've only got about half an hour. I need to get on the road, and I've got a special stop to make along the way."

"I'll take what I can get." She led them to the parking lot. "Meet you at the usual place."

When they were settled at an outdoor table, Daniel said, "How are you feeling?"

Brooke removed the lid from her coffee cup and blew on the hot liquid. "Is that a doctor question or a friend question?"

"The latter. From where I'm sitting, it looks like the change of scenery is helping."

She nodded. "It is. I just couldn't take losing one more patient, you know?"

"I do. Dana-Farber is a fabulous institution, and Lord knows we improve patients' outcomes and make extraordinary breakthroughs, but the morbidity rate takes a toll."

"Especially in peds. Losing a six year old before he gets to take his first bike ride. That just..." She didn't finish the sentence. She didn't need to. She knew Daniel understood. It's why she'd left the cancer institute for the quiet of Provincetown, and why he'd gotten himself reassigned from the pediatric floor to geriatrics.

Brooke decided it was time to change the subject. "Was I right about getting a weekend place out here, or what?"

"As always, you were right. I love it here. A beachfront cottage is a nice counterpoint to the rigors of the job, even though it's only an occasional reprieve. And Orleans is close enough that it's not a bad commute back to Boston and close enough in the other direction so that I can buzz out here to check up on my friend, about whom I've been worrying way too much."

She waved a hand dismissively. "You don't need to worry about me. I'm fine."

He leaned forward and regarded her intently. "You know you can't run away from the world, right? You've been out of circulation for months. Renting a house at the end of the Cape is an admirable way to escape, but what are you going to do next?"

She looked away. "I don't know. I need more time."

"What you're going to need is money. I know you invested wisely, but I also know that you couldn't have socked enough away as an oncology nurse to retire at fifty."

She hated that he was right. But every time she sat down to think about her future, she came back to the same thing—watching children suffer, even if she could positively affect their long-term outcome—took too much out of her. She'd lost three relationships to the job, three good women, all of whom left because she gave everything she had to the children and had too little left to give at home.

21

"Listen," Daniel said. "What if I had the perfect solution?"

She scoffed. "There is no such thing."

"Hear me out. Do you remember Dr. Lindstrom?"

"Nora Lindstrom? Of course. She's a legend. She did more to help us understand and treat childhood leukemia than almost any other researcher except for Sid Farber. The thing I most admired about her, though, was that she never hid herself away in the lab. She would show up on the floor and talk to the staff about the patients, and then she would visit with the kids to cheer them up. She was one of a kind."

"Right. She's the stop I'm making on my way back to Beantown."

"Dr. Lindstrom is on the Cape?"

"She bought herself a cottage on the harbor in Truro when she retired."

"Good for her. But, my God, she must be over ninety."

He walked to the trash can and deposited his empty cup before returning to the table. "Just turned one hundred last month."

"Wow! That's amazing."

"She's phenomenal. Living on her own and still sharp as a tack."

"Imagine the knowledge she has and the stories she could tell." Brooke polished off the last of her coffee.

"Come with me."

"What?"

"Come with me to see her."

"I can't just... She's not expecting me."

"She's not expecting me, either. But I'm here, she's my patient, and it'll save one of her neighbors bringing her all the way to DFCI to see me in the office tomorrow."

"Did you say she's your patient?"

"Yeah. End stage small cell lung cancer."

"Oh, no. That's horrible."

"It is."

"You know that breaks doctor-patient confidentiality. You shouldn't be talking to me about this without Dr. Lindstrom's permission."

"Unless I'm having a professional consultation."

She noted the glint in his eye. "What are you saying?"

"I told you. I have an idea."

22

"Whatever it is, count me out."

"Don't say that until you hear my proposal."

"Daniel—"

He pushed on. "I'm going to refer Dr. Lindstrom to hospice tomorrow."

"How sad."

"It gets worse."

"How in the world can it get worse than that?"

"She's all alone," he said softly.

Brooke recoiled in horror. "How is it possible that a woman like that has no one?"

"I can't answer that. She wanted to leave all the decision making to me. I told her she couldn't do that. I insisted she find a relative or loved one who would step in. In the end, grudgingly, she admitted that she has a great-niece who's a professor at Columbia University Medical School."

"Thank God."

"Yes. At least there'll be someone who can handle her affairs and carry out her wishes. But you and I both know that the great-niece won't be able to stay out here. Fall semester just started. I'm sure she's locked into teaching a full course load."

"Where are you going with all this, Daniel?"

He fidgeted in his seat. "Dr. Lindstrom is going to need expert care."

"Uh-huh. You just said you're going to have her invoke hospice."

"I did. But hospice can only do so much. She's going to need full-time care. There's no way she can live alone safely without it now."

"She could move into an assisted living facility or skilled nursing home and have hospice care there," Brooke offered.

"Maybe, but she's fiercely private and independent and wants to stay in her own home."

"But at an in-patient facility she'd have twenty-four-hour care."

"True, but with the perfect, full-time, private duty nurse on hand, she could maintain her dignity and live out what's left of her life in the comfort of her own home. Surely she's earned that."

"Let me guess. That's where I come in?"

"Exactly." Daniel leaned toward Brooke. "You have all of the necessary training, you're available, and she's a great patient. Yes, her body is failing, but her mind... Her mind is clear. You said yourself she's got so many stories to tell. Imagine being able to pick her brain."

She had to admit the prospect was intriguing. "What makes you think Dr. Lindstrom wants full-time assistance?"

"I guess we won't know unless you come with me and you ask the good doctor yourself." He stood and offered her a hand.

"That was manipulative."

"No," he said, as they headed toward their cars. "That was genius."

Nora sipped a cup of tea and tracked the progress of a lone sailboat as it navigated the harbor waters in the early-morning light. This expansive view through the floor-to-ceiling sliding glass doors and past the large wooden deck was the reason she'd bought this place.

It hadn't looked like this when she moved in, but she had a vision of what she wanted it to be and how she intended to live out whatever time she had left. True, she'd paid a pretty penny to update and renovate the interior, remove walls, tear down and rebuild the deck and the stairs that led down to the beach below, put on a new roof, and re-shingle the exterior, but it all had been worth it. Her only regret was that she was no longer strong enough or stable enough on her feet to walk through the doors and onto the deck as she used to. She'd also had to forego her morning walks on the beach.

Even so, at one hundred, she lived in her own home, which was, she knew, more than she had a right to expect.

"Well, all that's changing now, old girl."

It wasn't that she hadn't planned financially for her end-of-life care, she had. After all, that was prudent. Still, she'd always assumed her end would come as the result of a sudden, catastrophic event, not a lengthy, drawn-out illness. She hadn't meant to impose on anyone, especially not Diana.

As if on cue, the doorbell rang. "Come in," she called. She swiveled the wheelchair around to face her visitor.

This time Diana didn't hesitate at the door. "Good morning." She walked directly to her and kissed her on the cheek. "How did you sleep? How do you feel this morning?"

She patted Diana's hand where it rested on the arm of the wheelchair. "I'm fine; you don't need to worry about me. I'm not going anywhere just yet."

"I didn't mean..." Diana's face flushed red.

She smiled kindly. "I know you didn't. It's a little gallows humor, which I realize now might be misplaced. I apologize." After a moment of awkward silence, she changed the topic. "Are you hungry? My next-door neighbor is nice enough to shop for me once a week and put the groceries away. I've got blueberry muffins and cinnamon rolls."

"No, thank you. I stopped and grabbed a cup of coffee on my way here." Diana pointed toward the harbor. "You've got an incredible view. I don't know why I didn't notice it yesterday."

"Probably because you were nervous and a little wary about seeing me after so long. The scenery was the last thing on your mind."

Diana blushed again and Nora found it endearing.

"One of the great advantages of being this old is that I can get away with saying pretty much anything. Folks expect the elderly to lack a filter."

Diana laughed and Nora was pleased to see her finally relax a little.

"I've never met anybody your age, so I have no basis for analysis, but I suspect there are very few centenarians who are as mentally sharp as you are."

"You sweet-talker, you. Come, sit down." She motored over to the sitting area and indicated the couch.

"Did you want to get out of the chair?" Diana asked.

"I'm fine for now, thanks. Too much jostling takes the wind out of my sails." When Diana was settled in the corner of the couch facing her, Nora said, "I know all of this is a lot to take in. I imagine you have more questions. As I told you yesterday, I'll answer anything I can."

Diana crossed and uncrossed her legs, folded her hands in her lap and then apparently changed her mind and placed them palms down on her pant legs. She took in a deep breath. "I'm not sure where to start."

"How about if I help you? Would you rather start with family matters or focus on why I asked you here?"

"Your lawyer said you want me to handle your medical affairs and your finances."

"That's correct."

"Why me?" Diana crossed her legs again. "I mean, surely all these years later there must be someone who is closer to you than I am."

She nodded. She'd been expecting this question. "Honestly, I hoped I would never need to designate anyone. In fact, I asked my doctor if he couldn't just take care of it for me. He refused. He said I needed a family member or some such.

"As you might imagine, I've outlived just about everyone of consequence to me. But that's not why I chose you." She paused to collect herself. "Diana, I've lived long enough to have loved and lost, to have experienced tremendous elation and crippling regret. I need you to know that the hardest moment of all was having to say goodbye to you."

When she dared to make eye contact, she recognized the reflection of her own pain in her great-niece's eyes. "I'm sorry, Diana. I'm sorrier than you'll ever know. Nothing I…"

Before she could complete the sentence, Diana was by her side, hugging her, tears streaming down her face.

"I love you, Aunt Nora."

"I love you, Diana."

At that moment, they both were startled by a loud banging on the front door.

Diana stood and quickly wiped the tears from her face. "Are you expecting anyone else?"

"Not that I know of," Nora replied. She called out, "Who is it?"

"It's Daniel, Dr. Lindstrom."

"Daniel? Since when do doctors make house calls this far afield? Come in, come in."

The door opened and Daniel walked in, followed by a second person Nora thought she recognized from Dana-Farber.

"Hello, Dr. Lindstrom."

"Call me Nora, Daniel. How many times must I tell you? And I see you've brought me another colleague. How delightful. Please come in."

As Diana began to step away, Nora took hold of her hand and squeezed. "Dr. Daniel Goodwin, I'd like you to meet my great-niece, Dr. Diana Lindstrom."

"It's a pleasure to meet you, Dr. Lindstrom. I'm your Aunt Nora's physician, and please, call me Daniel."

"Nice to meet you."

The other person stepped forward and knelt by her wheelchair. "I don't know if you remember me, Dr. Lindstrom. It's been years since we've seen each other."

Up close, Nora was able to see the woman more clearly. Her face brightened. "Brooke? Brooke Sheldon? How in the world could I forget my favorite pediatric floor nurse? It's so good to see you." She grasped Brooke's hand. "Brooke, this is my pride and joy, my great-niece, Diana. She's a professor at Columbia University Medical School."

"It's a pleasure to meet you, Dr. Lindstrom."

"It's nice to meet you, too. Ms. Sheldon, is it?"

"Brooke, please."

"I'm Diana."

CHAPTER THREE

Diana stood outside on the deck overlooking Cape Cod Harbor. Although Aunt Nora had given her permission to stay while the doctor conducted his examination, it somehow felt inappropriate, like an invasion of privacy.

On the beach below, in the distance, she spied a small child making a sandcastle under the watchful eye of a golden retriever. The scene jogged loose a long-forgotten memory of an outing with Aunt Nora when Diana was just learning to swim.

The two of them had gone to Jones Beach as a special treat. She remembered spending the day happily bobbing in the waves in the safety of Aunt Nora's protective embrace. She learned to kick that day, and that the properties of saltwater helped you float. It was magical.

"I believe the ocean is a balm for the soul."

She jumped at the sound of the voice so close.

Brooke joined her at the railing. "I'm sorry. You were lost deep in thought. I should've given you more warning."

"That's all right. I was just reminiscing about Aunt Nora teaching me the concept of buoyancy. I couldn't have been more than five at the time."

"I bet Dr. Lindstrom was the neatest great-aunt ever."

"For the time she was in my life she was. She concocted the coolest experiments to teach me concepts I couldn't otherwise quite grasp."

Brooke turned from the water and faced her. "Forgive me for prying, but you said, 'For the time she was in my life.' I don't understand. Hasn't Dr. Lindstrom always been part of your life?"

Diana shook her head. "She disappeared when I was ten. I had no idea she was still alive until her lawyer called me last week."

"You didn't..." Whatever Brooke had been about to say, she obviously thought better of it. "I'm sorry for both of you."

One glance sideways at Brooke told Diana she really meant it. "So am I. I feel like I missed out on so much."

"If you don't mind my asking, what happened?"

It wasn't in Diana's nature to be forthcoming; her experiences had taught her to be private and guarded. But something in the way Brooke asked told her the question was borne of concern, not prurient interest.

"I wish I knew. I'm still trying to sort through it all. I haven't had enough time with her yet to get answers." She gave up any pretense of studying the harbor now. Here was someone who knew her great-aunt. Perhaps she could learn something that would help her put together the missing pieces. "Can I ask you a question?"

"Sure."

"You worked with Aunt Nora? Where, and for how long? What was that like?"

Brooke laughed, the sound light and easy. Diana bristled. Was Brooke making fun of her?

"I'm sorry. You said you had one question. Unless my math is bad, that was three."

"Forget I asked—"

"No." Brooke wrapped her fingers around Diana's forearm. "Please don't take that the wrong way."

Diana wanted to withdraw the questions, wanted to withdraw, period. She never should have opened herself up in the first place.

"When I met your Aunt Nora," Brooke began, "I was a young registered nurse doing an oncology rotation at Dana-Farber. I barely knew how to take blood, and here I was, face-to-face with this woman I'd heard so much about during my studies."

In spite of herself, Diana was intrigued and more than a little perplexed. "Why would you have learned about Aunt Nora in school?"

Brooke gazed at her wide-eyed. "You don't know who your great-aunt is, do you? I mean," she rushed on, "you aren't aware of all she's done, particularly for children with leukemia?"

Diana felt more at sea than ever. "My specialty is neuroscience. I've spent my adult life studying the brain, the nervous system, and the biological basis of learning, memory, and behavior. I never ventured as far afield as to study about or research how to cure cancer." Diana hated that she sounded defensive.

"That makes perfect sense," Brooke said. "And to be fair, like most women of her caliber, Dr. Lindstrom didn't get the big headlines or the credit she deserved for major scientific breakthroughs. Unless you were studying locally at Harvard or the University of Massachusetts where she often lectured, you likely wouldn't have heard of her. You would've heard of Sidney Farber, and of the folks at Memorial Sloan-Kettering, but pioneering women like Dr. Lindstrom were mostly relegated to the fine print in journal articles."

"It's safe to return, you two. We're all done in here," Daniel announced through the open doorway.

Brooke headed inside and Diana followed close behind. When she returned to the bed and breakfast tonight, she would spend some time with Google.

Nora liberated the cup of water from the wheelchair's built-in cup holder, grasped the straw with shaky fingers, took a long pull, and then returned it to its cradle. She would handle this situation with grace, by God, and face this last chapter with dignity and humor.

Two forms, backlit by the sun, strode into the room from the deck. Brooke and Diana. They were similar in height, though Brooke was sturdy where Diana favored the wiry build of her ancestors on her father's side.

Nora shifted her gaze to Daniel, who leaned against the wall that separated the living room from the kitchen. Although he had offered to do this, she preferred to handle it herself. It was, after all, her life, and this would be among the last decisions she got to make on her own behalf.

"Sit down, please." She motioned to Diana and Brooke to take their places on the couch.

She glanced again at Daniel. His eyes held such sadness. They had known each other a long time. He was more than her doctor. He was her friend. Beyond the medical facts, he understood her on a personal level. She knew that if it were in his power, he would have spared her what would come next.

She drew in a wheezing breath. *Collect yourself, old girl.* Exhaustion crept closer, as it did so often these days, but she was determined to have this part done.

"Although I'd like to think myself immortal and invincible, Daniel here reminds me that I am neither." She labored for another breath. "This is a good thing, for Lord knows I wouldn't want to mislead folks into thinking that with my age comes great wisdom."

She regarded first Diana and then Brooke. They were looking at her expectantly. She remembered a bit of advice Sid Farber once gave her when she'd been nervous about giving a lecture at Harvard. "By all means be entertaining," he said, "but do get to the point before the audience wonders if there is one."

Good, solid counsel from a man and colleague she most admired. "Right. On with it, then." She leaned forward in the chair, fumbled for the straw, and sucked in another mouthful of water before settling back to continue. "We all know what the diagnosis is here, and as medical professionals, we all understand what this disease does. And at my advanced age, I'm confident we can all agree on the outcome."

She paused again to regroup. "After Daniel and I discussed it just now, I am choosing to enroll myself in hospice. We agree that the progression of my disease is such that a six-month life-expectancy at this point would be generous, at best."

Although she said it matter-of-factly, she faltered when she caught sight of Diana. The expression on her face matched exactly the look emblazoned on Nora's heart from so long ago—the day she said goodbye to that little girl.

"Diana," she began, and then paused until she was certain her voice was stronger. "I'm sorry. I wish... Perhaps it would've been better for you to continue believing I'd passed away long ago. To have to lose me twice... I can't imagine how that feels."

Tears pooled in Diana's eyes. Brooke squeezed her hand briefly and then grabbed a box of tissues from the end table and placed it between them.

"Until this illness," she pushed on, "I prided myself on my excellent health and fierce independence. It seems God has another plan for me now. I am still of sound mind, however, and as such, able to make my wishes known."

"Do you want me to excuse myself, Dr. Lindstrom?" Brooke asked. "This is between you, your doctor, and your family. It doesn't really concern me and I don't want to intrude."

"Oh, no, my dear. On the contrary, I wish very much for you to stay, and you must call me Nora." She gestured toward Daniel. "Daniel tells me that you recently left Dana-Farber. Is that true?"

"Yes."

"Hmph. That's their loss and the children will be the poorer for it."

Brooke started to say something and Nora held up a hand to stop her.

"I know the toll such a job takes on a nurse's body and spirit, and I can sympathize with your choice." She coughed, unleashing a spasm that tore through her chest, leaving a trail of fire in its wake.

As she fought for breath, Brooke's soothing hands repositioning her body in order to open her constricted airway. Almost immediately, she experienced relief.

When she had sufficiently recovered, she patted Brooke's hand. "Thank you, my dear."

"We should get you to bed," Diana said. She was on her feet, concern etched in every feature.

"In a minute."

"You really should rest now, Nora," Daniel said. "Doctor's orders."

"In a minute," she repeated. "I want to finish first. I'll have the rest of my life to rest." She shifted in the chair to get more comfortable. "As I was saying... Brooke, Daniel tells me you haven't decided yet what your future holds and that you're at loose ends."

"I—"

"It appears to me we may have the perfect short-term assignment for you while you figure it out. As it happens, if I have any chance to stay in my home, as I hope to do, I will require full-time, qualified nursing care."

"I can—" Diana started to say.

"You most certainly will not." She was running out of steam. This needed to go the way she planned, and quickly. "I have ample

33

financial resources to cover the expense, and I will not have you interrupt your career to care for me. That is most certainly not why I had my attorney contact you."

"Aunt Nora—"

"No," She wheezed and plowed ahead. "At my direction, my attorney prepared, and I have signed, both a durable power of attorney for my financial matters and a durable power of attorney for my health directives. Daniel insisted that I needed someone I trusted with my life to fulfill that role when I am no longer able. If you are willing, Diana, and only if you are willing, I can't think of anyone I would trust more to handle my affairs."

"It would be an honor. But, Aunt Nora, even if Brooke agrees to take on the job, I just found you again. I want a chance to reconnect, a chance to know you. A chance to…" Her voice faltered.

"I'd like that too, Diana," she said softly. "I'd like that very much. But not in a way that interferes with your career."

Diana nodded. "Understood. I'm only teaching Monday through Thursday this semester. Could I come out on the weekends?"

"I'd like that." Nora turned to Brooke. "Well? What do you say? I've got a guest bedroom. You'd have your own bath and your privacy. I would pay you the going rate, plus room and board, and I'd try not to be too much trouble." She paused to take in a rasping breath. "We can arrange with hospice for a certified nursing assistant to help me twice a week to give you a little time off, and I have wonderful neighbors who take care of my shopping and other odds and ends. Beyond that, I truly like you and would enjoy spending the time in your company."

She hoped Brooke would accept. Not only was she fond of her, she trusted her, and she knew it wouldn't be long now before she would have to put her life in someone else's skilled, caring hands.

"If you need time to think it over—"

"I'll do it," Brooke said. "I'll do it."

✧✧

Once they'd said goodbye to Nora, Brooke, Diana, and Daniel huddled together outside.

"Will Aunt Nora be all right by herself?" Diana asked.

Brooke nodded. "Your Aunt Nora is stronger than you think. Her mind is sharp, and she has a phone by her bed. I made sure that it was within her reach when I tucked her in. That was a lot of activity for her this morning, probably far more than she's used to on an average day. Sleep is the best thing for her right now."

"Given her age and condition, she's a medical marvel." Daniel added.

"What can I expect?" Diana asked. "What happens now? How quick-moving is this form of cancer?"

"It's already progressed," he answered. "The good news is the cancer hasn't metastasized to her brain. The bad news is it has spread to her bones and her liver."

"What can we do to help her?"

Brooke's heart hurt for Diana. She'd seen this too many times. It didn't matter the age of the patient. The reaction of loved ones was the same—take action that will make a difference.

"You can love her, spend quality time with her, and we can, and will, do our very best to manage her pain and discomfort," Brooke said.

Daniel reached out and put a hand on Diana's shoulder. "We all love your Aunt Nora. While her hospice team will be local and I'll no longer see her at my office, I will remain, if that is her choice and yours, her doctor of record. I promise you that I will stop by as often as necessary. I have a weekend place about thirty minutes from here." He pulled out a business card and wrote on the back of it. "I'm giving you all of my contact information, including my cell number. If you need anything or have any questions that Brooke or the hospice staff can't answer for you, text or call me."

"Thank you."

"You're welcome. Brooke is the best there is. Your great-aunt is in excellent hands." He pulled his car keys from his pocket. "I've got to get going." He kissed Brooke on the cheek. "We'll talk soon." He held out his hand to Diana. "I wish we'd met under different circumstances."

When Daniel pulled away, Diana said, "I feel like I owe you an apology."

The statement caught Brooke completely off guard. "Why would you think that?"

"Aunt Nora really put you on the spot in there. She made it next to impossible for you to say no."

"Believe me, had I wanted to turn her down, I would've done so. I didn't feel pressured in the least."

"You are under absolutely no obligation—"

Brooke wrapped her fingers around Diana's forearm to forestall the rest of whatever she'd been about to say. "I know."

"Your career is every bit as important as mine..."

She released her hold. "Diana, as your great-aunt said, I'm between jobs. I resigned my position several months ago. I just couldn't stand to watch another child lose a battle to cancer. Not right now, anyway."

"I can imagine."

"When I walked away, I rented a house about fifteen minutes from here. I've spent the summer running on the beach, meditating, and trying to regain my equilibrium. I still haven't figured out what's next for me. Dr. Lindstrom was an inspiration in my career; I can't think of any better way to repay her than to help her now."

"If you're sure..."

"I am."

"Okay, then." Diana pulled out her phone and clicked on the calendar app. "I have a meeting scheduled with Aunt Nora's lawyer in Boston tomorrow morning at eleven. I plan to head back here when that's done. Maybe it would be useful for us to get together to iron out the details of her care?"

Brooke admired Diana's efficiency. She also recognized someone like Diana needed to feel useful. That was something she was happy to encourage.

"That's a good idea. Where are you staying?"

"I got a room at a B and B in Provincetown."

"Do you like lobster?"

"Who doesn't like lobster?"

"Exactly," Brooke agreed. "How about dinner tomorrow night at the Lobster Pot? It's that big place in the middle of town with the perpetual line outside."

"I've passed it. Want to say seven o'clock?"

"Done. I'll meet you there." Brooke unlocked her car with the key fob.

"Wait." Diana stepped between Brooke and her Subaru.

36

Brooke looked at her expectantly.

"What about Aunt Nora? I know you said she'd be fine by herself, but I'm still worried."

"Your great-aunt has been managing just fine until now. She indicated she's got neighbors who check on her regularly. We know that, so far, she's been able to transfer on her own from the wheelchair to the couch and back again. She's drinking plenty of water. I think it's safe to leave her to her own devices for now."

The look of consternation on Diana's face told Brooke she wasn't so sure. Brooke reminded herself that, although Diana was a scientist, this illness was far from her area of expertise. Beyond that, the patient was her family, and that added a whole other dimension to the situation.

"Dr. Lindstrom is still mentally capable of recognizing when she needs help, and although her physical strength and stamina are compromised, in my professional opinion, she's still safe to be unsupervised with periodic check-ins. Remember too, this is someone who is fiercely independent."

"I trust what you're saying, but the woman we just left was too weak to get from the wheelchair into the bed. I'm worried about her. I didn't realize how involved all this would be. I guess I didn't really think it through."

She wanted to find a way to ease Diana's concern. She knew that in Diana's place, with the same set of circumstances and Diana's lack of experience with this disease, she likely would feel the same way. She was so lost in thought that she almost missed Diana's next sentence.

"Unfortunately, I've got a teleconference this afternoon with the head of my department, and Aunt Nora definitely doesn't have Wi-Fi. I'd push the meeting if I could, but…"

Brooke calculated what it would take to rearrange the remainder of her day. It was a small price to pay to give Diana peace of mind.

"I tell you what. I'll come back and check on Dr. Lindstrom later this afternoon and then one more time before bedtime."

"You'd do that?"

"Of course."

Diana seemed to mull that over. "While I'm at the attorney's tomorrow, I'll have him put together a contract for your service and back date it to today."

She shook her head. "Not necessary." She met Diana's eyes and held her gaze. "This isn't a business deal for me. This is Dr. Lindstrom. That makes it personal."

"Still—"

"Still, nothing." She tried to rein in her growing irritation. It was insulting that Diana would think her concern was money-driven. Nursing had never been about that for her.

"Give me your cell number and I'll text you updates." She said it more sharply than she intended.

"I didn't mean to offend you. If I have, I truly apologize," Diana said.

"No offense taken." She reminded herself that Diana was only trying to do the right thing. She pulled out her phone and handed it to Diana. "It'll be faster if you input your own contact information."

"Right." Diana laid her phone in Brooke's palm. "Quid pro quo, if you don't mind."

"Not at all."

When they'd finished exchanging contact details, Brooke said, "You'll be hearing from me later. I hope your call goes well this afternoon."

"Thank you. And thank you, again, for keeping an eye on Aunt Nora today. I'm sure that wasn't in your plans."

"You're welcome."

As she drove away, she glanced in the rearview mirror and caught a glimpse of Diana standing in the middle of the driveway. She looked shell-shocked.

Brooke reviewed their earlier conversation on the deck. She couldn't fathom having to process all that Diana was dealing with right now. She would do whatever she could to make this as easy as possible for Diana and for Dr. Lindstrom. This was who she was. This was what she did.

CHAPTER FOUR

D iana scrolled through the thirty-two results for "Dr. Nora Lindstrom, Dana-Farber." How was it possible that this information had been as close as a Google search and she'd never thought to look?

"Probably because you thought she'd been dead for years and her work would've pre-dated the internet."

She clicked on an entry for a lecture Aunt Nora gave at Harvard in 1973 titled, "Surviving Childhood Leukemia: A Success Story."

"A YouTube video of a lecture from forty-five years ago? How cool is that?"

The quality of the video was grainy, but that didn't matter to her. For the next hour, she sat transfixed, as her great-aunt held the audience in the palm of her hand. Aunt Nora was so alive, so passionate about the topic, brilliant, and so beautiful. Diana did the math—Aunt Nora would've been fifty-five when this was recorded and in the prime of her career. Diana would've been an infant.

As the lecture ended, her phone went off, startling her out of her ruminations. She checked the screen to see a text message from Brooke.

"Your Aunt Nora is safely tucked in for the night. She ate a little dinner, did the New York Times *crossword puzzle, and took care of her own personal hygienic needs before going lights out. All is well."*

Diana nodded in approval. Brooke had done exactly as promised—she'd checked on Aunt Nora twice and reported to Diana in succinct, yet sufficiently detailed, messages. So far, Diana was impressed with her professionalism.

The phone sounded again. *"Oh, and she said to be sure to let you know that I locked the front door with a key she gave me for safekeeping. LOL."*

Diana chuckled and replied, *"Thank you for taking such excellent care of her. And especially thank you for locking the door! I know I'll sleep better for it, even if she won't."*

She debated whether or not to include an emoji. Was this a business text? In the strictest sense, it was. But clearly this wasn't business in the formal sense. It felt too comfortable for that. In the end, she selected the wink emoji and hit "send."

Less than ten seconds later, her text alert sounded again. *"You're welcome. Honored. And glad you'll sleep peacefully tonight."* Brooke included a return wink.

Another text followed. *"FYI, I know you said you have the lawyer tomorrow morning in Boston. Please don't worry about things here. I'll stop by early and check on her. You just focus on your meeting. And no, I don't need a contract for that. It's my pleasure. I hope your conference call went as you hoped today. Sleep well."*

She smiled at Brooke's thoughtfulness. *"You too. And thank you again. Goodnight."* She stared at the phone for a minute, waiting to see if Brooke would respond one more time. When she didn't, Diana found herself surprisingly disappointed.

Nora clutched at her nightgown and struggled to sit up. She fought for air and reached for the glass of water on the bedside table. Her hands shook so badly that she didn't dare try to pick up the glass one-handed. She checked the clock. 1:45 a.m.

Steady, old girl. Don't panic. Take your time. She sucked in two or three shallow breaths before finally managing to inhale deeply. The pain in her chest and airways receded, and she closed her eyes in relief.

These episodes were a nightly occurrence now. It was, as she thought of it, her "new" normal. The sensation of oxygen deprivation frightened her, not because she was afraid to die, she wasn't, but because suffocation seemed such a horrible way to go.

Finally convinced she wouldn't drop the glass, she picked it up with two hands, took a few sips, and set it down on the coaster. Then she settled back into the pillows, pulled the covers up to her chin, and waited for sleep to claim her again.

"You knew! You knew and you let it happen."

"No—"

"You let all those people die." Mary was red faced and angry, seemingly oblivious to the jubilant shouts outside the window. "Worse still is that you had me and all those other girls help you do it. You didn't even give us a choice." She pointed a finger at Nora's chest. "You're a murderer, and we're all accomplices."

"Darling, I was sworn to secrecy. I couldn't tell you or anyone else, just like you agreed not to share with anyone what you were doing here."

"Don't you dare compare us to you. We only knew we were making a difference. You knew exactly what we were doing and what would happen. You knew!"

"It was necessary. How many more of our boys would've died if we hadn't done what we did? We won. We won, darling. Focus on that."

"Ugh. How can you even think that way? Thousands of people are dead. Thousands of mothers, daughters, sons, and grandparents, are dead. People on their way to the store for groceries are dead. Children riding their bicycles in the street were obliterated. We did that. Us! Thanks to you."

"No, darling. That's the wrong way to look at it."

"How else would you have me see it?"

"We won the war. It's over. Our boys can come home now. The world is safe again."

"The world will never be safe again. Not now. Not ever." Mary plopped down heavily on her side of the bed, put her head in her hands, and cried.

Nora sat down next to her and put her arms around her.

"No." Mary stood up abruptly. "I don't want you anywhere near me. You sicken me."

"You don't mean that. You're just upset."

"I don't mean that? How dare you! I do mean that. I don't ever want to see you again. Do you understand me? Stay away from me."

"You don't mean that. You can't mean that. You can't..."

"Wait! Don't leave me. You can't..." Nora thrashed around, her legs tangled in the sheets. Her eyes popped open in mid-sentence. After several moments, her heartbeat settled once again into its natural rhythm. It was always the same. No matter how many times she relived the nightmare, the outcome never changed.

She turned her head to the side and gazed out the bedroom window. Dawn was breaking on the horizon. "I'm sorry, darling. I'm sorrier than you'll ever know. Wherever you are, I hope you've found it within yourself to forgive me. More importantly, I hope you've forgiven yourself."

Wearily, she pushed herself up in the bed and threw off the covers. The past would need to stay in its box for now. Brooke would be coming in an hour or so, and Diana later in the day. She needed to make a cup of tea and shake off the cobwebs.

Brooke checked her Fitbit and picked up the pace. She still had half a mile to go to hit her distance goal for the day. By the time she got back to her place, she'd have less than an hour to get ready if she was going to be at Dr. Lindstrom's cottage by seven thirty.

In the blink of an eye, or the space of a weekend, Brooke's entire life had changed. Two days ago, her only responsibility had been to make sure she got the recycling out to the street on time for pick up. Now... Now she was charged with overseeing the care of one of her professional idols. Everything in her life would have to shift to accommodate that new reality.

She knew in the core of her being that this assignment was exactly what she was meant to do in this moment. She didn't believe in coincidences, and the number of synchronicities that resulted in the current situation was too many to ignore or discount. She ran through them in her mind as her feet flew over the hard sand by the waterside.

Of all the places in the world she could've selected to rent a house and recalibrate her life, she chose Provincetown, ten minutes from Dr. Lindstrom's cottage.

Daniel had called her night before last, wanting to go for a morning run together. When was the last time that had happened? In hindsight, she realized the run must've been the pretext for getting her to accept this post.

And what of the fact that the patient turned out to be a woman whom she knew and revered? Nora Lindstrom was renowned at Dana-Farber; her research and tireless work had helped Brooke and others save countless children's lives. And now Brooke was the one who would have the honor of helping Dr. Lindstrom at the end of her life. It was mind boggling.

Brooke sprinted the last fifty yards and then slowed to a walk as she reached the path leading to the parking lot. The exercise felt good, and the sun on her face rejuvenated her spirit. It was time to get this new chapter in her life started.

Diana stared at the mahogany-paneled walls in the waiting room at the law firm of Fitzgerald, Osborn, and Chase on State Street in Boston's Financial District. Her hair was slightly disheveled from the ferry ride over from Provincetown, and she ran her fingers through it in a vain effort to put it back in some semblance of order.

"Dr. Lindstrom? Mr. Fitzgerald will see you now." The young man behind the pedestal desk pointed toward the glass doors and hit a buzzer to admit her. "Down the hall, last door on your right."

"Thanks."

She rose and tugged on the back of her suit jacket to settle it in place. She passed by small offices filled with busy-looking attorneys. When she reached the end of the hall, the corridor widened. A secretary sitting behind a desk said, "You can go in, Dr. Lindstrom. Mr. Fitzgerald is waiting for you."

Diana peeked around the thick wooden door, which was slightly ajar.

"Come in, Dr. Lindstrom." Charles Fitzgerald stood, and she was struck by his height. She was five-feet-nine inches tall, and he made her look short. Where she had imagined him to be a stodgy old man, it turned out the attorney was most likely in his early sixties, nattily attired in a custom-fitted suit, colorful tie, and crisp, white dress shirt.

She shook his hand and took the proffered seat across the desk from him.

"I'm glad you decided to see your great-aunt and take on this responsibility." He folded his hands and rested them on a stack of papers in the middle of his desk. "She wasn't sure you would, and honestly, she was most reluctant to ask."

Diana leaned forward. "To be perfectly frank, I'm not sure why she did, and I'd love it if you could answer some questions for me."

"Okay. I'll do my best."

She sorted through the myriad questions swirling in her brain. "What kind of financial shape is Aunt Nora in?" She chided herself for the way the inquiry must've sounded. "I'm… I don't mean to be indelicate…" She shifted uncomfortably in her seat. "I just want to be certain that we can ensure her the level of care and comfort she needs and deserves at this stage of her life. Does she have sufficient funds to pay for a full-time, private duty nurse? Is she in any danger of losing her home? Does she have adequate medical insurance coverage to take care of prescription drug costs?"

He nodded. "I understand your concerns." He retrieved a thick binder from behind him and set it before her. "When I spoke with Nora yesterday morning, she asked that I share some of the details of her living trust with you, including her financials, the status and disposition of her homes—"

"Did you say, 'homes'? As in plural?"

"I did. Nora continues to maintain her primary residence in Cambridge, as well as the cottage in Truro. There are no mortgages or other encumbrances on either property, so I can assure you that she is not in any danger of being homeless."

Diana watched him closely. Was he being facetious? She could have sworn she saw the ghost of a smile. But just as quickly, it was gone.

He reached for the binder and flipped to a section titled, "Real estate holdings." He turned it back to her and pointed to a line at the bottom of the page.

She realized her surprise must be showing. The Cambridge home was valued at $2.3 million. The quaint little cottage in Truro was worth another $1.1 million.

When she looked up, he was watching her. This time, the wry smile was unmistakable.

"Nora was a child of the Depression. She learned the value of a dollar at a very young age, and she was a saver with no dependents. She always said she wasn't a penny-pincher. She was simply frugal and prudent. To answer your larger question, she has more than enough resources to take on a full-time nurse. She's covered by Medicare, which pays for hospice, and she also maintains a generous private health insurance plan that came with her retirement from Dana-Farber. By the way, although Medicare's hospice benefit will take care of things like durable medical equipment and medications, it will not cover any cost related to private duty care."

"Noted." She paused to consider the wording of her next question. "You've known her a long time?"

"She was one of my first clients. I was just a young pup fresh out of law school." His eyes took on a faraway look. "I asked her once why she took a chance on me. She said she always insisted that three people be younger than her—her doctor, her financial adviser, and her lawyer."

Diana laughed. "That's funny. But it's excellent advice and sound strategy."

"I learned a lot from listening to your great-aunt. She's one of the kindest, most patient, nicest people I ever met." He sighed. "I shall miss her more than you can imagine."

A wave of sadness washed over her. Here was a man who was grieving the loss of an extraordinary woman—a woman clearly everyone admired—and she'd never really gotten the chance to know her. "I wish... I wish I knew her as well as you seem to."

"She wished with all her heart that things could've been different between the two of you."

Diana nodded and swallowed hard, working to keep her emotions in check. "Why wasn't it?" she asked quietly. It was the question she kept coming back to.

He smiled kindly at her. "That's something you're going to have to ask Nora yourself."

He patted the stack of papers in the middle of his desk. "I've got some documents for you. Some of these are informational, like the names of banks where Nora has accounts, account numbers, locations of safe-deposit boxes, contact information for her financial adviser, her life, health, and home insurance details, and a list of her healthcare providers.

"I've also included several certified copies of her durable power of attorney and her health care proxy. Take the power of attorney with you to the banks, etcetera, and have them file that information so that you can access her accounts and pay the bills.

"Give the health care proxy to her health care providers and make sure they have it on file so that they know you are authorized to make decisions for her." He swept all the documents up and placed them in another labeled three-ring binder with Diana's name on it.

She tried to take it all in. It seemed surreal to be sitting here, having this conversation, realizing that she was about to become responsible for every decision and every transaction for someone else—someone who obviously had been meticulous in planning and living her life. Aunt Nora was a stranger to her. How could she be sure Diana would make the right decisions for her?

"Are you all right?"

"Yes, just a little overwhelmed. I can't believe Aunt Nora trusts me with all this. She doesn't even know me."

There was that look again. Fitzgerald said, "You're wrong. She knows you far better than you think."

She wanted to ask him what he meant by that, but he stood, signaling the meeting was over. She stood as well.

"It's a pleasure to meet you," he said. "I'm glad Nora has you to rely on. If you have any questions or need anything, please feel free to reach out to me via phone or e-mail. My contact details are in the binder."

"Thank you." She didn't know what else to say.

"Please give Nora my love and tell her Emily and I will be out to see her as soon as we can."

"I will." She shook his hand and turned to leave.

"Dr. Lindstrom?"

"Yes?"

"Take good care of Nora. She's one in a million."

"I will," Diana said, and she meant it.

CHAPTER FIVE

The grandfather clock chimed and roused Nora from sleep. The grogginess lingered, and she felt herself suspended in that twilight netherworld, where she was never sure where "then" ended and "now" began.

There was her coffee table, and the Monet print on the wall, and today's paper opened to the crossword puzzle... And sitting across the way in one of the two chairs that faced the couch was Brooke.

"I'm not very good company, am I? I fall asleep without the slightest provocation."

Brooke laid aside the book she'd been reading. "You're excellent company, but I'm not here to be entertained. I stopped by to see how the rest of your morning went and you were napping. I didn't want to disturb you so I decided to wait."

"Oh, dear. I hope I wasn't out long. What a waste of a beautiful day."

"How are you feeling?"

"Like I'm one hundred years old."

"Fair enough," Brooke said. "Although something more descriptive about your state of health would be helpful."

"Right. My bathroom habits have been regular, I enjoyed a little toast and tea, and I had difficulty with fifty-three across in today's puzzle, which naturally made me wonder if I was losing my faculties. Otherwise, I have been as you found me, asleep at the wheel."

"Excellent." Brooke packed her book into a computer bag sitting on the floor next to her. "I imagine Diana should be here any minute."

"If she met with Charles, it shouldn't have taken too terribly long. He's a busy man."

"Is Charles your attorney?"

"Has been pretty much since the day he graduated law school." Nora smiled at the memory. "He was so young and idealistic back then."

"And now?"

"Now?" Nora laughed. "Now he's a big-shot managing partner, balding and still idealistic. I hope you'll get to meet him. He and his wife, Emily are wonderful people. He's taken good care of me over the years."

The doorbell rang and Nora called out, "It's open!"

Diana let herself in. "How did you know I wasn't a criminal?"

"Criminals don't ring the doorbell," she answered, as Diana gave her a kiss on the cheek.

"You never know. I might've been a very polite criminal." She sat in the available chair.

"You look very nice," Brooke said.

"Thank you. I rarely have cause to wear business suits in the classroom. I had to dig this one up from the depths of my closet."

"I take it you met with Charles?" Nora asked.

"Yes, I met with Mr. Fitzgerald this morning. He was very helpful."

"Good. Do you have everything you need?"

"I think so. Can I ask you a question?"

"Of course. Anything."

Brooke stood. "If you two don't mind, this seems like the perfect time for me to stretch my legs. I'm going to take a quick walk on the beach. I'll be back in about twenty minutes."

Nora appreciated Brooke's less-than-subtle attempt to give her and Diana privacy. "Take your time," she said. "It's a beautiful day out there and I'm not going anywhere."

Diana waited to speak until Brooke took her leave. "I'm just... I want to make sure you're comfortable with me paying your bills and taking care of your business."

"I am. I wouldn't have instructed Charles to provide you with the keys to the car, so to speak, unless I was."

"Who has been paying your bills up until now?"

She raised her eyebrows in surprise. "I have, my dear. Who else?"

"You still pay your own bills?"

"I do."

"But you don't seem to have access to the internet or own a computer."

She chuckled. "There are these things called billing invoices, checkbooks, checks, envelopes, and stamps. Old-fashioned notions in today's world, I realize. Nevertheless, they do still exist."

"You pay everything with a check?"

"I do. Although occasionally I use cash if I'm at a store."

"What about credit cards?"

"What about them?"

"I didn't see any credit card account information."

She shook her head. "I ripped up my last credit card the day I retired. Haven't used one since."

If she hadn't thought it would offend Diana, she would've laughed at the incredulous expression on her face. "When you don't buy beyond your means, you don't need a credit card. If I don't have the money for something, I don't buy it."

"I see," Diana said. "Do you want me to take over the responsibility for paying your bills now?" She shifted uncomfortably in the chair. "I mean... You're obviously perfectly capable of managing your own affairs."

"I am, but I suspect that won't be true for too much longer. Don't you think it would be best if you had a trial run before I am no longer able to help you?"

"That makes sense. I just don't want to sweep into your life and take over. I want you to maintain as much control over your affairs as you want to have."

"I appreciate your concern, Diana. That's very thoughtful of you. But I assure you, I'm perfectly comfortable with whatever choices and decisions you make on my behalf."

Diana jumped up and started pacing. "How are you so unfazed by all of this? You don't even know me, and yet you are entrusting me with life-and-death decisions and all of your finances—everything you worked for your entire career. I don't get it."

She waited until Diana made eye contact with her. "Please, sit down. There's no reason for you to get yourself worked up."

Diana sat on the edge of her chair.

"That's better. Please understand. I've had my life. I've finished everything I'm going to accomplish, made my living, and taken care of my financial needs and affairs. I am at peace with whatever comes next. As you are now aware, I have sufficient resources to carry me through the rest of this life with enough to spare, thank God. Whatever you do on my behalf, Diana, I know you will do with love, because that's who you are. I am in the best possible hands. What more could I ask for?"

Diana frowned. "You could ask for someone who knew the first thing about you to take on such an important role."

She sighed. She was tiring again, but she refused to give in to sleep until she had eased Diana's mind. "As I explained to you yesterday, while others may know the details of my life more fully, no one better knows my heart, Diana. It's where you always have lived and where you live still."

Diana's face reddened. "You had a funny way of showing it. Most people who feel that way don't evaporate into thin air never to return."

What should she say? What could she say without venturing into truths she hoped to keep to herself? "Your parents were your gatekeepers, Diana. You were a child. It was their right—"

"Their rights were not more important than me."

She closed her eyes against the angst of that ten-year-old child who had clung to her pant leg. Clearly, yesterday's conversation was insufficient to ameliorate Diana's pain. "What did your parents tell you? What did Grandpa Bill tell you?"

"Which day?" Diana asked, her frustration clear. "One day you were traveling the world on some top-secret business and couldn't be contacted. Another time you no longer wanted to be part of the family."

She gasped.

"Then there was the famous, 'Aunt Nora is too busy to be bothered with us.' The list went on and on, until finally, when I wanted to invite you to my graduation when I received my doctorate, Mom and Dad told me you were dead."

Nora swallowed hard as some of the missing pieces of the puzzle fell into place for her. She'd experienced some of their cruelty, but this last bit...that they would lie with such viciousness... She'd thought that beyond even them.

"Why do you seem surprised by that? You already knew I thought you were dead."

"That's true. But I was unaware of the timing or the details of whatever lies you were fed. I'm sorry." She felt her energy draining away and tried to focus. "I know you want answers. I wish I had more stamina. If you would be kind enough to exercise patience with me, I promise I will respond more fully to your question soon. Can you accept that answer for now?"

"Yes, of course. I don't mean to tax you."

"Thank you. I know you're disappointed, Diana. In the meantime, please look in the end-table drawer. There's a picture frame in there. It's facedown. Would you be so kind as to retrieve it?"

Diana did as she was told.

Nora gestured to the picture. "Turn it over and see for yourself."

Diana turned the frame, gazed at the picture, and recognition dawned. "Where did you get this? Where did you get a picture of me receiving my diploma?"

"I took it myself."

Diana slumped heavily into the chair. "Are you saying you were there that day?"

Nora fought to stay awake. "I was. Your parents didn't know it. Nobody did." Her words were beginning to run together. "I never missed a big occasion, Diana. Never. I was so proud of you that day. Still am..."

Brooke paused at the top of the steps and checked to be sure her feet were free of sand. She estimated she'd been gone about half an hour—hopefully long enough for Nora and Diana to discuss whatever it was they needed to discuss.

"I'm back. I hope I'm not too earl—" Brooke took in the scene before her. Diana sat mutely in the chair, tears running down her cheeks. She held a picture frame loosely in her hands. Nora remained on the couch. Although she was sitting up, her eyes were closed and her head was tipped back.

Brooke glanced from one of them to the other and back again. "Are you all right?"

Diana nodded.

"What happened?" When Diana didn't answer, she strode the few steps to the couch and gently shook Nora's shoulder. "Nora? Dr. Lindstrom? Can you hear me?"

Nora stirred briefly and Brooke relaxed ever-so-slightly. "Nora, I'm going to get you into the chair and get you to bed. Is that all right?"

"Mmm."

"Okay. Give me one second." She glanced back at Diana, who hadn't moved. "Are you going to be okay for a minute?"

Diana nodded again. Brooke didn't like her color or her demeanor, but that would have to wait until she could get Nora settled. Once she'd done that, she returned to the living room. Diana was sitting in the same position she'd been in when Brooke had walked through the sliding glass doors from the deck minutes ago.

She knelt by her side. Gently, she laid her hand on Diana's arm and spoke softly. "Nora's fine. One of the inevitable facts of this disease is that it completely zaps her. She can handle short bursts of energy and focus, but she requires a lot of down time. It's not at all unusual for someone in her condition to drop off to sleep without warning. I know how alarming and unnerving..."

Diana shook her head. "It wasn't that." She rose, placed the picture on the chair, and grabbed the tissue box from the end table next to the couch.

Brooke caught a glimpse of a younger Diana in a graduation gown. She was being hooded. Brooke wondered why she didn't look happier; it should've been one of the proudest days of her life.

"Getting my doctorate from Columbia." Diana wiped her eyes and took a deep breath. "I'm sorry, by the way. I've been more emotional these past two days than I think I've ever been in my life."

Brooke stood and faced her. "You have nothing to apologize for. I can't imagine how head-spinning all of this must be for you. I think you're doing great."

"It sure doesn't feel that way. I'm trying to process all of it, but so many things don't add up."

Emotions swirled in Diana's eyes, and they shifted from blue to green depending on the light. Belatedly she realized Diana was waiting for her to say something. "Maybe we could talk through it. I often find that when I say it out loud, things click into place." Diana shrugged noncommittally.

"Are we still on for dinner? If you feel like it, we could talk about it then."

"Sure."

Brooke glanced at the grandfather clock. It was nearly five. "Nora's likely to sleep for a while yet. I can stay and fix her an early dinner and then get her settled for the night. That should give you plenty of time to unwind and change into something more comfortable." Even as the words came out of her mouth, she tried to reel them back in. She blushed crimson. "I didn't—"

Diana burst out laughing. "Oh, my God. You should see the look on your face."

"My word choice is usually more judicious and less unintentionally suggestive than that."

"I wouldn't have noticed except that you called attention to it."

"I should've quit while I was ahead."

"Too late for that now."

"Apparently." She regarded Diana quizzically. She certainly didn't seem disconcerted by the turn the conversation had taken. Was she gay? Brooke guessed it was possible, but she'd learned long ago about making assumptions, and it didn't seem appropriate to ask.

"Okay," Diana was saying. "Would jeans be appropriate for this restaurant?"

"You'd be overdressed."

"My kind of place. I'll see you there at seven? Do you think Aunt Nora will be sufficiently settled by then?"

"Absolutely."

"Right. I guess I'll just get going." Diana picked up the picture and looked at it wistfully one more time. She tucked it in the end-table drawer face down.

Brooke had so many questions, but Diana turned and strode toward the door. She turned back only long enough to wave. "See you in a bit."

"Right." She heard the car pull out of the drive. She took one step toward the end-table drawer and hesitated. Diana had a right to her privacy. If she wanted to open up and confide in Brooke, that was fine, but it was hers to do.

She changed direction and headed down the hallway toward the guest bedroom. There was no telling exactly how long Nora and Diana would need her, but she might as well use her time wisely and get familiar with her new temporary digs.

⊰⊱

Diana turned sideways and regarded herself in the mirror. These weren't her favorite pair of jeans, but they'd have to do. Was the shirt too tight? Maybe she should go with the black one instead. She yanked the shirt in question off the hanger and held it up against her.

What was wrong with her, anyway? When was the last time she'd been this insecure about her appearance? Besides, this was a business dinner—a discussion about the parameters of Brooke's assignment—not a date.

She ripped off the green blouse and pulled on the black. No more second-guesses. She fluffed her hair one last time, snagged her wallet off the table, and headed out. It was a glorious night for a stroll and she was early enough that she didn't need to rush. That left her mind free to turn over the new information.

Aunt Nora had seen her receive her doctorate. She'd been there. Not only that, she'd preserved the memory in a picture frame. Did that picture normally sit out where she could see it? Had she put it away because Diana was coming?

"Hey. Watch where you're going!"

"Sorry." Diana steadied the young woman she'd plowed into. The woman went on her way without acknowledging the apology.

Diana tucked away her ruminations for the moment and checked her surroundings. "Oh, for God's sake." She turned around and retraced her steps. She'd overshot the restaurant by two blocks.

She arrived at the hostess station seconds ahead of a raucous group of eight young lesbians. They were loudly discussing the merits of various gender-neutral pronouns, a sliding scale of gender identity, and their own preferences.

"It's a brave new world out there, isn't it?"

Diana started as Brooke materialized next to her. She looked fabulous in a white linen shirt and worn jeans. The scent of her spicy perfume wafted Diana's way and she breathed it in. Brooke had asked her a question, hadn't she? Diana struggled to remember what it was.

"How many?" The hostess saved Diana the embarrassment of asking Brooke to repeat herself.

"Two. Something by the water if you have it," Brooke said.

"Right this way."

When they were seated, Diana placed the napkin in her lap. "I could get used to views like this. It's so picturesque."

"I love the water. It's therapeutic—revitalizes the spirit. That's one of the major reasons I chose Provincetown for my retreat from the world."

"Do you miss it?"

Brooke regarded her quizzically. "Do you mean the noise and bustle of Boston? No. I prefer quiet and less hectic settings. In the city, everyone seems to be in a hurry to get somewhere else. I'd rather relish the moment."

Diana wondered. Had she ever truly enjoyed being fully present? She certainly was enjoying being here right now. The angle of the sun infused Brooke's eyes with light, shading them to blue, matching the hue of the water below.

"How about you? I know you work at Columbia. Do you live in Manhattan?"

"Me? No. Manhattan is too pricey for me. I rent a small condo in the suburbs. It's an easy train commute and shuttle from there."

"Would you prefer to live in the big city if you could?"

"Not really. I like being close enough to cultural attractions to have them in easy reach, but I'm not a constant noise fan either."

The server took their drink orders and hustled off to the next table.

"What do you usually have here?" Diana asked.

"Everything is good, but I'm a lobster and mussels fan, so the clambake is my go-to choice."

"Works for me." She pushed the menu away. "Before we get started, I want to thank you for everything you've already done for

Aunt Nora these past couple of days. You didn't have to do that, but you stepped up without hesitation anyway."

Brooke waved the words away. "As I told you, I love and respect your great-aunt. It's been my pleasure and privilege to help." She selected a fresh roll from the basket the server deposited on their table along with their iced teas. "These are heavenly, by the way. Unless you're gluten free, you really should try one."

"I'm not." Diana picked up a roll, buttered it, and took a bite. The bread melted in her mouth. "Oh my God, that's good."

"Told you."

The server took their dinner orders and left them alone once again.

"In terms of Aunt Nora's care," Diana began, "I've done some research, and it seems to me that, depending on your location, in-home private duty nursing care costs in the neighborhood of fifty to seventy-five dollars per hour."

Brooke fidgeted with the salt and pepper shakers. "I'm not going to hold you to market-value figures for Nora Lindstrom's care."

"Oh, yes you are."

"Oh no, I'm not." Brooke's jaw set defiantly.

Diana put her elbows on the table and leaned forward. "I've never heard anyone argue to get paid less than what they deserve."

Brooke mimicked her posture. "You've never met me before."

They were practically nose to nose. Diana felt Brooke's breath caress her face.

"More iced tea, ladies?" the server interrupted. "Your dinners should be up in just a couple of minutes."

She blinked, sat back, and took in an uneven breath. "Yes, please." What was it about Brooke that so unnerved her?

"How about if we settle on a weekly flat fee for my services and call it good?" Brooke asked. "I know Nora said she had the funds to cover a full-time in-home nurse, but I seriously doubt she had any idea how much that would cost."

"What if that arrangement short changes you?"

"What if it does?" Again, Brooke played with the salt and pepper shakers.

Finally, it dawned on her. Brooke was uncomfortable talking about money. "You know, you went to school for this, you trained for it, and you have tons of experience working with oncology patients. Asking for proper compensation on the basis of all that isn't a crime. You shouldn't be embarrassed—"

"Who said I was embarrassed?"

"I-I'm sorry. I just thought…"

"Here you go, ladies. Two clambakes."

Diana was so grateful for the server's timing, she thought she could've kissed him. How had this conversation gone so far off the rails? Had she misread Brooke's body language? And what in the world was she going to do to get things back on track? Everything seemed to go smoothly, except when they talked about the business of Brooke caring for Nora.

"This looks great." Easy, neutral.

"It does." Brooke teased a mussel from its shell and dipped it in melted butter.

"I don't want to argue with you about this." Diana used the nutcracker to break open a lobster claw. "You set the rate. Make it hourly or weekly. I trust you to be fair to Nora, to me, and most of all, I hope, to yourself. We'll set up a weekly pay schedule and reevaluate if we need to, depending upon the level of care Aunt Nora requires. Fair enough?"

"Fair enough," Brooke agreed.

Diana put down her fork. "I know I asked you and Daniel this yesterday, but we didn't have time to get into any detail. What should I expect? How will Aunt Nora's disease progress?"

"I can wait to explain this to you until after dinner, if you want. This isn't exactly polite mealtime conversation."

"No. I need to know, and I'd rather hear it from you than from the hospice liaison nurse tomorrow."

"Let's finish eating first and I'll talk you through it afterward."

They engaged in small talk for the remainder of the meal and split the check.

"How about we walk off dinner with a stroll on the pier?" Brooke suggested.

"Sounds good." Diana turned right out of the restaurant, and Brooke put a restraining hand on her arm. "What?"

"The pier is this way." Brooke pointed to the left.

"Thank God you're here or I'd be wandering aimlessly for hours."

"I gathered as much."

They meandered along, dodging foot traffic, until they reached the relative quiet of the pier.

"Okay," Brooke began. "What would you like to know?"

"I want to be prepared. Since I'm only going to be able to visit with Aunt Nora on the weekends, I want to know what kinds of changes I might see. I don't want to be shocked or caught off-guard by any kind of dramatic decline."

"Nora is already exhibiting some of the most obvious, typical signs of lung cancer—weight loss and loss of appetite. You've seen her cough up blood, heard her wheeze and struggle for air, and you know how easily she tires."

Diana nodded.

"All of these symptoms will remain for the duration and likely will become more pronounced and/or more frequent."

Diana sighed. "I hate that for her."

"It gets worse, and that's the hard part. I'd give anything to change it for her and for you, but I can't."

"I appreciate that." She regarded Brooke's profile in the moonlight. The muscles in her jaw were tense, but otherwise there was a softness about her. She was not fragile, exactly. Diana couldn't quite quantify it.

When Brooke offered nothing further, Diana said, "I imagine there's more. Please, tell me. I need to know."

"Normally, I wouldn't get into this level of detail at this point."

She nodded. "I understand. I'm not trying to make you uncomfortable. I just know myself—I'm much better off if I know all the likelihoods and possibilities. It's how I process and prepare."

Brooke hesitated. "All right. Other symptoms might follow, although it's impossible to predict which ones—hoarseness, difficulty swallowing, bone pain, perhaps some confusion—these are real possibilities."

"How long before…" She couldn't finish the sentence.

"It's impossible to say. On the one hand, Nora is one hundred years old. On the other, she's been in good health up until now. According to Daniel, she never smoked a day in her life."

"I thought you didn't have to be a smoker to get lung cancer?"

"True. Lots of people contract lung cancer without ever having smoked. But with this particular form of lung cancer, the patient almost always is a smoker. Why Nora has small cell lung cancer is a mystery."

They reached the end of the pier and turned around for the walk back.

"Thank you for your candor," Diana said. Lost in her own thoughts, she suddenly realized Brooke wasn't with her. She had stopped walking.

Diana backtracked.

"I need you to know, I will always be honest about what's going on with Nora, Diana. It does none of us any good if I do otherwise. But you have to ask. I won't simply volunteer information. If there's something you want to know, ask a question. I'll answer you truthfully every time."

She knew she should say something, but for a moment, she was transfixed by the earnestness in Brooke's features.

"Did you walk or drive?"

"What?" The question threw Diana off.

"Did you walk or did you drive here?"

"Oh. I walked. Why?"

"I know I don't have many data points yet, but it seems to me that you're somewhat directionally challenged."

She blushed. "I can't imagine what would give you that impression."

"Do you need help or an escort to find your way back to where you're staying?"

"I'll manage on my own, thanks." She shoved her hands in her pockets. She didn't need Brooke's assistance to find the B & B, but she wasn't quite ready for the night to end, either.

She spoke into the awkward silence. Time to get back on firm ground. "The hospice liaison nurse said she'd be at Aunt Nora's around nine o'clock. Do you have any idea how long the evaluation will take?"

"I wouldn't think it would take more than an hour or so."

"Good." Diana would have to get on the road right after that in order to get home at a reasonable hour and get any work done.

"I'm going to pick up a few things and head back to Nora's."

"You're going to stay there tonight?" She hadn't been expecting that.

"That's what you hired me for, isn't it?" Brooke winked and walked away. "See you tomorrow."

"Right. See you then."

CHAPTER SIX

Years of night shifts and being on call had conditioned Brooke to sleep lightly and hear anything out of the ordinary. By her calculation, Nora couldn't have gotten more than two consecutive hours of sleep at any point during the night. Although Brooke's direct intervention was never required, nevertheless, each time she sat up and kicked her legs out of the covers and over the side of the bed, ready to run in an instant if she was needed.

She hated to wake Nora now, especially because she finally had settled down and was sleeping soundly. But it was almost eight o'clock. The hospice liaison nurse would be here in an hour, and it would take time to get Nora cleaned up and ready.

"Nora?" She gently shook her shoulder. "Nora? It's time to get up."

Nora mumbled something unintelligible and pulled the covers higher.

"Dr. Lindstrom? Nora?"

This time, her eyelids fluttered open. It took her several seconds to focus. "Good morning. Have I slept the day away?"

"Not yet." Brooke smiled down at her. "But if you don't want to get caught in your nightie, we'd better get you showered and ready for company."

"That's right. The hospice person will be here at nine. We'd best make haste." Nora struggled to sit up and Brooke moved in behind her to help. "Thank you, dear Brooke. Where have you been all my life?"

"That's a long story for another day. How about we settle for a shower instead?"

"I'd rather listen to a story, but I accept the practicality of cleanliness as a necessity of the moment."

They used Nora's shower chair and made short order of the shower. They finished blow-drying her hair just as the doorbell rang.

"If you're okay here, I'll go answer that."

"I'm fine, dear. Remember, I've been dressing myself since before your mother was born."

Brooke found Diana at the front door, holding a bag of something delicious-smelling from the Portuguese Bakery in one hand, and a cardboard tray with three cups of steaming coffee in the other. She thought she'd died and gone to Heaven. "You're a sight for sore eyes."

Diana's eyebrows rose into her hairline.

"I mean, I haven't had a chance to shop for groceries for myself yet and I finished the muffins yesterday. Bringing me breakfast is an errand of mercy." She couldn't discern a way out of yet another uncomfortable exchange, so she simply stopped talking. Why was it that Diana brought out the awkward teenager in her? "Let me help you with that." She relieved Diana of the cardboard tray and carried it over to the kitchen counter.

"Thanks. How was your night? How was Nora's?"

She pointed back in the direction of the master suite. "She's just getting dressed now."

"She's already dressed, if you're talking about me," Nora chimed in. She maneuvered the wheelchair into the living room.

"Good morning." Diana gave her a kiss on the cheek.

"If my nose isn't failing like the rest of me, it smells like fresh coffee and pastries in here."

"Your nose is working perfectly," Diana said. "I didn't know if you two still had anything in the house for breakfast."

"That was very thoughtful of you. I don't have much of an appetite these days, so I'll leave those wonderful goodies for you two youngsters. I'll just have my usual cup of tea and piece of toast."

"I'll get it," Diana and Brooke said simultaneously.

"No need for you girls to fight over me. I can get it myself."

Brooke stood close by as Nora pushed herself up out of the chair and gripped the counter for support. She was shaky but managed to get herself to a stable standing position. It wouldn't be long before even this small effort would be too much for her.

In truth, Nora had passed the point where she should've been living by herself without a full support system, but Brooke understood her desire for independence and not to be a burden.

"Can I help you?"

"Damned infirmity," Nora muttered. "Be a dear and put this in the toaster for me?"

"Of course." She deposited the slice of bread and pushed down the lever. "Can I start the tea kettle?"

"Yes, please. The water's already in it and the tea bags are in that canister in the corner."

Brooke prepared Nora's toast and tea and settled her back in her chair. Out of the corner of her eye, she spied Diana. Her expression was a mixture of sadness, trepidation, and something else she couldn't quite identify.

Brooke's heart went out to her. In caregiver circles, they called this emotional whiplash. Certainly, there was more to the story...like that picture Diana held yesterday.

She'd wanted to ask Diana about the photograph and what had transpired between them. But the opportunity never arose, and Diana didn't seem the least bit inclined to bring it up.

"Malasada?" Diana offered.

"You bought fried dough? How can you possibly look the way you do and eat stuff like that?"

"Fast metabolism." Diana pointed to Nora. "And good genes."

"I would have to run for three days just to work off that one Malasada."

"I don't believe that for a second. You're in great shape."

"As if." Brooke was really famished and the smell of that fried dough made her mouth water. She sighed. "Yes, please, to the Malasada, but I'm eating this under protest."

"Whatever helps you sleep at night." Diana handed her a plate with the Malasada. "I hope you take your coffee black. You didn't have any at dinner last night, so I wasn't sure." She liberated a to-go cup from the carrier and slid it across the counter.

"I'm not sure whether I should be flattered or worried that you're so observant. Black is fine, thank you."

"I say we go with flattered and call it good."

Brooke swallowed and wiped the powdered sugar from her face with a napkin. She noticed Nora wore an amused expression. Before she had time to ponder that, the doorbell rang again. "Got it."

The hospice evaluator reminded Brooke of a nursing instructor she once had—brusque, efficient, and all the warmth of a hyena at feeding time. The good news, however, was that she would not be on Nora's regular care team. Her only job was to ensure Nora fit the criteria and qualified for hospice care, which she obviously did.

When she was gone, Nora broke the silence. "I'll give her credit for not wasting any of our time."

"No kidding." Diana threw out her empty coffee cup. "Are they all like that?"

Brooke cleaned up their plates and wiped down the counter. "No, thank God. In fact, they're never like that. Hospice workers are usually very gentle and empathetic. You needn't worry. She's only in charge of qualifying Nora for services. None of us likely will ever see her again."

Diana checked her watch. "I hate to do this, but I have to go. I've got a lot of prep work ahead of me for the semester, and I have to be in the office early tomorrow for a faculty meeting."

"I understand completely, and I don't want you driving in the dark." Nora hunched over as another coughing jag hit her.

Brooke handed her some tissues and helped her wipe away a smear of blood from her upper lip. She waited for Nora to catch her breath and made a mental note to talk to hospice about providing oxygen.

"Is she going to be all right?" Diana asked under her breath. "I can stay—"

"No, you will not," Nora wheezed.

"You get going. We've got this." Brooke stood up from where she'd been kneeling next to Nora's chair.

"You heard her. Nurse's orders."

"I'll go, but I don't have to be happy about it." Diana leaned over and gently hugged Nora and kissed her on the cheek. "I need you to stay out of trouble until I get back here on Friday."

"What kind of trouble could I possibly get into at my age?"

Diana took her leave and Brooke walked her to her car. "I promise I will take excellent care of her."

"You'll call me if anything changes?"

"I will. Remember, Diana, as long as Nora is able to make clear decisions, it's still her show. You've seen her—she'll fight to be as independent as possible for as long as she's able. You and I can advise, but she's in charge."

"I know." Diana fiddled with her key fob. "I appreciate you taking this on. I'm sure this wasn't how you imagined spending the next few months or however long this will take…"

Diana's voice broke and Brooke laid a comforting hand on her forearm. "Thank you for trusting me."

Diana cleared her throat. "I better get going." She stepped away and unlocked her car. "Would it be all right if I called to check in at night? Or e-mailed? Or something?"

Brooke laughed. "Pick your preferred method of communication. I'm fine with whatever you choose."

"Right. Well, then, I guess I'll talk to you tomorrow night."

"Drive safely." Brooke waved as Diana pulled away. When she got back inside, Nora's eyes were closed.

"Did she get off okay?"

"She did."

"She's a good girl."

"I can see that."

"We've got a lot to heal." Nora's words were slower now.

Brooke thought that an interesting choice of words. She tucked it away for later examination. "Can I get you more comfortable? Would you rather rest on the couch or the bed?"

"The couch is fine, dear. Then you're free to go and do whatever you need to do. I'll likely sleep the rest of the morning away."

"Okay. I'll put the phone next to you and program my number. Just press one in your preset numbers to reach me. Do you know how to do that?"

"Of course. What do you think I am, old or something?"

That startled a laugh out of Brooke. She supported Nora as she stood and pivoted onto the couch, put a pillow under her head and back, and then tucked her in with a blanket.

"Thank you, dear."

"You're welcome. I've just got to run a few errands and collect more of my belongings. I'll be back for lunch."

"No rush. I'm not going anywhere," Nora mumbled as she dropped off to sleep.

Brooke sent herself a reminder text. *Bring new book.* She suspected that she'd be spending a lot of time in the coming days and weeks watching Nora sleep.

⤜⤛

Brooke checked her watch. It was only eight thirty—too early for her to retire. She sat down to read in the upholstered chair facing Nora's bed, determined to keep vigil for at least another hour.

It had been a bad day for Nora. Apart from multiple episodes of shortness of breath, she had coughed up even more blood than usual and was visibly weaker. Brooke was glad Diana was gone and didn't have to bear witness.

"Don't go. Please. You mustn't..." Nora's voice trailed off and Brooke put her book down.

Nora was agitated, her head whipping side to side, her fingers restless on the covers. Brooke rose halfway from the chair. Should she wake her? She seemed in such emotional distress. On the other hand, Nora needed the rest.

"Mary! Come back!"

Nora thrashed and Brooke sprang into action. She knelt by the bed and lightly took Nora's hand. Tears streamed down the older woman's face. What could be causing her such consternation? Who was Mary? Did this have anything to do with Nora's comment about having so much to heal with Diana?

Brooke's touch seemed to calm Nora. Her breathing steadied and her features relaxed. Brooke wished she could dry Nora's tears. Instead, she remained as she was, afraid that any further movement would wake her.

Eventually, Nora's grip eased and Brooke liberated her hand. This was a good thing, as her fifty-year-old knees were rebelling. She stood and returned to her vigil.

Although the book was open in front of her, she had no idea what she was reading. The more time she spent with Nora, the more questions she had. Who was Nora, really? What kind of personal life had she lived? Had she ever married? Was she a widow? Why had she been estranged from Diana?

"You idolized this woman, and all this time, you knew so little about her." Well, maybe now she would learn about the personal side of Dr. Nora Lindstrom.

🖎🖎

"Am I catching you at a bad time?" Diana asked. "Is this too late for you?"

Brooke propped herself up against the headboard. "Ten o'clock? Never. I'm usually up until midnight. I was just lying here reading."

"The same book you were reading the other day?"

"No. I finished that one."

"So, what's this one? Anything good?"

"*The Stranger You Seek*, by Amanda Kyle Williams. Edgy and scary good."

"You can read something that gives you the heebie-jeebies right before bed?"

She laughed. "Don't tell me you're afraid of the dark and things that go bump in the night?"

"Are you kidding? I read scientific journals at bedtime. It doesn't get any scarier than that."

"Clearly you lead a life of adventure."

"Clearly."

She wrestled with her innate curiosity. Diana technically qualified as a client by virtue of her status as Nora's proxy. As such, Brooke should keep all of her interactions professional. Still, Diana was an enigma and she found herself wanting to know more about her.

"Speaking of science, can I ask what drew you to neuroscience?" *There. That was a safe question, right?*

"I knew from the time I was eight that I wanted to be a scientist. Aunt Nora would always say things like, 'I wonder what would happen if we mixed X with Y? What do you think, Diana?' And of course, that would be the beginning of a super cool lesson in physics, or chemistry, or whatever."

There it was again, that mixture of love, awe, and hurt in Diana's voice when she spoke of childhood memories involving Nora. *Tread carefully.* "So why the specialty in neuroscience, in particular?"

"That's a long story. But the short version is that my best friend from college got hit by a car while riding her bicycle on campus. The result was a traumatic head injury that affected her short-term memory, her ability to process speech, and her moods. It also left her to suffer with focal epilepsy—seizures during which she was fully conscious and aware, but unable to respond."

"That's horrible."

"The doctors tried all kinds of seizure medications, but none of them worked perfectly for her. She was twenty years old and she felt like her life was over." Diana's voice cracked with emotion.

"Oh, my God. I can't imagine."

"I promised her that I would dedicate my life to helping people like her. That meant becoming a neuroscientist. Teaching flowed out of that, and earlier this summer I finally was able to get a grant from the National Institutes of Health to research how these seizures propagate so that we can locate the originating foci and learn how to surgically remove them. There, that's the CliffsNotes version."

"That's amazing. So, if you're successful, it would mean that a patient eventually could be cured of epilepsy and seizure free?"

"That's my goal."

"I hope you get there."

"Me too."

She wanted to ask more about Diana's friend, like where she was now, but the time didn't seem right.

"Anyway, that's more than enough about me. How was Aunt Nora today?"

How should she answer that? Should she share with Diana the things she'd heard Nora say in her sleep? That felt like a violation of Nora's privacy.

"Brooke? Is everything okay?"

She chided herself for taking too long to answer. "Yes. Of course. Nora's fine. She's sleeping comfortably at the moment. We didn't have time to discuss it this morning before you left. She had a bit of a rocky night last night; you know, she was up a few times, restless. She had an equally rocky day today, but she managed to get a good long nap for one stretch and she seemed better for it." *There. That's the truth.*

"I'm sorry."

"For what?"

"That you likely got shortchanged on your sleep last night too."

She raised an eyebrow. Most people didn't think of the toll a night like that took on the caregiver. "It's okay. That's what I'm here for."

"Did you get a nap today?"

The question caught her off-guard. "Me?"

"Yes, you."

"No."

"In that case, I hope you get a full night's rest tonight." Diana's voice was softer.

"I'm sure I'll be fine."

"Can I call again tomorrow night?"

"Of course. You can call anytime to check up on Nora."

"By the way," Diana said, "there should be a technician coming out tomorrow morning."

"Really? For what?"

"I ordered internet for you."

"You did?"

"Yeah. After all, what are you going to do all day after you finish your book?"

"Thank you, Diana. That was incredibly thoughtful."

"You're welcome. Sleep well, Brooke."

"You too."

She sat still for a long time after the call ended. *Who are you, Diana Lindstrom? You're so...complicated.*

Diana gathered up her laptop and papers, loaded them into her computer bag, and exited the conference room. She knew she should be excited for the semester, a new crop of graduate students, and the promise of new and potentially groundbreaking research. But all she could think about was Aunt Nora.

Brooke's report last night was alarming. Diana knew Aunt Nora would have some good days and some bad, but it sounded as though the day went straight downhill after she'd left for home yesterday.

Her mind was filled with questions. Was Aunt Nora having a better day today? How did she and Brooke fare throughout the night? What were they doing now?

"Hey, Professor Lindstrom. You look particularly fetching today. How was your summer? Do anything fun? You didn't run off and find that someone special, did you? I'd be crushed if you did."

Diana never broke stride and barely looked at her colleague. Rosemary Neufeld was about as subtle as a bear at a landfill. Diana had dated her...so briefly she could've blinked and missed it.

Bethany had just left, along with half their savings, the car, and the house. Diana had been feeling low. Rosemary's fawning seemed like the antidote to her bruised ego and lack of self-esteem. She knew it was a mistake even before they arrived at the restaurant for dinner.

Four years later, she still was paying for that one night's bad judgment and moment of weakness.

"I landed an NIH R01 grant."

Rosemary stopped walking and whistled. "Look at you, big shot! That's impressive. Are you still thinking you're going to figure out how to surgically remove seizure foci?" Rosemary waved her hands outward. "I can see it now—Dr. Diana Lindstrom, the woman who single-handedly brought focal epilepsy to its knees."

"Very funny. As you know, there are many teams working to determine the dynamics of these seizures. It won't be just me. It will be a team effort."

"Speaking of which... Have you picked your research team yet? I can be very useful."

"Thanks, but I'm all filled up." Diana kept moving and escaped around the corner and into her office, where she closed the door and leaned against it. *Note to self, finish putting together the research team ASAP.*

CHAPTER SEVEN

B rooke closed the door behind the technician who'd just installed Wi-Fi in Nora's house. When she had handed him her credit card, he informed her that the invoice already had been taken care of, and the billing was set up in Diana's name.

"You certainly are efficient, Dr. Lindstrom."

The timing for the installation worked out perfectly, as Brooke had put Nora back in bed for a rest shortly before the technician arrived. Now she opened the bedroom door a crack and peeked inside.

"I'm awake."

"Did you have a good nap?"

"I did."

"Can I get you anything?"

"I wouldn't turn down a glass of water."

Brooke collected the empty water bottle from the night table, filled it with fresh water from the refrigerator, and returned. She grabbed a couple of pillows, helped Nora into a more comfortable position, and then handed her the water bottle.

"Oh, that's good. Whets the whistle, and a plastic water bottle is a much better idea than a glass. Good thinking."

"Thanks. How about some food?"

Nora shook her head.

"Do you want to get up?"

"Not just yet. Come. Pull up a chair and sit with me."

Brooke made sure she sat at an angle that made it easy for Nora to see her without having to turn her head. "Can I ask you something?"

"Seems everyone's got questions these days. Well, I've got nothing but time." Nora winked. "What do you want to know?"

"Everything," she answered honestly.

Nora chuckled. "We don't have *that* much time. Narrow it down a bit and I'll see what I can do."

She chewed on her lower lip. If she started by asking about something as clearly emotionally fraught and personal as Nora's lengthy absence from Diana's life or who this Mary person was, Nora might shut down. *I wouldn't blame her.*

"What brought you to Dana-Farber?"

"That's easy. Sid."

"Sid? As in Sidney Farber?"

"The same." Nora's gaze took on a faraway look. "He wrote this magnificent paper in 1948, for which he was excoriated. But I found his research and hypothesis fascinating. I believed he really was on to something. I wrote him a letter. That was the beginning of a beautiful friendship. We exchanged research notes and ideas for years. He asked me many times to come and work with him. Many times, I refused."

"What made you change your mind?"

Nora's smile turned into a pained frown, making Brooke sorry she'd asked the question.

"I lost a patient—someone I'd grown to care about over the years—and I realized that I needed to come home and get a fresh start."

"What year was that?"

"1972, the year Diana was born, and the year before Sid passed away. It was ironic, really. He was the reason I came, and then he was gone. He had a massive heart attack and died at his desk."

"That's horrible."

"Honestly, I can't imagine him dying any other way. He was driven by his work and helping the children." She took another pull from the water bottle. Her voice was growing hoarse.

"Am I tiring you out?"

"No. I'm enjoying the trip down memory lane. It's been forever since I've thought about these things."

"You mentioned Diana being born in 1972."

"She was a beautiful baby—had a shock of light blond hair and the greenest eyes I'd ever seen. They didn't really turn hazel until later. I held her when she was just hours old."

The love in Nora's eyes melted Brooke's heart. "She told me you were the reason she became a scientist. You got her excited about learning by coming up with experiments for the two of you to do."

"That's right. She was whip-smart and inquisitive. If I showed her once how to do something, she could replicate it on her own. Remarkable, really. I knew she was destined for great things."

Brooke saw her opening. "I hope I'm not overstepping. Diana also told me you left when she was ten and she never heard from you again. I can see how much you care for her. I can't imagine you simply disappearing like that without good reason."

Nora's brow creased; a pained expression was etched in her eyes and in the lines around her mouth. "She told you that?"

Brooke knew she needed to tread carefully. "Grudgingly, and then only because I was shocked that she was unaware of your accomplishments and professional work."

"What else did she tell you?"

"Nothing. She said she didn't have any answers."

"Mmm."

"If I might say so, even if you never share with me, I think it would mean a lot to Diana if she understood what happened."

Nora closed her eyes and inhaled deeply. The rattle in her chest was pronounced. When she opened her eyes again, they held a profound sadness. "I promised her an explanation and I intend to give it to her when she returns this weekend."

"That's great. I really think it will help her. She seems so..."

"Lost," Nora supplied.

"Yes."

"On some level, she's still that hurt little girl. She seems to have created a wall around her heart."

Brooke nodded. It was an apt observation. "Maybe so, but I think she has a hard time maintaining that distance where you're concerned."

"I know, and I fear all of this is causing her great pain. Perhaps I was wrong to have Charles reach out to her. Perhaps—"

"No. If I know one thing, it's that she'll look back and treasure the time she has left with you."

"Oh, dear. I certainly hope you're right."

"Just be honest with her. I think she needs to know the truth, whatever that is."

Tears formed on Nora's lashes. "Perhaps so." Her eyelids began to droop. "Perhaps so."

Brooke rose, removed the extra pillows, and pulled the blanket higher so that Nora's shoulders were covered. "Sweet dreams, sweet Nora." She crept out of the room, leaving the door open so that she could hear in case Nora needed her.

She wandered over to the sliding glass doors and gazed out at the water. In just a few short days, she'd become completely drawn into Nora's world, and to the mystery that was the Lindstrom family history.

That reminded her, she should text Diana and thank her for the Wi-Fi. She pulled out her phone. *"Many thanks for the access to the outside world. The technician was great. Very efficient. You didn't have to pay for that, you know."* She hit send and watched the blinking cursor. She didn't have to wait long.

"You're very welcome. Hey, we're still prepping for the start of the semester, no students yet. Would it be okay if I showed up tomorrow?"

She smiled. *"You bet! Nora will be so excited."* She hit send and then thought of something else she should've said. *"BTW, you never need to ask. You know that, right???"*

"Well, I wouldn't want to be in the way..."

"Never."

"Okay, then. See you both tomorrow. Should be there shortly after lunch."

"Great. See you then."

She stowed the phone in her back pocket, her heart unaccountably lighter.

Nora tried to breathe deeply and organize her thoughts. It was a wonderful surprise to have Diana back days ahead of schedule and yet, she hadn't anticipated needing to entertain Diana's question about her absence this soon.

She leaned forward and allowed Diana to fuss with the pillow that supported her back. She'd relocated from the bed to the couch. If they were going to have this discussion, Nora would be damned if it was going to be while she lay in bed like an invalid.

"Is that better?"

"Fine, thank you."

"Are you sure you're comfortable enough?"

"Positive."

"Can I get you anything else?"

Nora stilled Diana's busy hands. "I've got everything I need. Brooke and I have fallen into a very comfortable routine these past few days. She helped me shower before you arrived, made me lunch, and got me all settled."

"Why isn't she here?" Diana moved away and sat in the chair.

"I asked her to give us this time alone. She only snuck out the back way when we heard your car pull up." Nora studied Diana's face. There was something indefinable in her expression whenever the topic turned to Brooke. *Interesting.*

"I assure you, she's doing a fabulous job. I couldn't ask for a better nurse or companion."

"I'm sure she is. I'm glad."

"She's a lovely woman, isn't she?"

A blush crept up Diana's neck and stained her cheeks red. "Mm-hmm."

Nora cocked her head to the side. *Well now. Could it be? No time for that at the present, old girl.* Right now, while she had the energy, she needed to address the skeleton in the closet.

She sucked in a breath that resulted in a coughing jag and did nothing to calm her nerves. "You asked me a question when last you were here. I answered but not in sufficient detail to satisfy the hurt you carry within."

"Okay." Diana crossed her arms. "I'm listening."

She tried to draw in another deep breath. Where had all the air in the room gone? She chanced a glance at Diana. *She deserves to know.*

"In 1977, I was invited by a friend to be part of a contingent of fourteen individuals who attended a historic meeting in the Roosevelt Room of the White House."

"Wow! You've been to the White House?"

"Yes."

"Impressive."

"I thought so too, at the time. The press even covered the event, which came as a complete surprise to me. I assumed the gathering was a private affair." Nora took a sip of water. "The meeting was more symbolic than anything else, but I was proud to have been a part of it."

"What does that have to do with—"

Nora held up a hand. "I'm getting to that. None of this is easy for me. Please, let me tell the story my own way."

"I'm sorry."

Diana reminded Nora of a contrite child. "As I was saying, this meeting occurred in 1977, when you were five. Five years later, I was present at a party your grandfather threw for some old friends of his that were visiting from Washington, D.C. Bill particularly wanted me to meet one man—a photojournalist of some repute."

She folded her hands in her lap to keep them from shaking at the memory of events she had thought long past and buried. "I exchanged pleasantries with him and went on my way to mingle with the other guests. He stared at me for the better part of the evening, to the point where I felt terribly uncomfortable."

"What did you do?"

"I left." She took another sip of water. "Several days later, I was back in Boston when I received a call from Bill. It was unusual for us to speak that often, and more unusual still for your grandfather to reach out to me at work. He asked me to return to New York for the following weekend. I asked him if everything was all right—specifically, if you were all right. You were the apple of my eye, Diana. If anything had happened to you…" She shook her head. "I couldn't have borne it." She paused to gather herself.

"Bill assured me you were fine and that I would be able to see you if I came."

"What did you do?"

"What did I do? Why, I went, of course." She cleared her throat. The hoarseness was back, but she was determined to push through it.

"I arrived a little after lunchtime on Saturday." She smiled at Diana, picturing the little girl she'd been back then. "I don't know if you remember, but whenever I would come to visit, I would bring you a brand-new Kennedy half dollar."

Diana's face lit up. "I still have them."

"You do?"

"Yes. I keep them in my safe-deposit box."

She put trembling fingers to her lips. Diana had held onto the keepsakes after all. "I'm glad."

"They were a piece of my relationship with you, Aunt Nora. I never planned to part with them."

"If you did, I wouldn't blame you. I have no idea what they're worth in today's dollars, but I imagine it would be quite a bit." Diana shrugged, and Nora pushed onward with the story.

"In any event, that day when I arrived, you were busy riding your bike, so I didn't see you right away. Bill came out to meet me as I got out of the car. I could tell by the look on his face that this wasn't going to be a happy occasion."

Diana leaned forward. "I remember that day. I had asked my mother to let me know when you got there, but she didn't."

"I'm not surprised. Your parents came outside and stood behind your grandfather. He had a manila envelope in his hand." In her mind's eye, Nora still could see the tableau.

"Are you all right?"

"What?"

Diana knelt in front of her. "You're crying."

"I am?" She brushed her fingers across her cheek. They came away wet. She accepted the tissue Diana handed her and blotted her eyes.

"Maybe we should stop," Diana said.

Nora patted her hand. "No. I need to finish this. I'll be fine."

Diana wasn't mollified. She remained rooted to the spot.

"Anyway, your grandfather waved that envelope in front of my face. He asked me if I knew what it was. I told him of course I didn't." She balled up the tissue in her fist. "He opened the envelope and slid something out of it. It was a picture." She swallowed hard and stared off into the distance.

"Bill stuck it under my nose. It was so close I had to back up to see it." She wiped away another tear. "The picture was of me at that

White House meeting from five years earlier—the gathering I'd naively thought was private. I couldn't believe it."

"What did that have to do with anything?"

"That man from the party the previous week was the one who'd taken the picture. He told your grandfather he knew I'd looked familiar to him, so he went back and searched through batches of photographs from old assignments until he came upon this photograph. Then he sent it to Bill."

"Why was that a problem?" Diana grabbed another tissue and handed it to her.

Finally, she looked directly at Diana. This was something she'd never intended to discuss, something she'd never wanted to reveal. People of her generation simply didn't speak of it. And yet, surely of anyone, Diana would be sympathetic.

"The historic event at the White House was the first time ever a group of gay men and lesbians had been invited to meet with a representative of the president of the United States."

Nora waited and watched as a series of emotions passed across Diana's face.

"I don't understand."

Nora sighed. *Spell it out, old girl. Be brave.*

"Bill asked me point-blank if I had been at that meeting with *those* people. I told him I had. He asked me if I was with them. I said I was. Then he asked me if I was…" Her voice was practically a whisper. "…one of those sexual deviates."

Diana gasped. "That's what Grandpa called them?"

She nodded. "His tone of voice was so dismissive. Something within me snapped. I told him that if by that he meant that I was a lesbian, then yes, I was." She couldn't bear to look at Diana now. Instead, she gazed out the window at a cloud as it drifted by.

"He said he wouldn't have some sick, twisted queer hanging around his granddaughter, and he forbade me ever to see you again." Her voice broke on a sob. She fought for breath, determined to finish this once and for all.

"That was when you rode up and jumped off your bike. You grabbed me around the legs as Bill shoved me back toward the car. I-I didn't want to make a scene. I didn't want you to be hurt."

"It's okay," Diana said. She took her hand.

"I bent down and told you I loved you, and that you'd always find me in your heart. Your father pried you off my pant leg. You wouldn't let go." She couldn't see through her tears. "I couldn't bear to see your heart breaking like that, even as my own heart broke. And that was the last time you saw me."

She struggled for air.

"It's okay now. Relax, Aunt Nora. Breathe. Please, just breathe."

"I tried," she said. "As God is my witness, I tried to get them to change their minds—to let me see you. I sent letters and cards, but nothing worked. I'm sorry, Diana. I'm so, so sorry."

"Shh. It's all right, Aunt Nora. It's all right."

But Nora knew the truth. It wasn't all right. It never had been, and she could never make it so.

Diana shifted slightly. Her left arm was falling asleep where Aunt Nora's bony shoulder blade rested against it. She didn't dare move, though, lest she wake her.

Aunt Nora was a lesbian. Correction. Aunt Nora was a loving, doting great-aunt, banished by her family and cut out like a cancer simply because she preferred women.

Diana swallowed around the lump in her throat. Poor Aunt Nora. What must it have been like for her all those years ago? By Diana's calculation, Aunt Nora would've been sixty-four when that confrontation took place. How long had she known she was a lesbian? She'd been at that White House meeting in 1977, so certainly she'd known then. But surely she must've had a life before that?

As much as Diana wanted to ask all of these questions out loud, she'd seen how hard it had been for Aunt Nora even to say as much as she already had. As long as she lived, she never would forget Aunt Nora's anguished expression and the fear and shame that practically radiated from every pore of her being.

With her free hand, she fished her phone out of her pocket. She clicked on the Google app and typed with her thumb. *White House meeting 1977 lesbian.* She clicked on the first entry. "White House Meeting of 1977." She read the 2007 press release celebrating the thirtieth anniversary of the historic meeting, including quotes from

Midge Costanza, the aide to President Carter who had arranged the meeting.

When she finished reading, she clicked on the accompanying image. A large group of mostly men and a sprinkling of women sat around a massive rectangular table. She imagined the woman at the near end was Midge Constanza. She tried to enlarge the image to see the other participants. Would she recognize Aunt Nora among the faces? Was that her, third from the right? It was impossible to tell from the thumbnail-sized picture. She followed a link to more images, but the link was broken.

Nora stirred, and Diana quickly closed down the screen.

"Goodness. I'm so sorry. I didn't mean to fall asleep on you. Have I been out long?" Nora struggled to sit up.

"Let me help you." She gently lifted Nora so she was sitting upright against the back of the couch. She searched her face. "Are you all right? Can I get you something? Water? Food?"

"Not necessary." Nora averted her eyes. "I can only imagine what you must think of me now."

She measured her words. "I think you must have been a very courageous woman at a time when it wasn't easy to be different."

"I wasn't courageous. I simply told the truth. I'd learned long ago the cost of keeping secrets. That day I learned the cost of honesty. In the end, it turned out the price was the same."

What does she mean by that?

"Maybe I will take that drink of water, after all."

"Of course." Diana jumped up and refilled Nora's water bottle. She looked somehow smaller and frailer.

"Thank you."

"You're welcome."

They were like polite strangers. It was as if the revelations of a few hours ago had never happened.

Diana chewed her lip. Should she ask? *There might never be a better opportunity.* "I do have one question. I asked you this before, but you didn't really answer me."

Nora's eyes flashed briefly. "I imagine there's far more than one question I haven't answered. But I think one more answer might be all I have the strength for."

Her brows knit together. She needed to phrase the question carefully. The last thing she wanted was to be confrontational, but she had to know... "Why didn't you defy them?"

"Who? Your parents and my brother?"

She nodded. "I know you said they were my parents and my grandfather and it was their right to forbid you to see me, but..."

"I tried many times to change their minds in letters and phone calls. Finally, when none of that made a difference, I confronted them in person."

"What happened?"

"It was your eleventh birthday and they were having a party for you in the backyard. I showed up at the door with a present and demanded to see you. Your father blocked the doorway. I said I wasn't leaving without talking to you.

"Your grandfather came out to see what the commotion was. He grabbed me by the arm and led me to his car. He picked up a large, flat envelope off the passenger seat and waved it under my nose. He must've been expecting me to show up.

"When my eyes focused on the envelope, I could see it was addressed to my employers. I could just imagine what was inside." She cleared her throat and sipped the water. "Bill told me that if I ever tried to contact you again, even by smoke signal, he would send that package to my bosses."

Finally, Aunt Nora made eye contact with her. "It would've been the end of my career. All my hard work, my reputation, all that I could've done for the children, would've been wiped out in an instant. My brother knew that. He knew I'd never risk it. I couldn't." Her voice broke, and she held her head in her hands.

Diana wrapped an arm around her shoulders and lifted her chin so they were eye-to-eye. "I'm so sorry."

"I'm the one who's sorry, Diana. I wish I could've been stronger. I wish I'd stood up to him."

"I understand now why you didn't. It's okay."

Nora shook her head. "Nothing about this will ever be okay."

Listening to her gasp for air, Diana had to agree.

CHAPTER EIGHT

B rooke slid open the glass doors and listened. She hoped she'd been gone long enough to give Nora and Diana time to resolve Diana's questions. She cocked her head to the side. The only sounds were the grandfather clock ticking off the seconds and Nora's labored breathing. She moved farther into the cottage.

Diana was standing at the window, lost in thought. She looked at once pensive and sad. Brooke came alongside her and placed a soothing hand on her shoulder. "Are you okay?" she asked in a voice barely above a whisper.

Diana turned toward her. "I will be."

"Did you get the answers you needed?"

"I got the truth."

Interesting phraseology. "I'm here for you if you want to talk. I've been told I'm an excellent sounding board."

"I can believe that."

Diana's eyes were a vivid shade of green today. Belatedly, Brooke realized three things: her hand still rested on Diana's shoulder, she was staring, and they were in the middle of an awkward silence.

She dropped her hand to her side. "Does Nora need anything? How long has she been asleep?"

"Which time?" Diana shoved her hands in her pockets. "She dropped off for about an hour after our conversation. This may sound crazy, but honestly, I think it took so much out of her emotionally that her physical body simply shut itself down for a while."

"That makes sense."

"She drank some water when she woke up, but she wasn't interested in food." Diana sighed. "I tried."

"I know." She resisted the urge to touch Diana again. Another awkward silence ensued. Finally, she said, "I'm going to make an offer, and I hope you'll take me up on it."

Diana took her hands out of her pockets and crossed her arms, effectively closing herself off. Brooke pushed ahead anyway.

"You're planning to be here every weekend, right?"

"Yes."

"It's ridiculous for you to keep paying to stay at a bed and breakfast."

"Aunt Nora only has one spare bedroom—yours."

"I know. I was going to say, you're more than welcome to stay at my place." Diana stiffened, and Brooke rushed on. "I'll be here with Nora, so it's just unused space now. It makes perfect sense."

"Or I could give you a breather. You're going to need days off. I'll be here. I could stay with Aunt Nora and you can go back to your place for the weekend."

As tempting as the offer was, Brooke already had experienced Nora's nights. That wasn't a good option. "How about if we compromise? You stay at my place, we all can eat dinners together here, I'll take the overnight shift, and you can spell me for a bit on Saturdays?"

"Sold."

⊰⊱

Diana stood back as Brooke strode through her place, flipping on light switches as she went. "There's coffee in the cabinet, orange juice in the fridge, and granola in the pantry. What's mine is yours, so make yourself at home. The bed is pretty comfy. If you want a softer pillow, there's one in the linen closet. Extra blankets in there too."

"I'm sure whatever you've got will be fine." Diana trailed behind. So far, she hadn't noticed any personal touches. Then again, this was just a rental, so maybe Brooke's things were in storage somewhere, or maybe she still owned a place in Boston. Diana made a mental note to ask later.

In truth, she was starting to compile a rather long mental list of things she wanted to know about Brooke, starting with whether or not she was gay. Several times, she caught Brooke's gaze lingering, and the frequent soothing touches hadn't escaped her notice either. The latter Diana attributed to Brooke's compassionate personality. Then there were the double entendres. They didn't seem to be intentional, but what if they were a subconscious manifestation of her true feelings?

Diana also had an equally lengthy list of things she didn't want to examine too closely, like why her skin tingled whenever Brooke touched her, or why it mattered to her so much whether or not Brooke was gay. Brooke was here to do a job, and Diana would do well to remember and focus on that.

"…over here."

She tuned back in. Brooke was looking at her quizzically. Clearly, she had missed something that required her input. "I'm sorry. What did you say?"

Brooke stopped walking. "I'm the one who's sorry. I'm babbling. I'd tune myself out too."

"I wasn't…" She didn't finish the sentence. *I wasn't tuning you out—quite the contrary.* No, that was something she had no intention of admitting out loud.

"Anyway," Brooke said, "make yourself at home. I'll just leave you to it."

"Thank you. This is incredibly generous." She followed Brooke back to the front door.

"Easy stuff. I hope you sleep well."

"See you in the morning?"

"You know where I'll be." Brooke waved as she got into her car.

Alone in the house, Diana took her time wandering from room to room. Brooke's spicy scent lingered in the air. She inhaled deeply. *Not helpful.* She grabbed her bag off the living room floor, carried it into the lone bedroom, and set it down on the cedar chest at the foot of the bed.

She rummaged through the bag for her boxers and T-shirt, changed her clothes, snapped up her toilet kit, and got ready for bed.

Brooke had changed the sheets, but that did nothing to stop Diana's mind from wandering to places it had no business going.

Sleep was sure to be a long time coming. She pulled the covers up to her chin and prayed that it eventually would take her.

∾⃝↝

Nora lay awake staring at the ceiling, the past very much present in her thoughts. For years, she'd told herself that what happened back then could not be changed, and therefore didn't bear thinking about. She'd done her best to watch out for Diana, keeping tabs on her from afar, easing her path from the safety of the shadows when possible, and resigning herself to the truth that this was the way it had to be.

When she retired and the threat of exposure no longer held sway over her, she convinced herself that, as an adult now, if Diana wanted to find her, she would've done so. It wasn't her place to reappear out of nowhere. She never suspected that by the time Diana reached true adulthood, she already believed Nora was dead. If she had known that…

"So many regrets, old girl. It doesn't do to dwell on it." She shifted in an effort to ease the heaviness in her chest, but she knew the truth—the shortness of breath, the hoarseness, the rattle, the pain in her bones—the end was coming for her, and soon.

The real question was what she could do in the time she had remaining that could heal the deep wounds Diana carried within. She understood why her great-niece avoided lasting, meaningful attachments. She'd been abandoned too many times—first by her, then by Robert and Edwina, and most recently by that Bethany person, who obviously wasn't the right woman for her anyway.

Her mind alit on Diana's body language whenever the topic turned to Brooke. Nora might be old, but she still had eyes. She searched her memory. Had she ever seen Brooke with anyone? She was next to positive Brooke didn't have a husband, nor did she wear anybody's ring. Nora didn't remember her ever talking about going steady with anyone.

"You're an old woman. You can get away with asking questions others never would dare to ask." Tomorrow. Tomorrow Nora would probe Brooke on the subject.

∾⃝↝

"Diana should be here any second."

"Mm-hmm." Brooke finished off her bowl of yogurt and granola just as Nora's toast popped up in the toaster.

"Did I hear her say she would be staying at your place?"

"I thought it made more sense for her to take advantage of my empty house instead of paying to stay at a bed and breakfast."

"That was very thoughtful of you."

Brooke shrugged. "It's not like I'm there. She can have her privacy and a home-away-from-home."

"I'm sure she'd feel at home even if you were in it."

Her hand paused in the middle of buttering Nora's toast. *That was an odd thing to say.* "I don't know about that."

"She likes you. I can tell."

Brooke placed the plate in front of Nora. "I hope she thinks I'm doing a good job."

"I don't mean that. I mean, I think she's fond of you."

"She hardly knows me."

"You don't need to know someone a long time to know how you feel about them."

She turned away and busied herself washing her bowl. *Keep the conversation neutral.* "Well, I think she's very nice too."

"Mm-hmm."

Something about Nora's tone triggered alarm bells in her head. Where in the world was Nora going with this? If she didn't know any better…

"I don't remember ever hearing you mention a husband or boyfriend, and I'm sure I would've recalled if you'd introduced me to one."

Oh, boy. She kept her back to Nora and wiped the already-cleaned counter a second time.

"Is there a lucky fella in your life?"

There it was. The saving grace was that the question required only a simple yes or no. "No."

The tea kettle whistled, and she poured the hot water over Nora's tea bag and brought it to her.

"Thank you, dear." Nora patted the seat next to her. "Sit, please."

Reluctantly, she did as she was asked. Maybe she could redirect the attention away from herself and satisfy her own curiosity. "How about you? Were you married?" She kept her tone lighthearted.

"Heavens no. Who would have me?"

"Are you kidding me? You're the great Dr. Nora Lindstrom. Not only that, but you were a real looker. I bet the guys were lined up around the block for you."

Nora shook her head. "Not so I ever noticed."

"Surely there must've been someone?"

A shadow fell across Nora's features. Just as quickly, it disappeared. "I just wasn't the marrying kind, I guess." She blew on her tea.

Not the marrying kind...would that have been code for someone who was gay in Nora's era? Could this be where Mary came in? She regarded Nora critically. She supposed it was possible...

"So, if there isn't a man, is there a woman?"

"What?" Brooke was so shocked by the directness of the question, she was certain she must've misunderstood.

"Are you gay?"

She blinked. No, there was no misunderstanding. She'd never lied about her sexuality; she wasn't about to start now. "Yes."

She searched Nora's face. The revelation didn't seem to offend her in any way. In fact, it appeared as if the news pleased her.

"Do you have a girlfriend?"

Brooke's eyes opened wider. What had happened to reserved, polite Nora Lindstrom, and who was this woman sitting in her kitchen? "Not for a long time."

Mercifully, at that moment Diana appeared in the doorway. "Hi."

"Hi," Brooke answered, perhaps a tad too eagerly. She jumped up. "We were just finishing breakfast. If it's all right with you, I've got a few errands to run this morning. I should be back by mid-afternoon."

"No problem," Diana said. "By the time you get back, Aunt Nora and I will have conquered today's crossword puzzle."

"I bet you're right."

She escaped to her bedroom, changed clothes, snatched the car keys off the dresser, and made a hasty exit. She didn't want to risk Nora asking any more personal questions, especially in Diana's presence, and she didn't want to examine too closely why that bothered her so much.

తఃసౌ

Diana and Nora watched Brooke leave. "Was it something I said?" Diana asked in jest.

"More likely something I said," Nora replied.

She regarded her curiously. "You haven't scared her off, have you?"

"I certainly hope not."

She stared a minute longer. Clearly, something had transpired between Aunt Nora and Brooke before she arrived. "Is everything okay?"

"Fine."

"Right." What else was there to say?

"If you're serious about helping me with that crossword puzzle, we'd better get started, hadn't we?"

Nora motored over to the couch and Diana assisted her with the transfer. "Pen or pencil?"

"What kind of question is that? Pen. Always a pen. One must approach a puzzle with confidence."

They worked through the puzzle together with several breaks. Nora fell asleep occasionally, and twice her body was wracked by coughing spasms.

She was asleep now. She appeared to be deteriorating right before Diana's eyes. Did Brooke think so too? Diana wished she were here. She was so much better at this caretaking thing. It wasn't simply that she was a nurse either. Diana admired her compassionate nature, patience, and calming presence, all qualities she knew she lacked.

"Diana?"

She half-rose from the chair. "Yes? Do you need something? Water? Food?"

"Relax, dear. I don't need anything from you at the moment. Thank you for offering, though." Nora adjusted her position so that she was sitting up higher on the couch. "Actually, I have a question for you."

Diana sat forward. The hoarseness in Aunt Nora's voice was making it hard to hear her. "I'm listening." She also was trying to decipher the expression on her face.

"Were you aware that Brooke is gay?"

Her pulse jumped. "Was I...?"

Nora's lips curled up in a mischievous grin. "Did you know or was that a happy coincidence?"

She knew her mouth must be hanging open, but she couldn't help it. There it was—confirmation that Brooke was gay. But how could Aunt Nora be so sure?

"Judging by the look on your face, I'll take that as a no. She is, you know."

"H-how..." She cleared her throat and tried to rein in her galloping pulse. "What's your source?"

Nora laughed. "How very scientifically put. Always searching for reliable data. Good for you."

"Well?"

"Brooke told me, of course."

"She..."

Nora waved a hand. "She didn't just blurt it out, naturally. I inquired directly."

"You asked her point-blank?" She ran her finger under the collar of her polo shirt as heat radiated up from her chest to her neck and beyond.

"I did."

"You seem awfully pleased with yourself."

"Wouldn't you be?"

Diana sat back. Brooke was a lesbian. She'd confirmed it to Aunt Nora. Brooke definitely was a lesbian. "Huh."

"What was that, dear?"

She hadn't realized she'd uttered that out loud. "That explains why she shot out of here like her hair was on fire. You put her through an inquisition."

Nora laughed. "I told you it was something I said."

"You did." She couldn't fault her for that. She frowned, thinking about how uncomfortable Brooke had been earlier.

"Oh, stop worrying so much. She'll be fine."

"Am I that transparent?"

"Yep. Written all over your face."

She jumped up to pace. "I didn't know Brooke was a lesbian, to answer your question." She pivoted and walked in the other direction. "I don't think that was such a good idea, Aunt Nora. What if you offended or embarrassed her?"

"What if I didn't?"

She reversed direction again. "I don't know. She sure seemed uncomfortable to me."

"Stop fretting."

"Easy for you to say. You do remember that she's your primary caregiver, right?"

"I do. Please, Diana. Sit back down. You're making me dizzy."

Reluctantly, she did as she was told.

"She's really quite fetching, don't you think?" Nora finally asked.

"What?" Diana felt her face flush again. "I don't know."

"You don't? I have a hard time believing that. You have eyes, don't you?"

She tried to hold onto a thought as hundreds of them flitted through her mind. "Did you tell her you were…"

"Like you two? Heavens, no."

"Did you tell her I was?"

"No. Though I do think you should ask her out."

"I should…"

"Ask her out on a date. She's single, you know."

She held her head in her hands. This couldn't be happening. She wasn't having this discussion with her hundred-year-old great-aunt. "Aunt Nora…"

"What, dear? She's single. You're single. She's a looker and a catch. Such a lovely woman. I think you'd make the perfect, dashing couple."

She couldn't believe her ears. "Where is all this coming from? Yesterday, you could barely look me in the eye and tell me about yourself. Now you're giving advice to the lovelorn."

"That was different. That was about me. This is about you. I thought women your age were more open these days?"

She shook her head. "Please, whatever you do, I beg you, don't have this same discussion with Brooke. You've already done more than enough."

"I'm sorry if I've embarrassed you, dear. That was never my intention. I just want to see you enjoy yourself. Seeing you in love would make me happy. You deserve that, Diana, whether you believe it or not."

At that moment, Diana's phone buzzed, indicating an incoming text. Her heart skipped a beat as she read.

"Sorry, I'm running a little bit later than I expected. I stopped at the market to pick us all up dinner. Any special requests?"

Well, at least she knew Brooke was coming back.

CHAPTER NINE

N ora caught herself grinning and adjusted her expression. She would need to be mindful not to overplay her hand. Diana sat on one side of her, Brooke on the other. Neither of them had made discernable eye contact with the other throughout the entire dinner, but she could feel the shift in the air.

"Pass the salt, please."

"Of course."

"This is a wonderful dish," she ventured. Clearly, it would be up to her to break the awkwardness. "Wherever did you learn to cook, Brooke?"

"Believe it or not, it was my father who was the chef in our family. My mother saw meals as a necessary evil. My father believed the perfectly prepared meal was tantamount to a sure invitation to Heaven."

"This is very good. Thank you for cooking," Diana added. "I'm with your mother. I cook because I have to sustain myself, not because I enjoy it."

"Were you much of a cook, Nora?"

"Not really. I usually ate at my desk while catching up on reading journals or the latest studies."

Diana speared a cube of sweet potato with her fork and corralled a piece of chicken, a sliver of red pepper, and a strand of pickled onion to go with it. "Truly, this dish is amazing."

"I can't take the credit for it. It's a *New York Times* recipe. I just followed the directions."

"Don't be so modest, Brooke dear. Learn to take a compliment." Nora wiped her mouth and pushed her plate away. "Diana's correct.

This was nothing short of brilliant. I wish I had the appetite to eat more."

"Are you all right? Do you need to go lie down?" Diana's brows knit in concern.

Nora calculated. If she said yes, it would leave Brooke and Diana alone together. That might be advantageous. On the other hand, she was enjoying the company. It likely wouldn't be long before she couldn't do that anymore. "I'm fine for now, thank you."

"By the way, I've been meaning to tell you, Aunt Nora... I watched a video of one of your lectures from the 1970s on YouTube."

"You did?"

"I did. Don't look so surprised."

"Well, first, I had no idea such a thing was possible. Second, I can't imagine you wanting to sit through an entire lecture. I'm sure it was the educational equivalent of watching paint dry."

"On the contrary, I was transfixed. You were a rock star."

Nora laughed. "I'm sure Elvis is spinning in his grave at the comparison."

"Diana is right," Brooke said. "Yours were the only lessons in which I forgot to take notes. I was too caught up in what you were saying."

"You two flatter me."

"As my wise Aunt Nora says, 'Learn to take a compliment.'"

"Touché, my dear." She felt the heaviness settle in her chest and she fought for breath. *Damned infirmity.*

"Nora? What's going on?" Brooke stood over her.

She raised a trembling hand and patted her chest.

"Okay. Hang on. I've got you."

She closed her eyes as pain blossomed and threatened to engulf her.

"Here you go."

She opened her mouth so that Brooke could administer the morphine and a dose of Ativan under her tongue. Seconds later, Brooke placed the oxygen cannula in her nostrils and threaded the tube around her ears. She struggled to breathe. It was several minutes before she felt relief.

"Better?"

She nodded. She didn't trust her voice. *That was a bad one, old girl. Steady as she goes.*

"How about if we get you ready for bed?"

She was dimly aware that both girls were standing over her. She wanted to comfort them but didn't have the strength for it. Instead, she nodded again as Brooke and Diana helped her transfer to the wheelchair and then onto her bed.

❦

"Will she be all right?" Diana shook her head. "That's a stupid question. I mean, is this typical at this stage?"

Brooke smiled kindly and touched her briefly on the hand. "There are no stupid questions. The oxygen and morphine will help ease the sensation of shortness of breath, and the Ativan will help her relax. We'll do our best to keep her as comfortable as possible. To answer your question more directly, yes, episodes like the one you just witnessed are not unexpected and likely will occur with more frequency now."

Diana jammed her hands in her pockets. "Yeah, I was afraid you would say that."

"I'm sorry."

"I know." Diana stared at her feet. Everything about Aunt Nora's situation sucked. Belatedly, she realized Brooke was clearing the table and doing the dishes by herself. "I can do that."

"I've got it."

"That's not fair. You cooked. I should do the cleanup."

"Whose rules are those?"

"Emily Post."

"She said no such thing."

"Well, she should've." Diana nudged Brooke aside. "Really, I've got this. You should check on Aunt Nora."

Brooke pointed to the baby monitor on the corner of the kitchen counter. "I can hear her perfectly fine from here."

"When did you install those?"

"Yesterday. This way Nora can have her privacy when she wants it, and I'm available to her any time she needs me without my having to be on top of her."

"Smart."

"Only on the third Wednesday of every month."

"Very funny."

She took advantage of Brooke's attention on the dishes to observe her more closely. Aunt Nora was right—she really was very pretty, although not in the conventional sense. It was more the way all of her features came together. She had a great smile, inviting eyes, and an air of accessible warmth…

"…does that sound okay to you?"

Oh, no. She'd been caught again. "I'm sorry. What was the question?"

Brooke cocked her head and regarded her far too closely for her comfort. "Where in the world were you?"

"Nowhere," she answered too quickly. "I couldn't hear you over the clanging of the dishes." *Lame. So, so lame.*

"Uh-huh." Brooke's tone was skeptical. "I asked if you wanted to step outside and get some air? It's a beautiful night out there. We can take the baby monitor."

"Oh. Sure." She led the way onto the deck. In the stillness of the evening, she could hear the sound of the water lapping against the shore. A plethora of stars twinkled overhead. Under different circumstances…

"It's magical, isn't it?"

"What?" Could Brooke read her thoughts?

"The night sky. The stars are so much brighter out here without the clutter of big city lights."

Brooke was leaning against the railing, her hair blowing gently in the breeze from the harbor. In the shadows created by the full moon's light, she looked like some ethereal being sent straight from heaven.

"Yes." Her voice came out huskier than she'd intended. It was time to change the topic. "Imagine how many nights like this Aunt Nora has seen in her lifetime."

Brooke turned around so that she was facing her. "I can't even fathom it. One hundred years. It's hard to wrap my brain around that much living. So much has changed in her lifetime."

"I wonder sometimes if people weren't better off in some ways when Aunt Nora was our age. Life must've been simpler then."

"In some ways, you're probably right. But think about all of the marvelous inventions and advances that have occurred. A cure for so many diseases that were lethal when Nora was a child, technology that allows for robotic surgery, organ transplants…"

"Television."

Brooke laughed, the sound full and rich. Diana's stomach flipped. "Yes, television."

"I'm glad I could make you laugh."

"Me too. Seems like it's been forever since I did."

"That's too bad. Laughter looks good on you." Diana knew she was skating dangerously close to flirting.

"Yeah, well—"

"No!" Nora's strangled cry rang out in the night, the sound distorted through the baby monitor.

They ran toward Nora's bedroom. When they arrived at the side of the bed, her eyes were open but unfocused, and wide with fear and anguish.

"Nora?" Brooke sat on the side of the bed and gently massaged her arm. "Nora? It's Brooke and Diana. You're all right. You're safe."

"No!" Nora cried once more.

Diana felt frozen to the spot. She'd never experienced anything like this. Brooke took her hand and pulled her toward Aunt Nora.

"It's okay. Talk to her. It will help calm her down."

She moved up to the head of the bed and leaned over. "Aunt Nora? It's Diana. Brooke and I are right here." When that got no response, Diana said, "I love you, Aunt Nora."

Nora blinked and her eyes focused. She glanced from Diana to Brooke and back again.

"That's our girl, Nora. Take a deep breath." Brooke motioned to Diana. "Could you please get her some water?"

"Sure thing." She grabbed the empty water bottle from the night table and filled it. "Here you go."

Brooke smiled at her reassuringly and nodded her thanks as she propped Nora up and added another pillow for support behind her back. She handed her the bottle and encouraged her to drink.

"Better?"

"Yes, thanks." She cleared her throat and handed the bottle back to Brooke. "Dying isn't for sissies, I can tell you that."

Diana took Nora's hand and perched on the edge of the bed. "Hang in there, please. I just found you again. I'm not ready to lose you."

"I'll always be with you, dear. You have only to look inside your heart."

"Are you ready to go back to sleep?" Brooke asked Nora.

"I imagine so."

"I'll be right outside if you need anything." Brooke pointed to the monitor on the night table. "Remember, I installed this monitor so that all you have to do is speak out loud and tell me you need something. I'll come running."

"I'm certain a brisk walk will be more beneficial for your knees than running, dear."

Brooke chuckled and fussed with the pillows one more time. "Have I mentioned lately how much I appreciate your sense of humor?"

"I don't think so."

"Well, I do." Brooke stepped back and touched Diana on the shoulder. "I'll leave you two alone. Let me know if you need me."

"Okay. Thank you for taking such good care of Aunt Nora."

Brooke turned around, a smile playing on her lips. "That's what you hired me for."

Diana watched her retreating form as she disappeared through the doorway. When she returned her attention to Nora, she was grinning like a Cheshire cat. "Stop it."

"What?" Nora blinked.

"Don't give me that innocent routine. I can see right through you."

"I have no idea what you're talking about."

She shook her head. As she did so, she caught sight of the seemingly innocuous object standing sentinel on the table. Brooke could hear their every word. She would do well to remember that.

"Do you think you'll be all right now?"

"I do. Please don't fret over me, dear. I'm not afraid to die."

"I know. But I'm afraid to lose you. Not the same thing." Aunt Nora's hand went lax in hers. She was asleep.

Carefully, Diana extricated her hand and crept out of the room. Brooke stood out on the deck, just as she had been earlier. Diana's

heart fluttered happily. *Stop it. You're only thinking about Brooke that way because Aunt Nora is trying to set you up.*
Brooke must have sensed her presence because she turned to face her now.
Diana swallowed hard. *Right. Keep telling yourself that.*

The chill of the late-night breeze seeped into Brooke's bones. She checked her watch: 11:17 p.m. She should head inside and go to bed. Nora's breathing sounded labored but regular through the monitor, and Brooke knew from experience that she should take advantage of the quiet times to get some rest. If only her brain would cooperate.
She trudged through the house, locking doors and turning off lights, reviewing the events of the day as she went. What a long, strange trip it had been, beginning with Nora's blunt questions about her sexuality and love life, and ending with Diana's hasty departure less than an hour ago.
Several times during dinner, she thought she'd seen odd looks pass between Diana and Nora. Then again, it might have been her overactive imagination.
Speaking of an overactive imagination, why was it she couldn't stop herself from envisioning Diana's shy smile and wishing she could see more of it? She imagined Diana tucked into her bed, the covers pulled up to her chin, reading some scientific journal. Since when were scientific journals sexy?
Her phone dinged, signaling a text, and the sound startled her. She pulled the phone from her back pocket and glanced down at the screen.
"Just wanted to make sure Aunt Nora's sleeping well and wish you a good night. Thanks again for everything."
She ran her fingers over the words. Diana certainly was sweet and thoughtful.
"You're welcome. All is well here. You really should put down that article and get some shuteye. Nurse's orders." For good measure, she added a wink emoji. She waited, as the telltale three dots appeared immediately.

"LOL. And YOU really should put down that book. Doctor's orders." A blown kiss emoji followed.

She grinned. *"Touché, I will if you will. On the count of three. One..."*

"Two...," Diana typed.

"Three...," Brooke answered.

"Good night, sweet Brooke."

"Sweet dreams, Dr. Lindstrom." She tapped the phone against her thigh and returned it to her back pocket. She headed down the hall to get ready for bed. Sweet dreams, indeed.

Nora opened one eye and peeked across the room. Brooke and Diana had their heads bent close together, working on a jigsaw puzzle Nora suggested they all start that morning. This was phase two of her plan.

Now that she'd given Diana the necessary facts about Brooke, it was time to help her get to know Brooke better. A collaborative effort that required proximity was a good start. *Don't break your arm patting yourself on the back just yet, old girl. A spark still needs to be fanned into a flame.* She cleared her throat loud enough for Diana and Brooke to hear.

Diana jumped up. "Are you all right?"

"Welcome back." Brooke swiveled her chair around to face Nora. "Did you have a nice nap?"

"I did."

"I'll get you some water." Diana took her water bottle to the refrigerator and refilled it.

"Are you hungry?" Brooke asked.

"I'm afraid not, dear." She struggled to prop herself up, and both Diana and Brooke stepped in to help. "You two don't need to hover." When she was better settled, she said, "I have an idea. Charles and Emily will be here in a few minutes. I'll be well supervised. Why don't you girls go get some fresh air and some lunch?"

Diana crossed her arms. "I'm not going anywhere. I have little enough time with you as it is."

Brooke wrapped her fingers around Diana's wrist. "Charles is Nora's attorney. Perhaps she wants to discuss a business matter with him in private."

Diana pulled away from Brooke's grasp and seemed as though she would balk.

Nora knew she needed to do something. "Exactly so, my dear. Very perceptive of you. It's nothing to concern yourself about, Diana," she rushed on, seeing the wounded expression on her great-niece's face. "Just tidying up some last-minute details."

Diana finally lowered her arms to her sides. "You'll call us if you need us?"

"I promise." Nora crossed her heart with her fingers. "I'll even keep the oxygen on."

The doorbell rang and Nora called, "It's open!"

Charles' tall form filled the doorway. "Come in, come in, dear Charles. It's so good to see you. You brought Emily?"

"I'm here." A petite woman with a winning smile playfully pushed past Charles.

"Ah, excellent. You see?" Nora said to Diana, "I'm in wonderful hands. Charles, you've already met my great-niece, Diana. This is my dear friend and caregiver, Brooke Sheldon. Brooke, this is my favorite attorney, Charles Fitzgerald, and his wife, Emily."

"I'm your only attorney, Nora."

"Don't quibble with me, Charles. I'm paying you a compliment."

"It's a pleasure to meet you both," Brooke said.

"Nice to meet you too," Emily answered. "And you, Diana."

"Nice to meet you."

"Diana and Brooke were just on their way out to lunch," Nora supplied. "Have fun, girls. No need to hurry back. Take your time."

Diana looked questioningly at Brooke, who nodded. "Right. Call us if you need anything."

"Don't be such a worrywart. I'll be fine."

Diana grabbed her car keys off the table, and she and Brooke headed toward the door.

Brooke circled back. "If you have any questions or Nora needs anything, I'll write my cell number down for you." She grabbed a notepad and pen off the counter and scribbled down her number.

"We'll take good care of her, we promise," Emily said.

"We'll be back in about an hour." Diana and Brooke took their leave.

"Sit down, sit down, you two. It's wonderful to see you both." She did her best to sound upbeat, although her energy was waning again.

Charles put down his briefcase, brought over a kitchen chair for Emily, and pulled up another one for himself. "You look fabulous as always."

She chuckled and it came out as a wheeze. "You're a horrible liar, Charles. It's one of the reasons I always knew you were giving me true advice. If you hadn't been, I'd have known it."

"I'm deeply wounded."

"And here I thought all lawyers had thick skin." She fought for another breath. "I'm so glad you were able to come."

Emily took her hand. "Are you kidding? Wild horses couldn't have kept us away."

"She's a good one, Charles. Hold on tightly to her."

"I plan to."

She nodded. They were good together. Diana and Brooke would be good together too, she knew. She just needed to give them a push.

She stirred as gentle hands settled a blanket over her. Had she fallen asleep? She struggled to open her eyes. Charles and Emily were standing over her, their faces a vision of sorrow and worry.

"You two look like you've been to a funeral." She smiled, hoping it would lighten the mood. "I'm sorry. I seem to have trouble keeping my eyes open these days."

"No apology necessary. We don't want to wear you out."

"Nonsense. I'll have plenty of time to rest later. Right now, I need you to do something for me, Charles."

He sat down and pulled his chair even closer. "Anything for you, my friend."

"Did you bring your computer as I asked?"

"I did."

"And my will is on that thing?"

"It is."

"And you said you could print something on the spot?"

"I can. I have my portable printer right here." He patted the briefcase.

"Excellent. I need to make a few changes to my will."

He raised an eyebrow. "We can do that, but are you sure?"

"I'm sure you'll tell me a codicil in this case would be ill-advised, and that revoking the existing will and replacing it with a new one is preferable." She winked at him. "You see? All these years you thought I was ignoring your advice. Do I need witnesses?"

"You do."

She nodded. "My next-door neighbors will be home. I'll see if they can come over after we've got it down on paper. "I, Nora Lindstrom, being of sound mind and body…""

CHAPTER TEN

The moon played peek-a-boo with the water as the prevailing winds blew the clouds across the darkened sky. Tonight was even chillier than last night. Fall was settling in to stay.

As had become their custom, Diana and Brooke stood side by side on the deck after dinner. They'd tucked Nora into bed and then washed and dried the dishes together.

"I can't believe I have to leave again tomorrow." Diana said the words softly, almost to herself. "I thought it would get easier. Instead, every time I walk out that door I panic that it might be the last time I see her alive."

Brooke wanted to touch her, to smooth the worry lines from her brow and reassure her. But Diana was right. Nora's condition was worsening. She was deteriorating rapidly, and at this rate, Brooke estimated Nora's life expectancy had dwindled to days and weeks, rather than months.

"You know I'll do everything I can to keep her comfortable."

Diana nodded. "I know. I just…"

Now she couldn't help herself. She covered Diana's hand where it rested on the railing. "I promise I'll keep you in the loop every step of the way."

Diana didn't pull away. She searched Brooke's face. "You'll be honest with me?"

Brooke maintained the eye contact. "Always." They were talking about Nora, but she meant the comment to be all-encompassing.

"I trust you."

The air around them stood still as Diana leaned forward, cupped Brooke's jaw with her free hand, and brought their mouths together.

105

Brooke's heart pounded in her ears as she leaned into the gentle pressure. She heard a gasp and wasn't sure whether it belonged to her or to Diana. Warmth spread throughout her body, and then, abruptly, cold air rushed back in. She opened her eyes. Diana stood a few feet away, wild-eyed and breathing heavily.

"I'm sorry. I shouldn't have... I had no business... I didn't mean..."

"Please don't finish that sentence," Brooke choked out.

Diana stuffed her hands in her pockets. "I have to go." She gave Brooke a wide berth as she made her way through the sliding glass doors. "Tell Aunt Nora I'll stop by for breakfast on my way out of town."

Before she could answer or move, Diana was gone.

She leaned back against the railing. Her hands shook and her body trembled. Part of her understood why Diana apologized. She was Nora's nurse, and any involvement with Diana, while not technically inappropriate, certainly would complicate things.

But the rest of her felt bereft. The sensation of Diana's lips, soft and supple, hungry but not demanding, was seared into her being. What was she supposed to do about that?

Diana paced back and forth in the living room of Brooke's house. "Stupid, stupid, stupid. What were you thinking?" She turned and paced in the opposite direction. "You weren't. That's the problem."

She still could smell Brooke's perfume in her nostrils and taste the sweetness of her lips. None of that was helpful. What was she supposed to do now? Pretend nothing had transpired between them? No. She should address the issue head on.

"And say what? I couldn't help myself? How lame is that?" But that was the truth. She hadn't meant to lose control—hadn't meant to act on her impulse. It just...happened. And now it couldn't un-happen.

Finally, she plunked down in a chair and dropped her head into her hands. What a cluster this was. Then again... "It's not like she didn't respond to you." She touched her lips. She still could feel the tingle of excitement.

That was also true. Brooke had met her overture without hesitation and matched her fervor. She felt Brooke tremble against her.

She jumped up and again began to pace. "It doesn't matter whether the kiss was welcome or not. Your Aunt Nora is dying, and you're acting like a horny teenager. Not only that, but Brooke is her nurse. Now you've screwed up everything."

What was Brooke feeling right now? Was she appalled by Diana's behavior? Was she packing her bags? Had she determined it was impossible to work for her after tonight?

Diana swallowed the lump in her throat. If Brooke walked away now... "Stop it." Brooke was a woman of great integrity. She'd never abandon Aunt Nora when she needed her most.

Besides, Brooke didn't work for her—she worked for Aunt Nora, who was sharp as a tack and fully capable of making such decisions. She was paying her salary. There was no employer/employee dynamic between her and Brooke.

Diana caught a glimpse at the clock. Two thirty in the morning? How had it gotten so late? Breakfast at Aunt Nora's was less than six hours away. The thought of coming face to face with Brooke again made her go weak in the knees. Still, she couldn't avoid her forever...

≈≈≈

Nora glanced from Diana to Brooke and back again. The tension between them was palpable. Neither woman had made more than cursory eye contact with the other, and the usual lively conversation had been replaced by stony, uncomfortable silence.

"Please pass the salt."

"Sure."

"Thank you."

"You're welcome."

What in the world had happened overnight? She couldn't imagine, but this simply wouldn't do. She cleared her throat. "Is everything all right between you two?"

Brooke blinked, and Diana looked as though she'd gotten caught with her hand in the cookie jar.

"Everything's fine. Why wouldn't it be?" Diana answered.

"Of course," Brooke said, at the same time.

If she'd had the energy, she would've probed further. But her strength was waning. Air. Why couldn't she get any air?

"Is she okay? What can I do?"

Nora heard the concern in Diana's voice. She wanted to reassure her, but the words wouldn't come. The room faded away. She felt someone's gentle hands lift her and then a soft surface beneath her. It felt comforting and warm…

∽৯৵

"How am I supposed to leave when she's…" Diana ran her fingers through her hair and pointed at Nora's still form in the bed.

"I promise I'll let you know if there's any change." Brooke kept her voice even and calm. She had done everything she could to open and relax Nora's airway and improve her oxygen flow. Then she'd administered morphine to make her more comfortable.

"She could die and I wouldn't be here to hold her hand."

"Conversely, she could linger like this for days or even weeks. She could rally again and improve for a bit. It's impossible to say."

"Is that supposed to be reassuring?"

Brooke closed her eyes against the harshness of Diana's tone. "It's the truth. It's all I can give you. I'm sorry."

"Me too. About a lot of things."

"What's that supposed to mean?" She knew she shouldn't react. Diana understandably was unnerved at the sight of watching Nora gasp for air and black out.

But Brooke was human. The situation already had been emotionally charged after last night, and Diana had barely given her the time of day at breakfast.

It wasn't as though she'd begged Diana to kiss her, or even signaled her interest. Diana was the one who'd made a move on her, not the other way around. Now she was acting as though the kiss was the biggest mistake of her life.

"Never mind," Diana said. "Please keep me informed. I'll leave my cell phone on overnight."

"Fine."

"I'd like a minute alone with Aunt Nora."

"Please remember to turn the monitor back on when you're done."

Brooke turned on her heel, snatched up her corresponding monitor, snapped it to the waistband of her jeans, and kept walking until she was out on the deck. The cold wind stung her face, but she barely noticed.

Several minutes passed and then she heard the front door click shut. Diana hadn't even bothered to say goodbye. "Argh!" Brooke screamed in frustration, but the wind swallowed the sound whole.

She trudged back inside. The remnants of their aborted breakfast sat on the kitchen table. She scraped the food from the plates into the garbage can, washed the dishes, and wiped the table.

The monitor was quiet, save for the rattle in Nora's chest every time she breathed. She felt compelled to do a visual check just in case. Nora's mouth was slightly open and her hands fluttered over the covers. Other than that, she seemed peaceful and comfortable.

A rap on the front door nearly sent Brooke into orbit. She crept out of the bedroom and approached the door warily. "Who is it?"

"It's Daniel, Brooke."

"Daniel?" She swung the door open so fast that he practically fell over the threshold. "What are you doing here?"

"I missed you too." He laughed easily. "Did you forget I told you I'd stop by on my way out of town this weekend?"

She closed her eyes. In fact, she had forgotten. His text had come in just as she and Diana were leaving the restaurant after lunch yesterday. She'd been so focused on what Diana was saying that she'd let the text go.

"Well? Can I come in?"

She shook her head to clear it. "Of course. Honestly, I'm glad you're here."

"Why? What's going on?" He was all business now.

"Nora suffered a severe episode of dyspnea a little while ago. I followed protocol and she's resting relatively comfortably now, but this one was bad. It took quite a while to get her breathing back under control. In general, her symptoms are worsening. She tires easily, and she's not rebounding like she did before."

"Is she complaining of joint or back pain?"

"You know Nora. She's not complaining about anything. But her appetite is diminished, her energy levels are down, as is her strength, and she's sleeping most of the time."

"How's her mind?"

"She's still remarkably sharp." Brooke furrowed her brow. "There is one thing, though. She's been having vivid, terrifying nightmares almost nightly."

"What does she say when you ask her about them?"

"She doesn't. I asked her once and she blew me off. I haven't asked again."

He nodded. "Let's have a look at her, shall we?"

When he was done with his exam, he bid Nora goodbye and motioned for Brooke to follow him out of the room. His face was grim.

"You look about the way I feel," she said.

"No matter how many times we bear witness, this never gets any easier."

"It's especially hard when it's someone we both love and admire."

"Mmm. Stick with the morphine/Ativan combination for as long as it works, and if you think we need to change it, let me know."

"Do you agree with me that we're within a week or two?"

"I'd say we're closer to the former than the latter," he said. He glanced around. "I thought Diana would still be here."

"No." She knew she answered too quickly by the expression on his face. "I mean, she left just after breakfast."

He crossed his arms. "Something you want to tell me?"

"No." She averted her gaze. She'd never make a good poker player.

"Brooke Sheldon." He drew out her name.

"What?"

He frowned. "What's going on?"

Daniel was her best friend. If she couldn't talk to him about it, who could she talk to? She sighed. "Got time for a cup of coffee?"

"I thought you'd never ask."

They sat at the kitchen table and waited for the coffee to finish brewing. He waved away the cinnamon roll she offered him.

"I've known you a long time, my friend. The last time I saw you this upset was when Ellen forced you to choose between her and your job. That was six years ago, but I remember how lost you looked. It's the same haunted expression you're wearing right now."

She swallowed hard. The breakup with Ellen had brought her to her knees. But now was not then, and one kiss from Diana Lindstrom was not seven years of a committed relationship being ripped to pieces.

The coffee finished percolating and she selected two mugs from the cupboard, filled them, and sat back down. "I'm sure you can imagine how tough it is watching Nora slip away."

"Of course I can. But I sense there's more to what's up with you than that. I mentioned her great-niece and you practically jumped down my throat."

"Did I?"

"You're stalling."

"Am I?"

"You are."

"Okay." Brooke squared her shoulders. It was time to come clean. "She kissed me last night."

His brows rose in surprise. "And?"

"And, what?"

"A kiss doesn't usually result in this much angst."

"Well, the kiss wasn't the thing that caused the turmoil...at least not for me."

"I'm listening."

She resisted the temptation to shred her napkin or otherwise fidget. "It's not like I gave her an engraved invitation. I didn't."

"So, the kiss was unwelcome?"

"What? No. Yes. I don't know." She blew out an explosive breath.

"Well, that's clear as mud."

"I know. I'm not sure how I feel."

"Conflicted?"

She nodded. "We were standing out on the deck after putting Nora to bed and Diana leaned forward and...you know." She blushed.

"Okay."

"The first thing she did was apologize, like she wished she hadn't done it. Before we could even talk about it, she left. This morning, she treated me like I was some stranger or the hired help. Then Nora had her episode.

"When I finally got all that squared away, Diana went back to being the ice queen, asked for a minute alone with Nora and then snuck out of here without even saying goodbye." She slapped her palms on the table in frustration. "What the hell's wrong with her?"

He took a sip of coffee and sat back. "Sounds to me as though she's conflicted too."

"I get that. I'm Nora's nurse and she's dying. The timing's not ideal to start a relationship."

"How did you feel about it?"

"The kiss? The timing? Or what happened afterward?"

"Let's start with the kiss."

She stopped short of touching her lips as she recalled the delicious pressure of Diana's mouth on hers.

He chuckled.

"What?"

"If the dreamy expression on your face is any indication, I'd venture to say you enjoyed the kiss just fine."

She stiffened. "I didn't say that."

"You didn't have to." He squeezed her hand. "It's okay. There's no crime in exploring an attraction with Diana."

"She certainly acted as though there was. For God's sake, it was like high school all over again. We're grown women!"

"You're grown women in a challenging, emotionally difficult situation. Has it occurred to you that Diana might be worried about what you'd think of someone who would be acting on an attraction while her great-aunt lies dying in the next room?"

"Yes."

"Maybe she's concerned about optics."

"I should be more worried about the ethics of a relationship with Diana than she should be. I'm the hired caregiver here. It's up to me to keep professional distance."

"Is that what you want to do? Keep your distance from her?"

Her gut twisted. Staying away from Diana was about the last thing she wanted to do.

"Uh-huh."

"Uh-huh, what?"

"Don't ever play poker for money."

112

"I already knew that." Her tone sounded peevish, even to her own ears, but she really hated being so transparent. She sighed heavily. "I'm sorry. I don't mean to take it out on you."

"I'm a big boy. I can handle it."

"The point is, you shouldn't have to. I just don't know what to do or how to make this right. It's not like we can undo it."

"No, you can't."

"Got any words of wisdom or recommendations?"

"Well, assuming you're not planning to quit—"

"Quit taking care of Nora? Absolutely not." She pounded the table for emphasis.

"Easy there, tiger." He held up his hands palms outward. "I'm not suggesting you would or that you should."

"Good." She crossed her arms defensively.

"You can either continue to tip-toe around each other and endure Diana's cool distance—"

"Not acceptable."

"Right. Or you can address what transpired, acknowledge that although the timing is unfortunate, the feelings are real, and see where it goes from there."

She turned that idea over in her mind. On paper, it made sense. In practice... "What if the earth didn't move for her?"

"I imagine she wouldn't have felt compelled to kiss you if she wasn't wicked attracted to you. And why wouldn't she be? You're a catch."

"Sweet-talker."

"Truth."

"Still..."

"Brooke, you're never going to know unless you have a discussion. I guess you'll just have to be cool with it if she says she's not interested."

"Ugh." The notion that the kiss meant nothing to Diana made her sick to her stomach.

"Relax. Smart money says Diana's sweating this out the same way you are."

"I wish I shared your confidence."

He checked his watch. "I've got to get on the road. The rest of the world is going to be heading back to civilization any second now, and I'm allergic to bumper-to-bumper traffic."

They stood and she gave him a hug. "I'm so glad you stopped by. I don't know what I'd do without you. You're a good friend, you know that?"

"I do. Good to know you recognize that too."

"Get out of here before your head doesn't fit through the door anymore."

"Here's your hat, what's your hurry," he joked. "You keep me informed about Nora's condition. Check in as often as you need to. If you have any questions or need me to come out, say the word."

"I'll do that. I can't stand the thought of that brilliant mind and buoyant spirit leaving us."

"I know. She's a rare commodity, a truly beautiful human being. I'm going to miss her."

"Me too."

"Cherish the time you have left with her, and advise Diana to do the same." He gave her one last hug and headed out the door.

She and Diana had to get past this awkwardness. Otherwise, Diana forever would regret the kiss, as it meant lost time with Nora at the end of her life. If that happened, there would be no chance for them going forward, if there even was a chance now.

CHAPTER ELEVEN

Diana gathered her papers off the lectern and stuffed them into her computer bag, along with her iPad, laser pointer, and her hard copy of Dale Purves et. al.'s, *Principles of Cognitive Neuroscience*. She fished in the front zipper compartment for her cell phone and turned it on. There was no message from Brooke.

She hadn't received more than a dutiful nightly report on Aunt Nora's condition all week, so it shouldn't have surprised her. Still, she missed their playful interchanges, Brooke's warm, comforting, upbeat words, and their easy rapport.

"It's your own damned fault. If only you'd exercised a little self-control, you wouldn't be in this mess now."

"Dr. Lindstrom?"

"What?" she snapped. She didn't bother to look up from the phone.

"If this is a bad time—"

Her head jerked up. "Oh, my God. No. No. Now's fine."

Alexander Montrose, the Dean of the Faculties of Health Sciences and Medicine stood in front of her at the foot of the stage, eyebrows arched and arms crossed. "Is everything all right?"

"Yes. Yes, of course." She thrust the phone into the pocket of her dress slacks.

"If you'll come with me, I'd like to show you something I thought you might find interesting."

She scrambled off the stage, snatched up her computer bag, and followed him out of the lecture hall. What could he possibly want? Was she in some kind of trouble? Yes, she'd been distracted of late, but she had good reason.

Tom Dalton, the Head of Department, was well aware of the situation with Aunt Nora, and so far, had been very understanding and flexible about excusing Diana from extended office hours. She'd asked permission on those occasions when she'd left early to travel to Truro. She'd presented fresh materials in lectures and overseen all clinical laboratory work by her graduate students.

When she tuned in to her surroundings, she realized they were headed toward the University's Butler Library. "We're going to the library?"

"As I said, I have something to show you that I believe might interest you. It certainly interests me."

She struggled to keep up with his long strides, as he led them inside the library and to the elevator, where he pushed the button for the sixth floor. The sixth floor, Diana knew, was home to the University Archives. What the dickens?

The research librarian greeted them as they exited the elevator. "Hello, Monica. Do you have what I asked you to pull for me?"

"Yes, sir. Right this way."

"Follow me, Dr. Lindstrom."

Monica led them through a series of doors into a climate-controlled room. She handed them each a pair of white gloves, put on a pair herself, and then placed two large boxes on an empty conference table. From the first box, Box 41, she removed two folders, one titled, "Atomic Energy Commission," and a second titled, "Atomic Bomb Discussion."

Diana read the outside of the box—George Braxton Pegram papers. She knew the name, of course. George Braxton Pegram was a professor of physics and Dean of the Graduate Faculties at Columbia. He also was the man responsible for the historic meeting between Franklin Roosevelt and American nuclear scientists that led to the creation of the Manhattan Project.

But what did any of this have to do with her?

She examined the second box. It had neat typing that identified it as "Historical Subject Files, Box 6." From that box, Monica extracted another folder: "Atomic Energy Research, 1930s – 1980s."

Diana wracked her brain, trying in vain to make a connection.

"Thank you, Monica. I'll take it from here," Dean Montrose said.

Monica left them and he turned his attention to Diana. "Tom mentioned to me that your great-aunt is in failing health. I'm sorry to hear that, by the way."

"Thank you, sir."

"When Tom told me her name, I couldn't believe it. I can't imagine how I didn't know you were related. As a graduate student, I did my dissertation on the manufacturing process for Uranium-235."

"The fuel for the atomic bomb we dropped on Hiroshima?"

"The same."

"I'm sorry, sir. I'm not following you."

"Your great-aunt played a pivotal role in the manufacture of the fuel."

"My Aunt Nora? Are you sure?"

He smiled. "I'm positive. That's why I had these materials brought over. I thought you might want to see for yourself, if you didn't already know."

"I-I didn't." None of this made any sense. Aunt Nora spent her career curing childhood leukemia. She had something to do with the atomic bomb?

He opened the Atomic Bomb Discussion folder and scanned the contents until he found what he was searching for. He turned to the page and slid the folder in front of her.

There, in black and white, was a list of scientists working on the Manhattan Project and their assignments. Under the heading Oak Ridge, Tennessee, 1943 – 1945, was "Lindstrom, Nora. Physicist. Oversight of the Calutron Uranium Enrichment Operators, or 'Calutron Girls.'"

Diana pulled her phone out of her pocket. "Can I take a picture of that?" She would ask Aunt Nora about it when she saw her this weekend.

"I don't see why not." He perused one of the other folders, the one titled, "Atomic Energy Research, 1930s – 1980s." Again, he trailed a finger down the table of contents until he found what he sought. He opened to a page and rotated the folder so that she could see it.

The heading on this document read, "Atomic Bomb Casualty Commission – Radiation Effects Research Foundation (RERF) Radiation Health Studies." She skimmed the document. RERF, a joint effort of the American and Japanese governments and based in Hiroshima, apparently had been formed shortly after the bombings of Hiroshima and Nagasaki with the aim of conducting a long-term study of the effects of the radiation exposure suffered by the bombing victims, their children, and future generations descended from those survivors.

Again, she wondered what Aunt Nora's connection could be to such an endeavor. She glanced up, a question in her eyes.

He peered over her shoulder. "Keep reading. You're almost there."

Three-quarters of the way down the page, she saw it. "Dr. Nora Lindstrom will oversee the team conducting the Life Span Study, and will have secondary responsibility for the F1 (Children of the A-Bomb Survivors) Study. She will report directly to the Advisory Committee of the Atomic Bomb Casualty Commission, or ABCC, in Washington, D.C."

"May I?" She held up the phone again.

"Of course. None of this is classified anymore."

She snapped several photos. She wished she could take the documents with her and read them at her leisure. There was so much more she needed to know about Aunt Nora.

What was it Grandpa Bill and Dad used to say when she was a child? *"Your Aunt Nora is off doing top-secret work out of the country. We're not allowed to contact her."*

"Your Aunt Nora is working for the government and travels constantly. She's made it clear she has no room in her life for the likes of us. She's too focused on her career."

The excuses meant nothing to her as a child; the bottom line was that Aunt Nora had disappeared from her life. But now, in light of these new discoveries...

"Dr. Lindstrom?"

Diana blinked. "I'm sorry. You'll have to excuse me. It's a lot to take in."

"Your great-aunt never talked about her work? Once Tom connected the dots for me and I realized who Dr. Lindstrom was to you, all the pieces fell into place. I assumed her career was the impetus for you being a scientist, and particularly for your choice of Columbia, where the Manhattan Project began to take shape.

"I contacted her when I was working on my dissertation. Over the years, we kept in touch. Her sage advice often guided my career choices. She was a giant in the field, and a mentor to me and many others."

She measured her words. "Aunt Nora was my inspiration, but I only recently reconnected with her. I hadn't seen her since I was a small child."

"Oh. I'm sorry. I didn't mean to pry."

"It's okay."

"Perhaps it's a conversation you can have with her now?"

Her heart lurched. Brooke's updates hadn't given her any reason to believe Aunt Nora's condition had improved since she'd left on Sunday. "I'm not sure she's still at a point where she's capable."

"I'm sorry."

"Me too."

He checked his watch. "I've got a meeting."

"And I've got office hours. Thank you for showing me all this."

"You're welcome. That's quite a legacy she's left you."

"Yes." She nodded thoughtfully. "Yes, it is."

Brooke straightened the blanket at the foot of Nora's bed. She hadn't roused since early this morning, when she'd awoken only long enough to take a sip of Ensure and pat Brooke on the hand. The unsolved *New York Times* crossword puzzle sat on the hospital tray by the bed. That made Brooke saddest of all.

"Knock, knock."

"Hi." She wheeled around to greet Anita, the affable certified nursing assistant hospice assigned to provide care twice a week.

"How's she doing?"

"Not good."

"So, no shower assist today?"

"No. But I'm certain she would welcome a sponge bath and a change of sheets."

"You've got it." Anita moved efficiently around the room. "Why don't you take a short break? I've got this. I'll text you when Miss Nora and I are done here."

Reluctant as Brooke was to leave Nora's side, she really did need an hour or so to clear her head. "If you're sure you're all right, I'd love to take a quick run and have a shower."

"Absolutely. We've got this, haven't we Miss Nora?" Anita gently massaged Nora's arm and she opened her eyes. "Are you ready to get cleaned up?"

Nora nodded her approval.

"Okay, then. Let's take care of you."

Brooke signaled her thanks and headed down the hall to change for a run.

The beach was deserted, as she expected given the dampness of the cold wind and the charcoal-gray sky. She spent several minutes stretching and started off at a light jog, increasing speed as she warmed up. It felt good to be outdoors and to remember that she was healthy and alive.

Between managing Nora's care during this precipitous decline and the stilted communications with Diana, she was mentally and emotionally spent.

Diana. She would be here tonight. How in the world would that go? She frowned. Their text exchanges were polite, clinical, and distant. The only discussion of consequence stemmed from a question Diana posed out of the blue.

"What do you know about Aunt Nora's career before she came to Dana-Farber?"

"Nothing, except that she told me Sidney Farber recruited her personally to come to Boston, and that she finally accepted after losing a patient that really mattered to her."

"Okay. Thanks. So, she hasn't said anything more specific about what she was working on?"

"As I said, no. Only that she admired Dr. Farber and that they'd been corresponding since 1948."

"1948? You're sure?"

"I'm very sure."

"Okay, thanks."

"You're welcome."

And that had been that. Diana hadn't explained her interest in Nora's early career, and Brooke hadn't asked her to illuminate. She considered asking Nora in one of her more lucid moments, but truly there hadn't been enough of those to allow for such questions.

120

She checked her Fitbit. It was time to head back. In the end, what happened from this point forward between them would be up to Diana. Brooke was done trying to figure out her intentions or mindset. If Diana wanted something more from her than a professional interaction, that would be up to her to initiate. Brooke didn't have the time or patience to play games.

⋙⋘

Diana sat on the side of the bed holding Aunt Nora's hand. "Aunt Nora? I'm here. It's Diana."

Her eyelids fluttered, but otherwise she did not respond. Diana shifted her gaze to Brooke, who was standing in the doorway, leaning against the frame. She looked impossibly beautiful, but her makeup couldn't hide the signs of exhaustion around her eyes. Diana resisted the impulse to tell her to get some rest. That would've been too personal, and she was determined not to go there again.

"She's been like this all week?"

"She's had short stretches of consciousness during which she's been quite lucid, but those have been few and far between."

"I see. Will it… Do you think she'll have any more times like she had before, when she was interacting with us?"

"You mean will she be able to sit up and have a normal conversation?"

She nodded. It sounded silly when Brooke said it that way. "I guess that's unrealistic."

"Not at all." Brooke pushed off from the frame and took a step toward the end of the bed. It was as close as she'd come to Diana since she'd arrived an hour ago.

"In my experience, patients in the end stages of the dying process often have what I call a 'rally,' where all of a sudden they appear to be getting better—stronger. Sometimes this phenomenon lasts a few minutes, and sometimes as long as a few days. It just depends."

Diana absorbed that bit of information. What she wouldn't give to have one more discussion with Aunt Nora. After spending several nights researching "The Atomic City" and the "Calutron Girls," she was hungry to know more about Aunt Nora's role in all of it. That Aunt Nora played such a critical part in one of the defining moments in the history of World War II intrigued Diana to no end.

"Do you have any more questions for me?"

She started. She'd nearly forgotten that Brooke still stood there. "I guess not."

"Right. Take all the time you want. I'll be in the living room if you or Nora need anything. I'll turn the monitor off to give you your privacy."

"Thanks." She didn't know what else to say. She'd left her office too late in the afternoon to arrive in time for dinner. Instead, she'd texted Brooke to tell her not to wait for her for dinner and grabbed a lobster roll at the beginning of the Cape.

Was Brooke relieved to eat alone? Or disappointed? Did it matter at this point?

Nora moaned and Diana stroked her hand. "It's okay. Rest now. You've earned it."

She stayed with her for another half an hour, but Nora never opened her eyes. "I'll be back in the morning. I love you, Aunt Nora." She kissed her on the forehead and closed the door on her way out of the bedroom.

Brooke was sitting curled up on the couch, her eyes closed. The sight took Diana's breath away. In repose, she was even prettier. Without the worry lines, she appeared as Diana imagined she'd looked straight out of nursing school—young and ready to save the world.

She hated to wake her, but there was nothing for it. She cleared her throat and Brooke jumped.

"Sorry. I must've dozed off."

"No problem. I didn't want to disappear and not say goodbye."

"Right."

"Well, goodnight."

"Right."

This was crazy. She should say something more. "Brooke?"

"Yes?" Brooke looked at her expectantly.

"Thanks again for taking such good care of Aunt Nora. I know you're doing everything you can."

"You're welcome. That's what I was hired to do. I take my responsibilities very seriously." Her expression, so open in sleep, was a closed book now.

"Well, I suspect it's more than that to you, and I want you to know that I recognize that and appreciate it."

"Thanks."

She shifted awkwardly from foot to foot. "Anyway, I'll be back first thing in the morning. Should I bring anything for breakfast?"

Brooke shrugged. "Nora isn't really eating much these days."

"I meant for you," she said quietly.

"Oh. That's not necessary. I can take care of myself."

"I know that." She opened her mouth to say something more and then thought better of it. "Okay. I should be here around eight. Is that too early?"

"Eight is fine. Truly, you're Nora's family. You can, and should, come and go as often as you like."

"I don't want to interrupt her care."

"You won't."

Diana pulled the keys from her pocket and palmed them. "See you at eight, then."

As she headed toward the door, Brooke rose, turned the monitor back on, and strode in the direction of Nora's room. Diana stared after her retreating form. She wanted to tell her to come back so they could talk about what had happened between them, so that they could get past this insufferable politeness. But she couldn't bring herself to say the words. Tomorrow. Tomorrow they could talk about it. She closed the door softly behind her.

CHAPTER TWELVE

Nora blinked and the world came into focus. Sunshine streamed in through the bedroom window and exploded in a rainbow prism of light across the covers. From the angle of it, she judged that it was mid-morning.

What day was it? And where had her mother gone? She'd been here just a minute ago, urging Nora to get ready. It was almost time to go. But she was so tired. Maybe she could close her eyes for a few more minutes...

"I love you, Aunt Nora. I wish we had more time."

She fought her way up to the surface. "We have all the time in the world, dear." She struggled to open her eyes.

"What? Did you say something?"

She cleared her throat and tried to project her voice. "We have all the time in the world."

"She's awake!" Diana's face, lined with stress and sadness, swam into view.

"How long have I been asleep?"

Brooke strode into the room. "Not too long." She approached the other side of the bed. "I gave you a dose of medicine a little over an hour ago. Would you like to sit up?"

She nodded. "And would you be a dear and get me some water?"

"Of course." Brooke repositioned her and hustled out of the room.

Nora watched her go and waited until she was out of sight. "Have you taken my advice?"

"Excuse me?" Diana asked.

"Have you asked her on a date?"

"Who?" The tips of Diana's ears turned red and she evaded her pointed gaze.

"Playing dumb doesn't suit you, dear. Brooke, that's who."

Diana fussed with the corner of the bed covers. "No."

"But?"

"But, what?"

"I don't know. You tell me. There's something more, that's for certain. If not, you wouldn't be so uncomfortable with the subject."

Diana looked as though she would bolt and Nora wanted to laugh, if only she'd had the energy. She raised her eyebrows in expectation. "Well? What is it?"

"I... I kissed her." The words came out in a rush.

This time, Nora did laugh. She clapped her hands quietly in delight. "Excellent. That's progress."

Diana shook her head and bit her lip.

"Whatever is wrong? You didn't enjoy it?"

"What?" She shifted uncomfortably. "No. It isn't that. It never should've happened. It was inappropriate and the timing is all wrong."

"Poppycock." She waved away Diana's words.

"You're..." Her eyes filled with unshed tears. "Brooke is your nurse. Now is not the time—"

"Listen to me, Diana. There is no perfect time for love. You seize the moment when it presents itself, regardless of the timing. I give you my blessing."

Diana gripped the bedcovers tightly. "I can't—"

"You most certainly can. Do you love her?"

"I don't know. I hardly know her."

"Are you attracted to her?"

"Yes."

"Well, that's a good place to start. Get to know her. She's got a beautiful heart, you know."

"I know."

"Love is the most powerful tonic for all you've been through, dear. Open your heart to Brooke. Together you can heal those scars you're carrying."

"I'm not—"

"Oh, yes, you are. Diana?" She patted the bed next to her and Diana sat next to her hip.

"Yes?"

"Consider this an old lady's dying wish. I want you to be happy. I can't leave this Earth and not know that I've done something right for you, that I've made up for the love you didn't get to feel from me all these years."

"It's not up to you to solve my love life."

"You're right. It's up to you." Nora stared pointedly at her. She looked miserable. "Take it from someone who knows too much about this subject. If we've ever truly loved, at some point, we've been hurt and had our hearts ripped apart. But when we give up on love and close our hearts to new possibilities, we cease living."

Diana looked as though she would interrupt.

"Let me finish, please." She was parched. She wondered where Brooke was with the water, but she was determined to take advantage of the time alone with her great-niece.

"I've spent most of my life existing instead of living, alone and convinced that I didn't deserve love. I threw myself into my work, believing that by doing good things, I could make up for all I'd done wrong in my personal and professional life. I've had decades with too much time to regret, wishing away my life with could-have-beens and should-have-beens." She gripped Diana's hand. "Don't be me, Diana. Be stronger and better than I was. Live and love for me. Please."

"I—I will, Aunt Nora. I promise you, I'll do my best."

She nodded as exhaustion took her. She wished she could keep her eyes open, but she was losing the fight.

Brooke leaned heavily against the kitchen counter, Nora's water bottle held loosely in her right hand. She knew she should've gone into the living room and turned off the monitor. She'd meant to…

It's not as though it was on your person.

She shook her head disgustedly. *That's a flimsy bit of rationale and you know it.*

What should she do? Should she admit to Diana that she'd heard the conversation between her and Nora? To be sure, that would ease her conscience.

No. Diana would be mortified. Clearly, she'd forgotten about the monitor. Otherwise she never would've been so open with Nora. Besides, she couldn't even bring herself to talk about the kiss. How in the world would she react to knowing that an intimate conversation with her dying great-aunt had been broadcast for Brooke to hear?

"Are you okay?" Diana regarded her quizzically. "You look like you're a thousand miles away."

She clutched at her heart. "I-I didn't hear you come out."

"I gathered as much." She pointed at Nora's water bottle. "I don't think she'll be needing that right now. She's asleep again."

"Oh. I'll put it on the tray so it will be there next time she wakes up." Brooke pushed off from the counter.

"Wait." Diana stepped into her path, blocking her way. "I-I've been meaning to talk to you about...about the other night."

This was it. This was the moment. If she was going to share what she'd heard, now was the time.

"I know I've been acting like an idiot."

"Diana—"

"Please, let me say my piece, and then you can tell me whatever it is you want to say."

Her jaw clicked shut. She could see that this wasn't easy for Diana, revealing what she knew would only make it harder and more awkward.

"I want you to know, it's not in my nature to go around kissing women indiscriminately." Diana glanced up at her from underneath long lashes. "In fact, I can't remember ever taking a chance like that before."

"I'm not sorry you did," she said softly.

Diana nodded. "I'm very attracted to you. It's just..." She sighed and shoved her hands into the pockets of her jeans, a gesture Brooke had come to recognize signaled embarrassment or discomfort. "I should've thought through the implications before I acted impulsively. You're Aunt Nora's nurse, and apart from wanting to avoid any hint of impropriety, Aunt Nora is dying, and the timing of that kiss was problematic for me. I was disappointed with myself for not exercising better self-control. I can't imagine what you must be thinking about me."

She couldn't stand still any longer. She covered the few steps between them and lifted Diana's chin with two fingers. Her eyes were a vivid green today, and Brooke's breath caught in her throat.

"I think you're a woman of principle, caught in a difficult…no, make that a nearly impossible…situation, watching helplessly as someone you love dies. It's wreaking emotional havoc on your heart. It's a wonder you can tie your shoes in the morning, never mind deal with complicated issues like attraction and what to do about it."

"That's very kind. Thank you."

"You don't need to thank me for stating the obvious. The real question isn't about what happened, but about where we go from here. I promise you that I don't think any less of you for acting on your feelings, and that I have no problem discharging my duties where Nora is concerned."

"I never doubted that you would continue to give Aunt Nora your very best. No one could be better suited to this assignment, nor would I trust anyone else with it."

"Good. For the record, in case you're wondering, I'm wicked attracted to you too, Diana Lindstrom."

Diana's mouth formed an "O."

"So, now what?" Brooke asked.

"I wish I knew."

"How about if we focus on Nora now, and agree that if we still feel the same way later, we'll explore 'us' at that time?"

"That sounds like a great plan." The crease in Diana's forehead eased. "I'd like to tell you I won't be tempted to kiss you until then, but I never lie."

She laughed easily. "I wish I could resist you, but that wouldn't be the truth either."

"Right. Okay, then?"

"Okay," she agreed. They stood inches apart. She knew it would take nothing to lean forward and… "I'd better go check on Nora."

"You do that."

As she retreated, she felt Diana's gaze on her. She smiled.

Diana whistled to herself as she walked along the beach. The bracing cold felt unaccountably refreshing against her overheated cheeks. Aunt Nora's place was necessarily warm for the patient's comfort, and Diana didn't envy Brooke for having to adapt accordingly.

Brooke... Now that they'd cleared the air, Diana allowed her imagination free reign. Aunt Nora was right. Brooke could easily steal her heart right out from under her if she wasn't careful. Then again, that was the thrust of Aunt Nora's advice, wasn't it? Cast caution aside and let the heart have what it wants. Diana never had been particularly good at that. She'd always been cautious by nature, and her life experiences had made her even more so.

Aunt Nora's words tumbled around in her head, and she pondered their meaning. What was it she regretted so deeply? Who had broken her tender heart? And what did she mean about professional mistakes? Was she referring to the atomic bomb stuff? Diana had so many questions. Would she get an opportunity to get answers?

Brooke had said most end-stage patients rallied. Aunt Nora did exactly that this morning, if only for an hour. Would she do it again? So far, she'd shown no signs of it. In fact, she hadn't regained consciousness since their discussion this morning. Still, Diana kept a watchful eye, not wanting to miss one last chance to ask Aunt Nora everything she wanted to know.

Brooke practically shoved her out the door and told her to get some air. Sitting vigil, she said, was hard on the soul. It was important to take breaks in order to revive the spirit. What about Brooke's spirit? Diana couldn't imagine the toll caring for sick and dying patients must have taken on her.

She hadn't given it much thought until now, but Diana could see why Brooke had walked away from Farber. What would she do after Aunt Nora was gone? Would she stay in nursing? Suddenly, Brooke's choices mattered a great deal to Diana.

Don't get too far down the road. Attraction doesn't always equate with compatibility or love. You don't even know if you're right for each other.

She checked her watch—1:15 p.m. She probably should head back. What if Aunt Nora was awake? She pulled the cell phone from her back pocket. Brooke promised her that if Aunt Nora regained consciousness, she would alert her right away. She also had cautioned that such opportunities were most likely to occur earlier in the day; many patients shut down as the day wore on.

Of course, there must be exceptions to every rule, and Aunt Nora was nothing if not exceptional. She was so strong, with a will of steel. She'd lived to be one hundred years old and maintained her independence right up until the end. You didn't achieve that by being weak. If it was possible to will oneself back to consciousness and lucidity, Aunt Nora would get the job done.

As if on cue, Diana's cell phone buzzed with a text message.

"She's awake and eating some Jell-O and a little soup. She's quite alert and looking forward to seeing you." Brooke included a thumbs up emoji.

Her heart pounded hard. Aunt Nora was awake. She took off at a run.

Diana ran into the room as though her hair were on fire and came skidding to a halt next to the bed. "Hi."

"Hi, yourself," Nora said. "Brooke was telling me that you took a walk on the beach. Oh, how I miss being able to do that."

"I'll leave you two alone to visit." Brooke squeezed Nora's hand. "If you need anything, shout. You've got fresh water here," she pointed to the hospital tray, "and you're not due for any more medications for another two hours."

"I'm sure Diana and I will be fine, dear. Won't we?" She patted the side of the bed in invitation and Diana sat.

"We will," Diana answered. Her gaze lingered on Brooke as she exited the room, a development that didn't escape Nora.

"Do I sense progress?"

"You are incorrigible, you know that?"

"Well, it's not as though I have anything else to focus on, dear. Allow an old lady some vicarious living, why don't you." She winked.

"You're embarrassing me, so how about if we talk about something else, please."

"As you wish."

"Can I ask you a few questions?"

"I guess that depends. What's the topic?"

"Your past."

She raised an eyebrow. "I thought we already covered that."

"I'm confident we barely scratched the surface."

"I don't think I have the strength to rehash an entire century." She covered Diana's hand with hers. "I wish we had more time too, dear. You must feel as though you've been robbed. It's so unfair to give you such a narrow window. That's my fault and again, I apologize."

"Seems to me the blame lies with Grandpa Bill and my parents," Diana said.

"Is that what you want to discuss? Do you still have unanswered questions?"

"About why you left? No, it's nothing like that. I want to talk about things that happened long before I was born."

She began to feel uneasy.

"I came across some documents in the archives at Columbia. They had your name in them."

Now her heart skipped a beat as her mind scrolled through myriad possibilities of what Diana had uncovered.

Diana fished her phone out, searched for something, and then held the screen so that Nora could see it. "According to this employee roster, you worked as a supervising scientist at Oak Ridge during World War II. You were in charge of the uranium enrichment effort."

She closed her eyes as the memories came flooding back—the sucking sound of her boots being swallowed by the ever-present mud, the bustle of the girls heading to the plant in time for their shifts, the rows upon rows of Calutron machines, the endless calculations and adjustments, and the hum of activity in town on a Saturday night.

"Aunt Nora?"

She opened her eyes. "Technically, the town was called Clinton Engineer Works back then. It didn't become Oak Ridge until after the war."

"So, this is accurate? You were there?"

She sighed heavily. "I was."

"You oversaw the production of the fuel for the atomic bomb?"

"No. I supervised the girls who operated the Calutron machines that separated the isotopes." At Diana's blank look, she added, "It was my job to make sure the girls kept the needles on the meters exactly where they needed to be in order to ensure maximum fuel production."

"You were a woman."

She smiled wanly. "An apt observation."

"In a supervisory position in the 1940s. A physicist who played a major role in ending the war."

"I did my job. We all did. They wanted the girls to be supervised by a woman. They thought it would help with morale and communication."

"You won the war for us."

Tears pricked her eyes, and she fought to tamp down the shame and regret that threatened to drown her. "I was responsible for the deaths of more than one-hundred-thousand people, Diana. Please don't romanticize it. I spent the next thirty years of my career trying to make amends."

Diana took her hand. "You didn't make the decision to drop the bomb, the president did."

"What I did—what I had the girls do—made that possible. I've had to live with that all these years, and so have they," she added quietly. "Some of them never forgave me." Her voice broke. "I haven't forgiven myself."

"Breathe, Aunt Nora. Please, slow down and breathe."

She saw the panicked look on Diana's face. She struggled to take in air.

"Brooke! Brooke, help!"

The panic in Diana's voice broke Nora's heart.

"Nora? Nora? It's Brooke. Can you hear me? I'm going to give you some medicine. Nora? That's it. Take it easy. I'm going to lay you back now. Focus on a breath. That's it."

"I did this. I upset her." Nora heard Diana's strangled lament. "I never should've pushed her for answers."

"Shh. It's okay, Diana. You didn't do anything wrong. Talk to her. She can hear you."

"But she's in so much pain."

"The meds will kick in soon. Talk to her. Tell her what you want her to know. Tell her how you feel."

"Aunt Nora? Aunt Nora, it's Diana. I'm sorry. I'm so sorry. I didn't mean to upset you. You're my hero, Aunt Nora. You always were, and you're more so now. I love you. Please, please forgive me. Please forgive me."

Nora felt the pressure of Diana's cheek against her hand. With effort, she lifted that hand to caress her great-niece's face. "I…" She injected more force into her voice. "I forgive you, dear. There's nothing to forgive. I love you, Diana. Always in your heart. Remember…"

A tremendous pain split her chest in two and she gasped, her eyes flying open. As they did, she saw Diana standing over her. Brooke's arm was wrapped around her, holding her protectively.

Nora smiled as light filled her and the pain receded, replaced by a joy unlike any she had ever known. It was time to go.

CHAPTER THIRTEEN

D iana stared unseeing out the kitchen window. She could hear Brooke and the hospice nurse talking in low tones in Aunt Nora's bedroom as they waited for the funeral home to finish securing the body and readying it for transport.

In the end, everything had unfolded so quickly. One second Aunt Nora was alert and answering her questions, and the next, she was...gone. She closed her hands and balled them into fists to keep them from shaking. She'd never watched someone die before.

Dead. Aunt Nora was dead. The idea of it left a gaping hole in her heart. Strange. She'd spent most of her life believing Aunt Nora was dead. Why was it so different now?

The answer was quite easy, really. Before, she had held a child's distant memory of a favorite relative. Now... Now Aunt Nora was alive in her heart and mind and still larger-than-life. There was Aunt Nora hunched over a crossword puzzle, pen tapping rhythmically against her chin, eyes filled with intelligence and life. And there was Aunt Nora, her posture regal even at one hundred, imparting wisdom about love and giving her dating advice.

Beyond all that, now Diana had a more detailed picture of her great-aunt. She was a glass-ceiling-breaking war hero, a champion of children with leukemia, a dedicated research scientist, an accidental lesbian activist, and a captivating lecturer. More importantly, she was a loving great-aunt.

"How are you doing?" Brooke came up alongside her, close enough to touch, although she refrained from doing so.

She shrugged. "What happens now?"

"Nora pre-arranged and pre-paid for everything. The funeral home will take care of the cremation and call you when her ashes are ready to be picked up."

"Oh."

"I called Daniel. He'll sign the death certificate electronically."

She nodded dumbly. She was having trouble holding on to details.

"Maybe you should call Mr. Fitzgerald?"

"Who?"

"Nora's attorney. I imagine she gave him all of the pertinent information and instructions."

"That makes sense." She checked her watch and was shocked to see that it was only a little after six. It felt more like midnight. "He's probably eating dinner."

"I'm sure he wouldn't mind the interruption under the circumstances."

"Okay."

"Would you like me to do that for you?"

"No. I'll take care of it." She pulled out her phone. "Will you stay with me?"

"Of course."

She placed the call, surprised when Mr. Fitzgerald answered on the first ring.

"Hello, Dr. Lindstrom."

"I'm sorry to disturb you, Mr. Fitzgerald." Her voice cracked. "It's…" She paused to gather herself. "Aunt Nora is…"

Brooke took hold of her free hand and squeezed it gently. "It's okay," she mouthed silently.

"Aunt Nora passed away a little while ago."

There was a pause on the line. "I see. I'm very sorry for your loss, Dr. Lindstrom."

"I'm sorry for your loss too."

"Thank you. They broke the mold when they made our Nora."

She smiled through her tears. "Truer words were never spoken."

"Are you all right? Do you have someone with you?"

"Brooke is here." She squeezed her hand in return and then broke contact.

"Good."

"Mr. Fitzgerald?"

136

"Charles, please."

"Charles? I'm not sure what to do next. Is there something I should be doing?"

"The only thing you need to focus on right now is you. Your Aunt Nora was well prepared for this day. She left very clear, very specific wishes and instructions."

"That's what I mean—"

"All of which I will share with you, but not tonight. Tonight, you rest and take care of yourself. How about if I stop by tomorrow morning, say, around ten o'clock, would that be all right with you?"

"Sure."

"I'll bring Nora's instructions with me, and we'll take it from there."

"Okay."

"Dr. Lindstrom?"

"Diana."

"Diana? It would be helpful if Ms. Sheldon was present tomorrow."

She raised an eyebrow. "Hold on, I'll ask her if she's available." She held the phone to her chest. "Can you be here to meet with me and Mr. Fitz—um, Charles—tomorrow morning at ten?"

Brooke nodded. "Anything you need."

She put the phone back to her ear. "Okay. She'll be here."

"Perfect. I'll see you both tomorrow. Again, I'm very sorry for your loss."

"Thank you. See you in the morning." She ended the call and faced Brooke. "Thanks for agreeing to that. I'm sure you have better things to do."

Brooke shook her head. "Actually, there's no place I'd rather be than wherever you are. I'm here for you, Diana."

Diana knew that she meant it. "What now?"

"Are you hungry?"

"Not really." She couldn't even think about food.

"Tired?"

"Physically? Or emotionally?"

"Yes," Brooke answered.

"Fair enough. I'm exhausted, but I don't think I could close my eyes."

"Feel like going for a walk?"

137

She glanced out the window. "It's dark outside."

"Ever practical, Dr. Lindstrom. You do know they have this invention called the flashlight?"

"I'd heard tell of such a thing, but I've never seen one in action." She appreciated Brooke's effort to distract her with levity.

"They even include it as an accessory on your phone."

"No kidding."

"Would you like me to show you?"

"Should we turn the lights out?"

"No," Brooke threaded her arm through Diana's, "I think we should take this experiment outside." She led them to the coat closet and grabbed their jackets.

"Where should we go?"

"I was thinking a walk on the beach would do you good."

"Should we check the tide?"

"The tide is out and so is the moon. I found a flashlight in the drawer the other day when I was looking for a can opener. We'll be fine."

"I thought you were going to demonstrate the flashlight feature on the phone?"

"I can if you want, but I'm thinking the beam from an actual flashlight might be brighter." Brooke nabbed the flashlight out of the drawer as she pulled on her coat.

They meandered along the shore for several minutes in silence. Brooke was right—the moon shone brightly in the night sky, and the beam from the flashlight added more than enough illumination to light their way.

Aunt Nora would've loved a night like tonight. The thought sent a searing pain straight to her heart. She gasped and pulled up short.

"What's the matter?" Brooke backtracked to her.

"I-I was just thinking..." She put her hand to her mouth as a sob broke free. "It's such a beautiful night. Aunt Nora would've loved to take a walk on the beach on a night like this." Tears flowed freely now, and she was powerless to stop them.

Brooke enveloped her in a warm hug. "That's right. Let it all go. That's right." She rubbed soothing circles on her back. Eventually, she kissed her on the top of the head.

Diana leaned into the embrace, soaking in the comfort. Finally, her tears subsided and she pulled back. "I'm so sorry. I got you all soggy." She wiped ineffectually at the wet spot on Brooke's jacket. "That's okay. It'll dry." She withdrew a packet of tissues from her side pocket and handed one to Diana.

"Thank you."

Brooke shrugged.

"No, I mean it." She searched Brooke's face. "You loved Aunt Nora as much as I did. You knew her better than I did. You spent every day caring for her, seeing to her every need. And yet, you put aside your own grief in order to take care of me. I don't know how you're even standing right now."

Unable to hold back any longer, she reached up and moved an errant strand of hair off Brooke's forehead. Her fingers lingered on the worry lines above Brooke's brow.

"You're amazing," she whispered. She stepped forward once again, her fingers never losing contact with Brooke's skin. Slowly, tentatively, she brought their lips together.

This kiss was gentle, their lips trembling in equal parts grief, desire, and uncertainty. After several seconds, Brooke broke the kiss and cleared her throat. "It's a really emotional time, and I need you to be sure about what you're doing, what you want, and why."

Diana opened her eyes. Her heart was hammering in her chest and she willed her libido to calm down. "I understand." She toed the sand with the tip of her boot.

"Do you?" Brooked asked softly. She shifted so that they were eye to eye. "Nothing's changed, Diana. I want to explore us. When the time is right."

"Agreed." She was glad the darkness covered her embarrassment. "That was a mistake."

"No. It wasn't a mistake. It was a natural reaction to a highly charged situation. I can't have you thinking that every time we kiss it's a mistake."

She opened her mouth to apologize again and thought better of it. She fought the urge to shut down. She'd done that once, and it hadn't gone well for either of them.

"Diana?"

"Yes."

"It wasn't a mistake. It's a question of timing. This is too important. *We're* too important. When this happens—and I really hope it will—I want you to be sure it's about us, and not about anything, or anyone…else."

Brooke was right, of course. Now was not the time. She still was in shock over Aunt Nora's death, her heart felt as though it had been put through a meat grinder, and neither of them knew what tomorrow would bring.

"Diana?"

"Yes?"

"Say something."

"I'm sorry. I'm just not firing on all cylinders. You're right. I'm completely shell-shocked and raw. I'm not thinking clearly, and the appropriate thing to do is to process this loss first, and then figure out what's next."

Brooke studied her for long seconds and she squirmed. Unable to stand it anymore, she said, "That look tells me either you don't believe me, or you don't trust me."

Finally, Brooke spoke. "It's neither of those things. I'm trying to avoid any confusion or a repeat of the way this past week went between us."

"I know."

"What happened in the aftermath of our last kiss—that didn't work for me."

"It didn't work for me, either."

"Okay, then."

"Okay, then."

They began walking again. "Just to be clear," Brooke said, "that doesn't mean I can't be there to comfort you."

"Agreed. And it doesn't mean I won't let you."

"Agreed."

They continued on to the cottage in companionable silence. When they reached the steps leading up to the deck, Diana froze.

"What is it?" Brooke asked.

"I don't think I can stay here tonight."

"You don't have to."

"Going back in there…"

"I completely understand." Brooke paused. "Why would you think you'd need to stay here tonight?"

"Because there's no reason for you to stay here now that Aunt Nora is gone. I assumed you'd be going back to your place."

"Honestly, I hadn't thought about it." Brooke sat down on the step.

"I'm sure I can get a room at one of the bed and breakfasts," Diana said.

"You'll do no such thing. You stay at my place. I can stay here as I've been doing."

The idea didn't sit well with her. She wasn't superstitious or afraid of ghosts. That wasn't it. It was just that, scant hours ago, Brooke helped someone she loved cross over. How would she feel in Brooke's place?

She knew the answer. It was the same reason she couldn't stay at the cottage tonight. "No."

"Diana—"

"No. Not tonight, at least."

"Then I guess we're at a stalemate."

She sat down next to Brooke. "What do you suggest?"

Brooke was silent so long Diana wondered if she would answer. Finally, Brooke said, "There's an obvious solution, if you're okay with it."

"What's that?"

"We could stay together at my place."

Brooke's suggestion hung in the air between them. "Or not," she added, as she rose and trudged slowly up the stairs.

"No. Wait." Diana put a hand on her arm. "There's only one bedroom."

"I know."

"But..."

"I'm not talking about making love, Diana. There's a couch in the living room. I'm suggesting that I'd sleep on the couch."

"It's your place and your bedroom. You should take the bed."

"No. I'm not the one who's been staying there, you are. Please don't fight with me on this. We're both tired and emotional right now. The couch is plenty comfortable. Trust me, it wouldn't be the first time I fell asleep there."

She weighed her options. If she continued to object, no doubt Brooke would insist on staying at the cottage. That was even less preferable than her bunking on the couch.

"Uncle," she said.

"Uncle?"

"I surrender. You take the couch."

"Okay. I'll just grab an overnight bag and meet you in the driveway."

"Right," she agreed. She took a deep breath. It's not like they'd be sleeping in the same bed, or even the same room. They could do this without crossing any boundaries, couldn't they?

Brooke regarded herself in the bathroom mirror. Deep purple circles had taken up residence underneath her eyes, which were dull and glassy. *You look as though you haven't slept for weeks.*

That was not far from the truth, as she hadn't slept an entire night through since taking over Nora's care. Part of her wanted to fall into her own bed now and sleep for a week. The other part of her was grateful Diana accepted her solution and acquiesced to her sleeping on the couch.

Still, the prospect of sharing space, even platonically, with Diana made her pulse race, and that was the problem. She wasn't interested in a fling. What she wanted with Diana went deeper than that, and, given their rocky beginning, waiting until the emotional dust settled was imperative to ensuring any chance of anything else.

You got yourself into this. Wrestle your libido under control and deal with it. She splashed cold water on her face and wiped it off, brushed her teeth, combed her hair, and dabbed on a little perfume. *Because you always put on perfume before you go to bed. Yeah, right.*

She paused as she passed the open bedroom door. Diana was awake, lying in the bed, hair splayed on the pillow, arms folded on top of the covers. Brooke swallowed hard. The sight of Diana in her bed…

"I'm not on your side, am I? Because if I am and it makes you uncomfortable, I can sleep on the other side—"

"You're not. On my side of the bed, I mean. I don't have a designated side. I mean, I don't have a firm preference. I mean…" She took a deep breath. "I think I should quit while I'm behind."

Diana's eyes held mirth. "I get the idea."

"Thank God." She wiped her brow in mock relief and motioned to Diana's empty hands. "What? No journal article to memorize?" Diana pointed to her empty hands. "What? No book to read?"

"Touché."

They were quiet for a moment.

"I want to say—"

"I wanted to tell you—"

They spoke at the same time.

"You go first," Diana said.

"No, you go," Brooke insisted.

"Okay. These past few weeks have been a blur. Honestly, I haven't even begun to figure out where to put all of my emotions around Aunt Nora—the missing years, her re-appearance in my life..." She ticked the items off on her fingers. "The one thing I know for sure is that I never could've gotten through any of it without you."

"That's not—"

"Don't interrupt me, please." She propped two pillows behind her and sat up in the bed. "It's true. You were my green wire—the one who grounded me when I felt untethered. Your compassion, your kindness, your caring, your steadiness... I came to rely on all of those things, and on you. Every day I knew Aunt Nora was in the best possible hands. And every night I looked forward to our exchanges like a kid anticipating her favorite bedtime story. So, thank you. Thank you for being there for me and for Aunt Nora. Thank you for everything." Her voice broke.

"You're welcome. Thank you for entrusting Nora's care to me, and thank you for brightening my days and evenings. As I told you at the outset, it was my honor and privilege to help you and Nora through this transition. Getting to know you has made this time even more special. With every interaction, I find myself wanting to know more." She searched Diana's face. Briefly, she allowed herself to imagine what it would be like to wake up to that smile and those eyes every day. "Well, I should..." She pointed in the direction of the living room.

"Good night, Brooke."

"Sleep well, Diana." Gently, she closed the door behind her.

⁂

Brooke awoke with a start. *Diana.* Diana was crying. She could hear her even through the closed bedroom door. Without thought, she threw off the blanket and scrambled off the couch. She skidded around the corner and hesitated only for an instant at the bedroom door. When her quiet knock went unanswered, she opened the door a crack and peered inside, allowing her eyes to adjust to the darkness.

"Diana?"

"I-I'm sorry if I woke you. I'm fine. Don't worry."

But she wasn't fine and Brooke knew it. She moved into the room and stood at the side of the bed. "You don't look so fine to me."

"It's just…"

Diana's shoulders shook, and Brooke couldn't restrain herself anymore. "May I?" She pointed to the bed.

Diana nodded.

She lifted the covers, slid underneath them, and opened her arms, relieved when Diana fell into them without hesitation.

"You don't need to be strong, Diana. It's healthier to let go and allow yourself to feel whatever you're feeling. There's nothing noble about being stoic in the face of death."

Diana buried her head against Brooke's neck and let the tears flow. When she'd cried herself out, she fell asleep on Brooke's shoulder.

Gentle puffs of air cooled Brooke's overheated skin. Poor Diana. Everything she thought she knew about Nora had proven to be a lie, and just as she and Nora had been making up for lost time, Nora passed away.

Brooke raised a hand to stroke Diana's face and let it fall away just short of making contact. She didn't want to take a chance on waking her. Rest and time. What Diana needed was time to heal.

And you. Isn't that what she'd overheard Nora tell Diana? That she was the ticket to making her heart whole?

Yet another reason to put on the brakes, she decided. How could she possibly know if Diana was acting on her own desires, or if she was following through on Nora's dying wish?

Diana moaned in her sleep, and Brooke brushed her lips against her temple. Diana settled down immediately and tightened her grip with the arm she had thrown across Brooke's midsection when she'd fallen asleep. *I will not react. I will not react. I will not react. Not now.* She breathed in the scent of Diana's honey shampoo and closed her eyes. It was late and she was exhausted. Her brain was on overload, and her body was warring with her common sense and defense mechanisms. How had life gotten this complicated? One thing was certain—in her current state she never was going to make sense of any of this.

CHAPTER FOURTEEN

Diana pried her eyes open. Brooke faced away from her, curled on her side. Her shoulder rose and fell with each soft snore and Diana resisted the urge to wrap herself around her and go back to sleep.

Vague snapshots of the night played in quick succession. Brooke showing up at the side of the bed. Brooke opening her arms to envelop her. Her arm carelessly tossed across Brooke's belly. Brooke nuzzling the side of her hair. Breathing in lungfuls of Brooke's intoxicating perfume. Awakening at one point with their mouths scant inches apart.

The memory of that last bit thrust Diana's imagination into overdrive and sent a bolt of warmth straight through her. *Okay. Time to get up. Right now.*

Slowly, carefully, she extricated herself from the covers and crept into the bathroom. A cold shower. That's what she needed. A cold shower would make all the difference in the world.

By the time she emerged, the bed was made and the smell of bacon and coffee permeated the air. She followed her nose down the hall and stood, mouth slightly agape, watching Brooke glide around the kitchen like a ballerina commanding the stage. How was it possible that flannel pajamas could be so sexy?

She should make a noise. She should do something to let Brooke know she was there, shouldn't she?

"Are you going to stand there all morning, or are you going to set the table?"

"What? Oh. Sure." Heat suffused Diana's cheeks. *Stupid. Stupid. Stupid.* Of course. Brooke could see her in the reflection of the range hood.

"I'll just…" She shimmied around Brooke to get to the silverware drawer. "That smells delicious." As if to emphasize the point, her stomach rumbled loudly.

Brooke laughed. "I'd ask if you were hungry, but I'm pretty sure I already know the answer to that."

"Sorry. I can't remember the last time I ate."

"Lunch yesterday." Brooke dropped two pieces of bread into the toaster. "Scrambled eggs okay? I don't have any cheese for omelets."

"Fine. Are you kidding me? I could eat your arm and be satisfied right now."

"Please don't." Brooke spooned the eggs out of the pan, added three strips of bacon, and presented the plate to her.

"Thanks." She put the plate down and finished setting the table. "I'm sorry about last night."

"Don't be. Are you feeling any better this morning?"

"I am for right now. I can't guarantee I won't lose it again."

"It's okay and normal if you do, Diana. That's to be expected."

"Well, for what it's worth, that caught me by surprise. But then, I don't have as much experience with death as you do."

"I'm glad for that."

"I hope I didn't drool on you. It's bad enough that I cried on you."

Brooke snatched the toast as it popped up and handed one piece to her and kept the other for herself. "You didn't. You might've snored a little, though."

"You too."

"We're even then."

Brooke turned off the stove and sat opposite Diana with her own plate.

"Thanks for making breakfast. This is great."

"You're welcome. You're sure Mr. Fitzgerald said he wanted to see both of us?" Brooke buttered her toast and took a bite.

"Yes."

"Why would he need me to be present?"

She wondered the same thing but hadn't thought to ask the question yesterday. "I don't know. I guess we'll find out."

"I guess we will." Brooke scooped up the last bit of scrambled egg from her plate. "Speaking of which, I'd better get in the shower if I want to be on time." She rose, rinsed her dishes, and threw them in the dishwasher. Next, she scrubbed the pans.

Diana joined her at the sink. "I'll finish up for you."

"I've got it. My hands are already wet."

Diana bumped her with a hip. "I said, I've got this. Hit the showers."

"Okay." Brooke dried her hands on a dish towel and headed in the direction of the bathroom.

Diana congratulated herself on not turning to watch her go. Instead, she buried her hands in the soapy dishwater and picked up the sponge.

She should make a list of items that would need to be taken care of before she headed home. First, she would send an e-mail to her head of department to explain the situation and organize a few days bereavement leave to take care of Aunt Nora's affairs.

Would a few days be enough? It wasn't as though Aunt Nora was a hoarder, but then again, Diana hadn't spent time snooping through her things. And she'd only seen the cottage. What about the house in Cambridge?

"Earth to Diana. Come in, please."

She blinked. "I'm sorry. Did you say something?"

Brooke stood a few feet away. She wore a pair of dress pants and a button-down blouse. Her hair was blown dry and styled, and she wore more makeup than usual.

"I asked if you were ready to go?"

"Oh." She glanced down at her own outfit and took stock. Should she change into something dressier? She really hadn't brought anything appropriate with her.

"You look fine." Brooke smiled and her eyes twinkled.

"Was I that obvious?"

"Yep."

"I can't help it. I feel like a slob compared to you."

"Well, you shouldn't. This is the Cape. Jeans are considered formalwear out here."

She frowned.

"If you feel that badly about it, I could loan you something."

"No. I'll suck it up."

"I'm sure Mr. Fitzgerald isn't going to care what you're wearing. If you want, I'll go back and change into jeans."

"No. It's okay. We'd better get going. I don't want to be late."
Brooke didn't move.

"What?"

"One car or two?"

"Oh." She hadn't given any thought to logistics. Truthfully, she hadn't considered anything beyond the mental list she'd made a few minutes ago.

Brooke picked up her car keys. "How about if we take two? Then you'll have the freedom to do whatever you want afterward."

"Right." She grabbed her car keys off the kitchen counter and stuffed her wallet into the back pocket of her jeans. "I'll follow you."

She didn't like the sound of her and Brooke going their separate ways. Hadn't Brooke told her last night there was no place she'd rather be? Was that only for last night? *Probably.*

While Brooke had made it clear she might be interested in exploring a relationship at some point, she'd also made it plain that that time was not now, in the midst of her grief.

So, where were they, then? Diana couldn't think of an excuse to interact with Brooke beyond the meeting, and Brooke had no obligation to help her now. *In other words, you're nowhere.*

She watched the bleak scenery fly by. The trees were leafless now, and the wind-whipped dunes left scattered sand across Route 6A. The sky was papered over with dense clouds. The landscape matched her mood. Most likely Brooke would disappear from her life, at least temporarily, and Aunt Nora...

Although she'd known from the first time Charles contacted her that Aunt Nora would pass away, her death still hit Diana like a two-by-four. How was that possible? It wasn't as though the outcome was ever in question.

"I miss you, Aunt Nora." She swallowed hard and fought back tears. Now was not the time to fall apart again. There would be plenty of time for that soon enough. No, she would go, hear what Charles had to say about Nora's wishes, say goodbye to Brooke, and focus on one task at a time.

※※

When Brooke turned into Nora's driveway, Mr. Fitzgerald already was waiting. She glanced in the rearview mirror. Diana was parking her car on the street. Brooke was worried about her. She looked so fragile and lost.

Mr. Fitzgerald opened the car door for her and helped her out. "I'm glad you could come, Ms. Sheldon."

"Call me Brooke, please, Mr. Fitzgerald. Honestly, I'm not really sure why I'm here."

"I promise to clear that up for you shortly. And please call me Charles."

"I'm sorry we're late," Diana said as she joined them.

"On the contrary, I'm early; you two are right on time. Shall we?" He motioned toward the cottage. For the first time, Brooke noticed that he carried a well-worn briefcase. He was casually dressed in a pair of slacks and an open-collared button-down shirt. unbuttoned at the top button.

Diana hesitated at the front door, and Brooke came up alongside her. "Are you okay?"

"I-I guess I didn't think even going inside would be this difficult."

"How about if I go first?" Brooke gently extricated the key from Diana's grasp and inserted it in the lock. She stepped inside and opened the wood blinds to let in the daylight.

Grief stabbed her in the heart. The house smelled like Nora. She half-expected Nora to call out, "It's open." But that never would happen again. Never again would Nora curse her "damned infirmity," or ask Brooke to help her make toast, or...

Diana handed her a tissue, and she offered her a pained smile. She hadn't realized until then that she'd been crying.

"Why don't you both take a minute? I'll get myself organized at the kitchen table."

She straightened up. "Thank you. I'm all right now."

"Let's move forward," Diana agreed.

Brooke grabbed three glasses from the cupboard and poured them all some water. She used the time to regroup. This wasn't about her grief. There would be time for that later. Right now Diana needed her.

"Again, let me offer my condolences. It's never easy to lose someone you love, and Nora, well, Nora was truly special." He shuffled through several folders, re-ordered them, and laid them on the table.

Brooke sat across from Diana with Charles between them. It occurred to her that she should ask if either of them wanted coffee, but this was not her house, and she wasn't the hostess. Serving water was as far as she was willing to go.

"I want you to know Nora loved both of you dearly."

Brooke raised an eyebrow. Nora appreciated her, of course, but she was being paid to do a job.

"Yes, you too, Brooke."

Belatedly, she realized she should've schooled her expression better.

"Nora confided in me the last time I saw her that, while she always admired you and your work at Dana-Farber, spending so much time in proximity to you these last few weeks showed her exactly who you were. She loved you for, as she said, 'your beautiful soul and big heart.'"

She squirmed. She never enjoyed being the center of attention, and both Diana and Charles were staring at her.

"Diana," Charles turned in her direction, "you were Nora's pride and joy. I know you had many questions when you came to see me in my office. I assume you were able to get some of your questions answered."

"Some." Diana crossed her arms, and Brooke recognized that she wasn't the only uncomfortable one in the room. "But I realized too late that I had more questions than answers." She shook her head. "There was so much more I wanted to ask. Now, I never—"

"Uh-uh," he cautioned. "Stop right there. Nora understood your curious nature more than you think. She anticipated you would yearn to know more, and she feared she wouldn't be here long enough to fill in the blanks." He tilted his head to read the label on one of the files. "She wanted me to give you this." He reached into the file folder, extracted a sealed envelope, and slid it across the table toward Diana.

She ran her fingertips across the neat, cursive writing on the outside of the envelope—Aunt Nora's unmistakable penmanship. "What's this?"

"It's a package she put together for you shortly after she was diagnosed. She gave me strict instructions that I was not to give it to you until after she expired."

Diana pursed her lips. "Did she do this before, or after, she had you contact me?"

"Before. At the point she created this, she still believed she would die alone, never having seen you again face to face."

Brooke shivered. The idea that Nora could've died alone and not surrounded by love was unthinkable. She reminded herself to thank Daniel the next time she saw him. Nora wasn't the only one for whom the last few weeks were life-changing. Being able to spend quality time with Nora was a gift to her as well.

Diana turned the bulky envelope over several times.

"Please don't open that yet. There are a few more things she asked me to share with you first. Diana, when you were in my office several weeks ago, I shared with you some of the details of Nora's living trust."

"Yes."

"Because all of her assets were titled to the trust, probate will be unnecessary. Nora did this purposefully in order to prevent your father and mother, and any other living relatives, from interfering with her wishes. She was adamant that no one would successfully contest the will."

He withdrew a sheaf of papers from another folder. He opened his mouth to speak again, and Diana held a hand up to stop him.

"Are you sure we should be talking about all this now? I mean, Aunt Nora hasn't even been gone twenty-four hours, and we're sitting here talking about the distribution of her assets. It seems…vulgar." She shuddered.

Brooke sympathized with her. One thing she knew without doubt—Diana wasn't in this for what she could reap materially. No, her love for Nora was unquestioned, genuine, and unencumbered by earthly possessions.

Perhaps some of Diana's discomfort had to do with Brooke's presence? Well, she could fix that. She rose. "Clearly, this is a private discussion. I should go."

"No," Diana said.

"On the contrary," Charles said. "This has quite a bit to do with you. Please, stay."

Reluctantly, she sat back down.

"I understand how you feel, Diana," he said. "But Nora was very specific about how all of this was to unfold, and, as you know, she was a persuasive woman, a force to be reckoned with. She had a lot of time to think about what she wanted, and she meticulously planned every detail, including the timing."

He picked up the top document on the stack of papers before him. "This is Nora's last will and testament. I brought a copy you can read through at your leisure, but she asked me to share several items she recently added, including a preface to the will."

He donned a pair of glasses and began to read. "I, Nora Lindstrom, being of sound mind and body, do hereby declare that the provisions contained within this will are my wishes, and mine alone. I have not been coerced or pressured in any way, and I have discussed my desires with no one prior to creating this legally binding document. I make these bequests of my own free will and with a full heart, and I ask those named herein to consider the contents of this document as my dying wish."

He flipped to the second page, scanned the contents, and lowered the paper to the table. "I'll spare you both the legal mumbo-jumbo. As I said, you can read the document in its entirety later. Instead, I'll share with you Nora's pertinent instructions and bequests.

"To Diana, my beloved great-niece, I bequeath via my trust, my primary residence in Cambridge, Massachusetts, and all the contents therein, with one exception. To Brooke, my trusted caregiver and friend, I bequeath via my trust, my cottage in Truro, Massachusetts, and all the contents therein to do with as she wishes."

"What?" Brooke exclaimed. She put her hand over her heart, which was beating wildly in her chest. Nora had left her this place? What could she have been thinking? She shifted her attention to Diana. Was this okay with her? Surely everything should pass to her; she was Nora's next of kin and chosen beneficiary. "That must be a mistake."

"It is not," Charles assured her.

"But Diana—"

"I'm fine with that, Brooke. In fact, I'm glad. This place suits you perfectly. Aunt Nora knew that." She smiled wistfully. "Leave it to Aunt Nora to know exactly the right thing to do."

She turned her attention to Charles. "You said there was an exception regarding the contents of the house in Cambridge. What was it?"

"I'm glad you asked," he said. He pulled out from his pile a third folder.

This one was thin and Brooke could see that it was marked, "Diana and Brooke."

He withdrew three sealed envelopes, all with lettering in Nora's precise script. One bore Diana's name, one Brooke's, and the third was addressed to both of them. He handed them each the envelopes addressed to them individually.

Brooke turned hers over.

"Please, open them and read."

"Now?" Brooke and Diana asked simultaneously.

"Nora's instructions," he said, as if that explained everything.

Brooke glanced over to see that Diana already had begun to read. She slit open the envelope addressed to her with a fingernail and teased out the letter.

My dearest Brooke,

If you are reading this now, it is because I have passed. First, I want to thank you for your compassionate, expert care. No one could have been in better hands than me. I am so grateful to you for all that you did for me.

Brooke swallowed hard and shook her head to ward off the tears that threatened.

But you were so much more than my nurse. You were my friend, my confidant, my companion. In you, I recognized the same extraordinary qualities I saw in someone I loved very much, many years ago, in a place far, far away. And for you, I hope for a much happier ending.

Brooke lowered the letter. Could Nora be referencing the Mary of her nightmares? Now she would never know.

By now, Charles will have read to you the portion of my will in which I leave to you the cottage. I know you, dear Brooke. You won't think you deserve such largess. But you do, my dear. You deserve every good thing.

Please know, I am not a sentimental person. Feel free to do with my possessions as you wish. Make this place YOUR home, not a museum or monument to me.

You are at a crossroads in your life, and you chose this area in which to heal. I did much the same when I retired here and purchased this place. It was my salvation. I hope it will be yours, as well. Consider it a repayment for your kindness, my dear.

Whatever choices you make in your life, please promise me you'll always choose love. Don't be like me, living with regrets for far too long.

Live, love, and be well, dear Brooke.

Affectionately, your friend,
Nora Lindstrom

Brooke cleared her throat to stave off the emotions welling up inside her, and slowly became aware once again of her surroundings. Diana was tucking her letter back into the envelope. Her expression gave nothing away.

What had her letter said? What words of wisdom had Nora imparted to her? It was none of her business and she would never ask. But that did not mean she wasn't curious. She imagined Diana was thinking similar thoughts. Perhaps later they would share with each other.

"Now that you're both done reading…" Charles removed a pair of key rings from his pocket. He handed one to Diana, and the other to Brooke. "As I said, there's no need for probate in Nora's case, so you both are free to treat the properties as your own. As Nora's executor, I'll file all the necessary paperwork to have the deeds transferred over and take care of disbursing the remainder of her estate. Everything is clearly laid out in the will. I'll leave you both a copy for your perusal." He handed each of them a folder. "Everything about each of your properties is in your respective folders."

He pointed to the third letter, the one addressed to both of them. It sat on the table between them. "Nora specifically asked me to leave you two alone to read that one, although she did ask that you read it simultaneously. So, this is where I exit, stage left." He stood, gathered his papers, and stuffed them back in his briefcase.

"But what about her burial wishes? She and I never discussed it," Diana said.

"She left instructions for that too." He tapped yet another folder. "You'll find everything you need to know about what to do next in this folder. If you have any questions, please call. And, of course, let Emily and me know once you've selected a date for the service." Charles turned to leave. "Oh, Diana? That thicker envelope that I told you not to open yet? Nora asked that you open it after the letter addressed to you and Brooke. You are welcome to open it in privacy or not, she didn't specify."

"Understood."

They walked Charles to the door. "Thank you for everything," Diana said.

"Yes, thank you."

"You're both welcome. Nora thought the world of you two, and I can see why. Take care of each other and yourselves. Remember, as long as you hold Nora's memory in your hearts, she'll always live within you."

They bid him goodbye and watched him drive away.

"Now what?" Brooke asked.

"Now I guess we follow Aunt Nora's next instruction and read the joint letter."

CHAPTER FIFTEEN

B rooke fidgeted with the coffee pot, opened and closed the cupboard twice without remembering to take out mugs or the bag of coffee, and then leaned against the counter. Her hands shook, and Diana restrained herself from going to her and putting her arms around her.

"I don't really need coffee. Please, come sit down."

Brooke turned and faced her. "I need you to know that I'm going to deed this place over to you."

"No, you're not."

"Diana—"

"I meant what I said before, Brooke. Aunt Nora knew exactly what she was doing, and she did the right thing leaving the cottage to you."

"I don't know how much this place is worth, but I priced homes here when I first came out after leaving Dana-Farber. I couldn't afford a shack, never mind something as lovely as this." She waved her hands to encompass the cottage.

"I don't care about the money. Besides, how many homes can I live in at one time? I've got my place in New York and now Aunt Nora's house in Cambridge. That's already one home too many."

"You could sell the cottage and—"

"No. I'm not going to do anything of the sort. Leaving this place to you was Aunt Nora's intention, and we're both going to honor that."

Finally, Brooke came back to the table and sat down heavily. "I can't fathom why she did that."

"And that's precisely why this is so perfect. You're not the kind of person who thinks good things should happen to her. You give of yourself without expectation, and Aunt Nora is right that you have a big heart. I'm so happy for you."

She wanted to take Brooke's hand, to smooth the worry lines from her face, to somehow make this okay. But she couldn't imagine what more she could say. Instead, she decided to change the subject. "How about if we open the joint letter and read it?" She pushed the envelope in Brooke's direction. "You've got nails. You open it."

Brooke slit open the envelope, removed several sheets of neatly folded note paper, and smoothed them on the table. Diana came up behind her to read over her shoulder.

"Can you see all right?"

"Tilt them up, will you?"

Brooke lifted the pages to a forty-five-degree angle. "This okay?"

"Perfect."

My dear girls,

I am so sorry to have left this earth with tasks undone, words unsaid, and questions unanswered. Who knew that was possible at my age?

Diana smiled at the gentle, self-deprecating humor so characteristic of Aunt Nora.

The one thing that gives me comfort and great joy is that the two of you have each other to lean on in this time of sorrow, and lean on each other I hope you do.

Charles would have told you both by now that the Cambridge house and all therein belongs to Diana, with one exception. No doubt you two are wondering what that might be. I won't keep you in suspense any longer.

In the attic of that home, you'll find an old, beat-up trunk (how trite).

Brooke glanced back at Diana. "Are you ready for me to turn the page?"

"Yes."

I mean for you, Diana, and you, Brooke, to explore the contents of that trunk together, never one without the other. I know, I know. This sounds like the contrived or eccentric wishes of an old and feeble woman. Yes, I am old but not feeble of mind, as I'm convinced you have discovered for yourself in these last weeks. So please, bear with me. I have my reasons for this stipulation.

Now for the rest.

Diana, I need to address something you shared with me when you first arrived here. There was a kernel of truth amongst the lies your grandfather and parents told you. I did spend decades of my life working on secret or classified projects. And I did, for a number of years, live outside the country, although I returned frequently to Washington as part of my work.

And that is where Bill's adherence to the truth ends and his fabrications begin. I returned to the states to live and work shortly before you were born. I never again worked overseas, and I most assuredly was never, ever too busy to be in your life. (You will discover proof of this when you open the thicker envelope Charles gave you, if you haven't opened it already.)

Diana remembered the first envelope Charles gave her—the one she had set aside for later. She spied the corner of it peeking out from underneath the folders he'd left.

"Do you want to open that now?" Brooke asked, following her gaze.

"No. Let's keep going. We can look at that afterward."

Brooke turned the page.

Brooke, dear Brooke... I awoke more than once in agitation, speaking a name quite clearly. On one such occasion, I noticed the expression on your face, and, much to my chagrin, it became clear to me that you heard me say this name in anguish. Yet never once did you ask me about it, even though I could see that you wanted to. You were the epitome of discretion, and for that I was, and am, most grateful.

Diana shifted so she and Brooke were face to face. "Aunt Nora was calling out someone's name?"

"Yes."

"Was it a man or a woman?"

"A woman. Mary."

"Why didn't you tell me?"

"I considered it, but I didn't want to violate Nora's privacy. Do you know who Mary was? A sister, maybe? Your mother or grandmother?"

She shook her head. "As far as I know, there were no Marys in my family."

"Well, whoever Mary was, she was really important to Nora, and something about the relationship haunted her."

She drummed her fingers on the table as she weighed the possibilities. "Mary could've been an old girlfriend."

"Girlfriend, as in a romantic interest?"

"You didn't know Aunt Nora was gay?"

"Not with any certainty, no."

"I asked her once if she'd shared that with you and she said she hadn't, but I thought maybe you'd figured it out on your own."

"No," Brooke said. "I mean, she asked me about my love life and didn't seem fazed by the fact that I was a lesbian. That made me wonder a little. Then she told me she'd never been married, which made me wonder even more. Once or twice I asked myself if maybe Mary was her lover, but it wasn't as though Nora set off my gaydar or anything." She sat back. "The short answer to your question is no."

"The plot thickens."

"I guess so." After a beat, Brooke asked, "How were you so sure I was a lesbian?"

Diana chuckled. "Aunt Nora made a point of telling me."

Brooke groaned and her cheeks turned a pretty shade of red. "How much did she divulge?"

"Nothing beyond the fact that you were gay."

"When was that?"

"I think it was on my second visit. She was quite adamant that I should ask you out. She browbeat me about whether or not I found you attractive."

Brooke nearly choked on a sip of water. "She did what?"

A blush crept up her neck. "The paraphrase goes something like this. 'Brooke is lovely, don't you think? And she's single. You should ask her out.' Or something like that."

"Oh, my God. Is that why you kissed me that first time? Because Nora thought we'd make a nice couple?"

"No." Her voice took on a husky quality. "I kissed you because I couldn't help myself. I kissed you because I find you fascinating and I want to know you better. I kissed you because it was all I could think about doing."

And it's all I can think about doing now. She stroked Brooke's cheek and allowed her fingers to wander to Brooke's lush lips. Brooke's eyes grew heavy lidded and Diana couldn't stand it any longer. She lowered her mouth to meet Brooke's and took her time exploring.

The taste of her was sweet and the texture of her lips and tongue so soft. She ran her fingers through the hair at the nape of Brooke's neck and deepened the kiss. This time, neither of them pulled away.

Diana's pulse thundered in her ears. No simple kiss had ever felt this exquisite. Her hand moved to the side of Brooke's neck, and then downward. She caressed Brooke's collarbone and...

"Wait." Brooke put a hand over hers. "Wait. Oh, God. Please wait before I can't think anymore."

She opened her eyes. Brooke's chest was heaving and Diana could see that her pulse was jumping too.

"I won't apologize this time," Diana managed.

"I don't want you to," Brooke answered, equally breathless.

She stepped back and returned to her seat. "I will, however, try to exercise better self-control. For now." She winked.

"Incorrigible." Brooke straightened her blouse. "How about if we finish reading Nora's letter?"

"Good plan."

Brooke picked up the pages again and moved her chair closer so that Diana could read too and so that she could maintain physical contact.

By now, you both are convinced I'm rambling, so I'll get to the point. Within the trunk I referenced, you'll both find answers that you seek. I am sorry that I'm no longer here to clear up any residual questions you might have, but God has granted me reprieve not to have to relive old memories that have caused me many sleepless nights, or to face the embarrassment of your discoveries and your scrutiny.

I hope by leaving you these records and writings to explore, you'll see my life as a cautionary tale. Please don't think less of me for my actions and choices. Instead, use my experiences to learn a different way to be.

Choose a different path, one guided by love. Please, my dear girls, do not close your hearts to love as I did. Instead, open your hearts and find the love that lives within. You both have a

163

tremendous capacity for love—it is my great wish that you use it to heal yourselves and each other.
Remember always that I am with you, and that I love you.
Yours,
Nora

Brooke reached over and took Diana's hand. "Are you all right?"

"I think so. I don't know about you, but I'm really curious about what's in that trunk."

"Me too. Right now, though, I could use some fuel. How about you? Lunch in town?"

"Deal."

⊰⊱

The Post Office Café was quiet now that the peak-season crowds had abated, and they had no trouble getting a table toward the back of the small space, away from the drafty front door.

Once they were seated and had ordered, Diana removed both the letter she read earlier and the unopened envelope she previously set aside. She placed the two on the table between them.

Brooke looked at her in question.

"If we're going to investigate Nora's past, as she seems to have given us license to do, we're going to need to be open with each other and share what each of us knows."

"Fair enough." Brooke produced her letter and laid it on the table on top of Diana's envelopes. "I'll go first." She removed the letter from the envelope and handed it to Diana. "I told you about Mary. Putting two and two together, the bit about me reminding her of someone she loved makes more sense. Maybe I reminded Nora of Mary."

Diana finished reading. "Sounds like a strong possibility. And maybe the regrets she references are about her relationship with Mary."

"Could be. I really hope there's something in that trunk that gives us definitive answers."

"No kidding. There's nothing worse than an unsolvable mystery." Diana returned Brooke's letter to its envelope and handed it back to her. She slid her opened letter across the table. "My turn."

As Brooke read, Diana said, "Aunt Nora obviously wrote this note at least a week ago."

"That would make sense, since I can assure you she wasn't in the kind of shape these past five days to write anything like this."

"Do you think…" Diana played with the condensation on the outside of her water glass. "Could I have caused Aunt Nora's death by bringing up painful memories?"

"What?" Brooke put the letter down. "Nora died of complications from lung cancer. Nothing you said…or did…killed her."

Her voice was soft and firm, and Diana wanted badly to believe her.

"Why would you ask that?"

"Right before she passed, I was questioning her about some historical documents I found in the archives at Columbia. It was about the Manhattan Project. She got very agitated about it and…" Diana couldn't go on. In her mind's eye, she watched Aunt Nora gasp for air, her hand movements jerky as she tried to grip the covers, and then…she was gone.

She shuddered, and Brooke briefly covered her hand with her own. "Don't do this to yourself. Your Aunt Nora passed away of natural causes. You brought her nothing but joy."

She shook her head. "It doesn't feel that way to me. I haven't been able to stop thinking about that last conversation, the one right before she died. I keep reliving it in my mind. I never should have asked her those questions, but I just had to know."

"I don't understand. You asked her about history and you think that caused her death?"

"Not just history—her role in history. And maybe I didn't cause her death, but I might've hastened it."

"No you didn't. What did Nora have to do with the atomic bomb?"

"Aunt Nora was part of the Manhattan Project. She was one of the scientists assigned to work with Robert Oppenheimer."

"Nora Lindstrom? The woman who helped Sid Farber cure childhood leukemia? Are you sure?"

"I'm positive, and Aunt Nora confirmed it for me right before she passed. Read the section of the letter about moral choices and science."

Brooke picked up the pages once again and scanned down. "You mean where she says, 'Diana, I've been following your work and your career. You are a brilliant scientist with a bright future. Please promise me you'll make more principled choices than I did. Ask questions. Always know and understand the end goal of your work. Trust your instincts. The moral imperative must at all times supersede the exigencies of scientific discovery and implementation?'"

"That's it, yes."

"What does that mean?"

"I wouldn't have understood the reference except for that last conversation with her. I found papers showing that Aunt Nora was in Oak Ridge during World War II and that she was a high-ranking physicist charged with overseeing the making of the fuel for the first bomb."

"Wow! That's amazing."

Diana thanked the server as he delivered her chef salad. She waited to speak until he'd handed Brooke her spinach salad and walked away.

"I had the same reaction as you, but it's like she was haunted by the experience. She helped win the war, but all she could think about was the Japanese lives lost."

Brooke took a forkful of spinach, strawberries, and pecans. She chewed and swallowed before asking, "Do you think that was what she meant when she urged us in the joint letter to use her life as a cautionary tale? And does it have anything to do with her living and working overseas?"

"Maybe. I'm hoping we'll learn more from whatever is in that trunk." She wiped her mouth. "As you can see, the rest of that note is just like yours—I'm free to do anything I want with the Cambridge house, etcetera, etcetera."

Brooke carefully folded the letter and put it back in its envelope. "We should put these away until after we finish eating."

"Right." Diana grabbed her two envelopes off the table and moved them out of harm's way as Brooke did the same with her letter.

"Aren't you curious about what's in the big one?" Brooke asked.

"I am."

"So why haven't you opened it yet?"

"I don't know. It's the last thing I'll ever hear from Aunt Nora that's meant specifically for me, you know? Once I read what's in it, that'll be it. I'll never hear from her again. I don't want to rush that." She set down her fork. "Does that make any sense?"

"It does."

"Still, I suppose I shouldn't delay any longer. Charles made it pretty clear that Aunt Nora was adamant and methodical about the order in which she wanted things done. I suppose I need to see what's in this one too."

"Do you want to be alone when you open it?"

"No." She smiled at Brooke. "I think I'd like you to be with me, if you don't mind."

They finished eating, paid the bill, and headed back to the cottage. Diana reached the front steps and stopped short.

"What is it?"

"This is your place now. I'm waiting for you to invite me in."

Brooke fumbled in her coat pocket for the key ring Charles gave her.

"You do remember that you already had a key that Aunt Nora gave you, right?"

"Oh. Right." Brooke looked flustered. "All this is going to take some getting used to." She unlocked the door and let them in.

After they'd put down their jackets, they returned to the kitchen table. Diana hefted the envelope in her hand. It was bulky and larger than the other letters.

"I guess I'd better get this over with." She tore open the seal and peeked inside. "Huh."

"Huh, what?"

She turned over the envelope and dumped out the contents. Four photographs spilled onto the table, along with another brief note in Nora's handwriting. Her hands shook as she picked up the first photograph. How had Aunt Nora gotten these? Her seventeen-year-old self stared back at her, graduation cap askew, as she gave the valedictory address at her high school commencement.

"Is that you?" Brooke asked.

She nodded.

"There's something written on the back." Brooke angled her head to read. "Diana, high school valedictory address, June, 1989."

Scrawled in black ink below the caption were the words: *Diana, dear, I took this photo with my Canon. Thank God I invested in that 300 mm zoom lens.*

Diana grabbed the next photo. There she was, giving her first big lecture at Columbia to a full complement of one-hundred-fifty eager first-year med students. She remembered the day with crystal clarity. She'd been so nervous, she'd thrown up before class. This snapshot was grainier, as if the lighting had been too dim.

"This one's captioned too," Brooke said. "Professor Diana Lindstrom, Columbia University. First lecture hall lesson." *Oh, my, I was so proud of you that day I could have burst a button.*

"Nora attended your first class? Did you see her there?"

She shook her head. She was dumbstruck. How could Aunt Nora have been there? Wouldn't she have seen her?

She recognized the next photo instantly. The local newspaper had captured twenty-year-old Princeton University ice hockey right wing Diana Lindstrom scoring the winning goal against arch rival Cornell.

"You played ice hockey?"

"Yeah." She stared at the back of the photo. *Although I was in attendance, the Associated Press photographer's photo was far better than anything I took, and when I wrote to him asking for a copy of the photograph and explained the circumstances, he was quite happy to comply. That sport was too violent, Diana. I always worried for your safety.*

"Isn't this one the same as the framed photo—"

"The one of my grad school graduation," Diana finished. "Yes."

"Nora wrote you a note." Brooke handed her the single sheet of paper.

My dearest Diana,

I hope these photographs are as meaningful to you as they were to me. Although I was forbidden to make contact with you, I never lost sight of you, as you plainly can see. I have always kept watch, even if you never saw me.

I am so proud of you. I watched you grow from a precocious, inquisitive child into a beautiful, talented, accomplished adult. Each step of the way, I cheered you on, applauding every success.

Diana, you have always had a place in my heart. No amount of time or distance has changed that. I shall remain, I hope, forever in yours, even though I likely will never see you again.
All my love and admiration,
Aunt Nora

Diana wordlessly handed the note to Brooke. She revisited each photograph and each handwritten comment. Aunt Nora had witnessed every important milestone, and she'd never known. She'd been practically close enough to touch, yet completely out of reach. So much wasted time. So many opportunities lost. So many things Diana wanted to tell her, and now she would never have the opportunity again.

When Brooke came around and opened her arms, she gratefully fell into them. The scent of her perfume was a balm to her battered soul.

CHAPTER SIXTEEN

Neither woman said a word as the sight of nearly bare trees whizzed past the car windows. It was just as well, since Brooke needed the time to sort through her emotions and try to bring some order to her scattered thoughts.

Since when have you become impulsive? When Diana announced she'd been given two weeks bereavement leave and asked Brooke if she'd go with her to the Cambridge house, Brooke hadn't even hesitated. She packed a bag with enough clothes for the two weeks and suggested that if they left now, they could be there before dark.

"What are you thinking?" Diana's tone was light.

She turned her head and regarded Diana's profile as she drove. It was amazing how much softer her features were when she relaxed. The sight made her smile. "Honestly? I'm wondering who is sitting in this car with you and what happened to practical, non-spontaneous me."

"I see. Were you being practical and non-spontaneous when you walked away from Dana-Farber and ran away to the Cape?"

"That's not fair. I was past the point of overload when I left, and I'd been considering it for the better part of a year when I finally pulled the trigger."

"Okay. When you agreed on the spot to take on the responsibility for Aunt Nora's care, was that practical, non-spontaneous Brooke?"

"All right. All right, already. You've made your point." She held up her hands in surrender. "But I want it noted that, up until very recently, I wasn't the least bit impulsive. I measured and weighed everything, including what kind of underwear to buy so that my panty lines wouldn't show. I actually did a scientific study."

Diana smirked. After a beat she said, "Well, now I know two things about you—you wear underwear, and you'll never suffer from unsightly panty lines. Good information to have."

Brooke slouched down in the seat as far as the seatbelt would allow. If she could've slithered under the floorboards at that moment, she would have. How was it that she was constantly embarrassing herself around Diana?

"So, which brand won?"

"I'm so not going to have the rest of this conversation with you. I stick my foot in my mouth every time I'm around you."

Diana glanced at her and then back to the road. "I think it's adorable."

She crossed her arms. "Yeah, well, you would. It isn't you who keeps digging herself a hole."

"Don't ever change, Brooke Sheldon. I find you charming."

In a bit of fortuitous timing, the GPS announced they were approaching their street. Saved by a disembodied voice with a British accent. If Brooke could've, she would've kissed her.

Less than five minutes later, they turned into the driveway of a stately old red-brick Colonial home just off Brattle Street. Diana cut the engine.

"Wow. Impressive place," Brooke said.

"No kidding. Holy smokes." Diana's hands remained on the steering wheel. The stress lines were back.

"You okay?"

"Yeah. I just…It's just…"

"A lot to take in?" Brooke offered.

"A lot to take in. I feel like I'm in some alternate universe. In a little while I'm going to wake up and I'll be in my classroom, teaching the next batch of Nobel-Prize-winning wannabes who are certain they're going to be the ones to cure all the world's diseases and syndromes."

"That will be true. You'll be back in the classroom before you know it. But you'll also be the proud owner of a fabulous and no-doubt historic home in one of the most desirable neighborhoods in the Boston metro area."

"This is a good neighborhood?"

She laughed. "You're a stone's throw from Harvard Square, the Mt. Auburn Cemetery is practically around the corner—"

"Being around the corner from a cemetery is a good thing?"

"Being around the corner from a really old, really historic cemetery is a good thing."

"Oh."

"You're less than fifteen minutes from Massachusetts General Hospital and four minutes from the Harvard campus. As they say, 'location, location, location.' You've hit the proverbial jackpot."

"Except that none of it means anything without Aunt Nora here."

"I can't argue with that. But I know this—Nora would never want you to stay sad for long. She told me more than once that she was ready to go. She'd had a long, full life. She was at peace with death."

"She might've been ready, but I wasn't."

Brooke reached across the expanse between them and took Diana's hand in hers. "I know. Death is most difficult for those left behind. A wise person who'd suffered a near-death experience once told me, 'Dying is easy. Living is hard.'"

"That's profound, and true, I guess." Diana ran her thumb across the back of Brooke's hand. "I feel like I got cheated, though, you know?"

"I do. You had so little time to get to know Nora."

"I barely scratched the surface."

"True. But the good news is, it seems like Nora left us a roadmap so that we can learn more about her and her life. What do you say we go inside?"

"Okay." Diana tightened her grip as Brooke pulled away. "Before we go in there, I want to say thank you."

"You're welcome. What are you thanking me for?"

"For coming with me. For not weighing and measuring first. For not leaving me to go through all this alone. For everything. Thank you for everything." Her voice broke. "It means the world to me."

"You're welcome. Thank you for sharing your grief with me, for trusting me enough to show your vulnerability, for wanting me to share this journey with you, and for giving me the privilege of discovering the mystery of Nora Lindstrom with you."

"You're welcome. Shall we?" Diana gave her hand one last squeeze before releasing her.

∽∾

Diana ran her fingers along the gumwood wainscoting. The hardwood floors, the wooden accents and brightly painted walls, the oriental area rugs... Everything was so clean and well maintained. Yet she knew Aunt Nora hadn't been here any time recently.

She could hear Brooke's footfalls on the tile floor in the kitchen, and the opening and closing of cabinets.

"Wait until you see this," Brooke exclaimed. "The entire kitchen looks brand new. Nora must've given this place a makeover sometime in the last few years. It's got professional-grade appliances and all updated fixtures. Amazing."

Diana joined Brooke. She was right. The entire kitchen looked like something straight out of *Better Homes and Gardens* or *Architectural Digest*. "Do you suppose Aunt Nora has a caretaker? Somebody's gone to a lot of trouble to do upkeep."

"Didn't Charles say all of the information we needed about each of our properties could be found in our folders?"

"That's right. I forgot."

"Did you bring yours?"

"I did. It's in my computer bag in the back seat."

"I'll get it," Brooke said.

She was gone before Diana could object. She wandered out of the kitchen and into the dining room. The table was covered with a perfectly creased, hand-embroidered tablecloth. A glass-front breakfront ran the length of the near wall. It was filled with fine china, crystal glassware, and highly polished pewter serving bowls.

She tried to imagine Aunt Nora sitting at the head of the table, entertaining erudite colleagues and friends.

"Got it," Brooke said. "Where are you?"

"In here."

Brooke appeared in the doorway carrying Diana's computer bag over one shoulder. She had a roller bag in each hand. "I know I only went outside for the folder, but I figured I might as well bring everything in before it gets full dark out there."

"Good thinking. I suppose we ought to figure out where we should bunk. We can check the folder after that." She relieved Brooke of her computer bag and suitcase.

They hadn't yet left the first floor and seen the sleeping quarters. From the size of the place, it was obvious there were multiple bedrooms and bathrooms, but none of them were on the main level. "All roads lead to the upper floors."

"It's your house," Brooke said. "Lead the way."

They carried their bags up the stairs to the second floor. Diana paused at the landing, trying to get her bearings. The staircase continued upward to a third floor. A brightly lit, airy full bathroom was directly in front of her. To the left was what appeared to be the master suite. To the right were an additional two bedrooms.

"Do you want to put your stuff in the master suite?"

Diana's heart turned over. "I can't stay in there, not tonight, anyway. Sleeping in Aunt Nora's bed seems...wrong."

Brooke patted her on the shoulder. "I get it. I'm not sure I could do that yet, either. I'm sure there are other bedrooms in this house."

"I think there are a couple that way." She indicated the open doors to the right. *And this is where it gets awkward.* There was no reason to suggest they share a bed tonight. But her body remembered waking in Brooke's arms this morning, and she knew she'd give anything to feel that sensation again.

"Probably. I'm going to check out the third floor." Without waiting for an answer, Brooke continued upward. "Hey. There are two more bedrooms up here and a sitting room that looks like it was Nora's home office. Mind if I choose one of the rooms up here?"

"No. Go ahead." Diana hoped her disappointment wasn't obvious. She dragged the suitcase behind her and headed toward the first room on the right. It was a guest bedroom with a queen-size bed, a comfy-looking chair in the corner, a vanity with an upright chair, and a pair of windows that overlooked the backyard. She set her suitcase and computer bag down and exited to explore further.

The next room on the right was another, smaller bedroom with a queen-size bed, a rocking chair, and a wooden dresser. This room featured a single window.

The only room remaining on the second level was Nora's, and Diana knew she couldn't put it off forever. She walked down the hall and entered through the French doors into a charming master bedroom suite.

The bedroom was large and featured a king-size bed with a solid-oak head and footboard, a matching dresser, and a bookcase chock-full of classics. Light streamed in through another doorway beyond the foot of the bed. She went to investigate.

"Whoa. Didn't see that coming."

"Didn't see what coming?" Brooke asked.

She jumped and clutched at her heart.

Brooke was less than an arm's length behind her. "I'm sorry." Brooke laid a hand on her shoulder. "I didn't mean to startle you. I thought you heard me knock on the door frame. Maybe I should wear a cow bell next time?"

Diana sucked in a deep breath and willed her heartbeat to settle down. She turned to face Brooke. "I guess it depends."

Brooke's fingertips grazed across her shoulder and down her arm before she withdrew the touch. "On what?"

"On whether I decide I'd rather be frightened to death or annoyed to death."

"Do I get a vote? If so, I prefer in all instances that you stay alive."

Brooke's voice was husky, and her breath smelled like peppermint Lifesavers. She was standing close—too close. Diana's gaze wandered to her mouth. If she leaned forward, their lips would meet. *Think of something repugnant. Think of something repugnant.*

"Diana?"

"Hmm?"

"What are you thinking?"

What should she say? "Why would you ask me that?"

"Because you have this really weird look on your face, like you just ate an entire lemon."

She barked out a laugh. "It worked. Ha!"

"What worked?"

"I was trying to think of the vilest thing I could imagine, and it worked."

"Why would you do that?"

"Because I was desperate to kiss you and I needed to distract myself so I wouldn't do it."

Now it was Brooke's turn to laugh. "You've lost your mind, you know that?"

"More than one person has suggested it." But she still had the irrepressible urge to sweep Brooke into her arms and kiss her breathless.

"Stop staring at me like that."

"Like what?"

"Like you're hungry and I'm on the menu."

"Oh, like that." Diana smiled sheepishly.

"Let's focus on your discovery, shall we?"

"Right."

She led them through the doorway and into a gorgeous sunroom with wrap-around windows. A settee sat in the corner. Floor-to-ceiling windows overlooked a lush back garden. A small desk filled the other end of the space, overlooking a shaded area with old-growth trees.

"Wow. This is a fantastic space. What a fabulous place to sit and read."

"Yeah." She could imagine Brooke curled up on the settee, reading a book while she wrote up her lecture notes at the desk. *Let's not get ahead of ourselves.*

Brooke breezed past her, oblivious to her fantasy, and popped her head into the master bathroom. "This clearly has been updated too. Nice granite, hers and hers sinks, cherry cabinets, a walk-in shower and what appears to be a new toilet."

"There's a custom walk-in closet in here," she called from the bedroom. She was surprised to find that the closet was empty. When had Aunt Nora cleaned out the closet? Or maybe she had someone do it for her?

"Nice," Brooke said.

"You have got to stop sneaking up on me."

"But it's so much fun to watch your reaction."

Again, Brooke was in her personal space. "You think so, do you? In that case, this is your fault."

This time, her instincts overrode her better judgment. She grabbed a handful of Brooke's sweater and pulled her close. Brooke's lips parted in surprise, and Diana claimed her mouth.

Brooke met her ardor and Diana felt her knees give way. Strong hands splayed across her lower back, holding her in place. Diana's hands flew into Brooke's hair, caressing, stroking, luxuriating in the velvety softness.

She groaned as Brooke's hands slid underneath her shirt and fingers deftly explored her overheated skin. "Oh, my God. I want you so much."

Even as the words came out of her mouth, she wanted to take them back. Not because she didn't mean it, she absolutely did. But because she felt Brooke's body stiffen in response just before she pulled away.

She closed her eyes. They both were panting, foreheads touching, breasts heaving, bodies shaking.

"That was…" Brooke trailed off without completing the sentence.

"Yeah." Diana was on fire, and the ensuing silence left her feeling exposed. What would Aunt Nora do? *She'd come up with some witty banter. She'd use humor to deflect.* But she wasn't Aunt Nora. Still, she could give it a shot.

"You do know we're standing in a closet. It's the ultimate lesbian cliché." She smiled to lessen the awkwardness.

Brooke cleared her throat and straightened up. "I don't know about you, but I came out of the closet years ago."

"Me too. Perhaps we should have a second coming…out." She stepped out of the closet and into the bedroom with Brooke close on her heels.

"Ha, ha. I give you points for cleverness, even though that was a groan-worthy pun."

"One can never have too many cleverness points." She decided to change the subject. "Didn't you go out to the car about one-hundred-years ago to get the folder so we could learn more about this place?"

"I did."

She led the way into the bedroom she had chosen for herself, with Brooke close on her heels.

"Nice room." Brooke snatched up the computer bag from the floor and thrust it at her. "But maybe we should take this somewhere safer, like the living room."

She couldn't argue with that. Being in the bedroom with Brooke was too distracting. Also, she badly wanted to tour the rest of the house, but for the moment, a little reading and research seemed the safest bet.

Once they were seated on the couch in the living room, Diana pulled out the folder labeled, "Diana – Cambridge House." The top document was a copy of Aunt Nora's will. She set that aside. Next in the folder were several sheets of paper stapled together. The top page was titled, "Important Information re: Cambridge House." This she began to read.

"Wait," Brooke said.

"What?"

"It looks like... May I?" Brooke relieved her of the document and an additional folded piece of paper tucked between the pages fell onto the coffee table. She handed the document back to her, along with the folded piece of paper. "Sorry. I saw the corner of this hanging out."

"Good catch." Diana opened the folded page.

Dear Diana,

I'm so grateful to have had the opportunity for us to get reacquainted before I passed. (Yes, I used past tense. If you're reading this, it means I've been mercifully relieved of my decrepit body).

When you first walked through the door of the cottage, I was afraid you would turn right back around and leave. I'm glad you stayed.

By now, you're also aware that I've left you the house in Cambridge. Please do not feel obligated in any way to inhabit the house. It is yours to do with what you wish. The same is true for the décor and my possessions.

Some time ago, when I realized I likely no longer would be able to travel back and forth between Cambridge and Truro, I took the liberty of hiring a caretaker for the house. I couldn't fathom renting the place out, and I didn't have the fortitude to sell it.

I do hope you'll find everything in good order and working properly. Note that I updated the kitchen and my living quarters just a few years ago when I looked around and realized that the rooms in which I spent most of my time were in dire need of a facelift.

You are under no obligation, of course, to keep the caretaker on, but this is someone I know well and trust. I've made provision for his continued salary in my bequest to you in case this is a path you choose to take.

Take good care of yourself, Diana. And, if you choose to keep the house, I do hope with all my heart that you'll fill it with love.

All my love,
Aunt Nora

Wordlessly, Diana passed the card to Brooke. She picked up the house document. It was a recitation of the facts of the house—its features, square footage, maintenance history, and a list of contractors, including professionals Aunt Nora had used for plumbing, heating, electrical, and general contracting. At the bottom of the page, in capital letters, was the name of the caretaker and contact information. She would be sure to get in touch with him first thing in the morning. She didn't want him to think there were intruders in the house, nor was she anxious to be surprised by someone with a key.

Next to her, Brooke's stomach rumbled. "I guess that means you're hungry?"

"Oops. Sorry about that."

"How about if we finish taking a quick tour of the place, grab some dinner in town, and hit the sack early? I don't know about you, but I'm exhausted."

"Sounds like a plan." Brooke stood and helped Diana up. "And for the record? I'll be sleeping on the third floor. Safer for both of us that way."

She heaved a heavy sigh. "Why must you be so practical?"

"Because one of us should keep a level head, and so far, it seems I've been elected."

"Now I have nothing to look forward to." She mock-pouted.

"How about this? First thing in the morning, we can go scouting around for the mysterious trunk."

"Well, at least that's something."

Aunt Nora's trunk, the object that might hold the key to the mystery of her past. Diana had to admit she was intrigued.

CHAPTER SEVENTEEN

The day dawned sunny and cold, and Brooke awoke to a splash of light creating an interesting pattern across the quilt. The room was so frigid she could see her breath. Diana would have to do something about the heat in this place. Or maybe they'd forgotten to turn it up before bedtime?

The latter was most likely. After all, they'd both been too preoccupied with trying to avoid the temptation of falling into bed together to worry about something as trivial as turning up the thermostat.

Brooke stretched and threw on a pair of sweats, a sweatshirt, and some heavy socks she'd thrown into her bag. She couldn't hear Diana from here, but that didn't mean she wasn't up.

When she reached the second level, she hesitated. Diana's bedroom door was open. She couldn't hear a shower. Would Diana shower in the master bath? Probably. She thought about knocking on the doorframe, but what if Diana was in there naked? It wouldn't do to start the day off aroused. It was bad enough she'd gone to bed that way. It took her forever to fall asleep.

They didn't have anything to eat in the house. She should find the car keys and go forage for food.

When she reached the landing, Diana called out, "I'm in here and I've got breakfast!"

Well, that answers that. She followed the sound of Diana's voice and discovered her in the breakfast nook. An untouched spread of bagels and cream cheese sat in the middle of the table, along with two cups of coffee, a fruit salad, and orange juice.

"How long have you been up?"

"Longer than you, apparently. I went out and got us breakfast."
Diana pointed to Brooke's head. "Nice hair, by the way."

Self-consciously, she smoothed down her cowlick. Diana was
fully dressed in jeans and a hoodie. Her hair was combed and neatly
ordered, and she smelled like lavender.

"Did you sleep okay?" Diana asked.

"Yes. You?"

"Better than I anticipated, although I wished we'd taken the time
yesterday to figure out the heating system."

She laughed. "I thought the same thing. I could see my breath up
there."

Diana wagged a finger at her. "Remember, I offered you body
heat."

"No, you didn't…not specifically, anyway."

"It was implied."

"Noted." She selected a poppy seed bagel and spread some
cream cheese on it and then spooned herself out a bowl of fruit
salad. "This mine?" She pointed to the coffee cup on the right.

"Yep."

"Thanks for getting all that."

"Hostess with the most-est." Diana took a bite of a cinnamon
raisin bagel. "I spoke with the caretaker this morning."

"He must've been up early."

"I texted him and he called me right back. Charles must've
talked to him, because he already knew that Aunt Nora was gone,
and he knew who I was."

"That's efficient."

"He'll be over a little later to walk us through some quirks and
idiosyncrasies." Diana made air quotes.

"In that case, I'd better jump in the shower." She gobbled down
the fruit salad and carried the bagel and coffee with her. "Be back
in a jiff."

She made short work of the shower, threw on jeans, a turtleneck,
a fleece, and her sneakers, and hustled back downstairs. When she
got there, all the food had been put away, and Diana was in the
kitchen talking to a really tall, thirty-something man dressed in
ripped jeans, a flannel shirt, and work boots.

"Brooke, this is Trent. Trent, this is Brooke," Diana said. "Aunt
Nora hired Trent as a teenager to watch over this place for her."

"Yes, ma'am. Miss Nora had me doing odd jobs at first, yard work mostly. Then I graduated to fixing things when they broke. Then I started working for a general contractor to learn the trades. When I told Miss Nora about it, she paid for me to go to a trade school and get my plumbing and electrical licenses. Now, I'm a general contractor myself."

He puffed out his chest, obviously proud of his progression. Brooke thought him utterly charming. And how in character for Nora to nurture a young man in whom she saw promise.

"Trent helped do all the remodeling. He installed the upgraded plumbing, brought everything up to code, and updated the heating and electrical systems."

"Yes, ma'am. Miss Nora trusted me with everything. I look back on it now and I was such a greenhorn. I don't know what she saw in me, but I sure am grateful to her. If it hadn't been for her, I probably would've gotten stuck working on cars down at the gas station. I'd do anything for Miss Nora, and that means I'll do anything for you, Miss Diana." He nodded, as if that was his bond.

"I really appreciate that, Trent. If Aunt Nora trusted you, then I do too. I have no idea yet how often I'll be able to get here, so I'm going to rely on you to do exactly what you did for Aunt Nora."

"Right. You can text me anytime and let me know you'll be coming to town. I'll make sure everything is set for you and stay out of your way. Otherwise, I'll stop by every day like I normally do and check on things, make sure the pipes don't freeze and the like."

"That sounds perfect, Trent. Did Aunt Nora pay you by check, or cash, or…?"

He shuffled from foot to foot. "She sent me a check once a month, ma'am. But heck, I'd do it for free for her. She was like a grandmother to me."

"I understand, but I'm going to pay you just the same as Aunt Nora. I think I have your address, but just to be sure, please text it to me."

"Will do, ma'am. Do you want me to show you how to work the wood stove and the fireplace?"

"Sure. Also, is there an attic in this place?"

"Oh, yes ma'am. I'll show you how to get up there after."

"Thank you, Trent." Diana winked at Brooke behind his back as they headed toward the living room, and mouthed, "Attic, trunk," and waggled her eyebrows.

Brooke smiled and nodded. If it had been her, she'd have stored the trunk in the attic too.

✥✥

Diana locked the door behind Trent and leaned against it. He was a nice, earnest guy, and she could understand why Aunt Nora trusted him. But boy, could he talk! She and Brooke got a primer not just on how to properly light and care for the woodstove and fireplace, but also the lowdown on the hot water heater, the breaker box, the water pipes, and the heating system.

"He was trying to impress you. Admit it. He was adorable, even if he bored you to tears," Brooke said.

"Was I that obvious?"

"Let's just say you went glassy-eyed after about the first fifteen minutes."

"But you were paying attention, right?"

"I hung on his every word."

"In that case, I'll have to keep you around in case anything goes wrong."

Brooke trailed her fingers playfully along Diana's jaw. "You've got Trent for that. You don't need me."

She moved out of range before Diana had time to respond, but every nerve ending was on high alert. Oh, she needed Brooke, all right.

"Are you coming?" Brooke called over her shoulder as she climbed the stairs.

"I have so many retorts to that."

"Get your mind out of the gutter, Dr. Lindstrom. I'm heading to the attic. Care to join me?"

She dutifully followed. They opened the door to the attic, climbed the narrow, rickety stairs, and ducked their heads to avoid the wooden beams, having learned the necessity of that the hard way earlier with Trent.

184

Brooke pulled the cord illuminating the single, naked lightbulb. "I thought I caught a glimpse of something that looked like a trunk down this way."

Diana pulled out her phone, accessed the flashlight feature, and pointed the beam so they both could see. They walked along the ancient floorboards until Brooke came to an abrupt stop. They were midway to the other end of the attic.

"Shine that over here." Brooke pointed to the right.

Five feet in that direction, a dusty canvas chair sat next to what appeared to be an old, weather-worn, wood and metal trunk. A battery-operated lamp was set conveniently nearby.

She shuddered. She half expected Aunt Nora to be sitting in the chair, a cup of tea at her elbow, visiting with the ghosts of her past and the memories that apparently haunted her for the remainder of her life.

"Shall we?" Brooke picked up the lamp and clicked it on. It didn't work. "You don't happen to have any double-A batteries handy, do you?"

"Stay here. Trent has some tools in the garage. I thought I saw some batteries there. I'll be right back."

She hustled down the three flights of stairs and into the garage, found the package of batteries she'd seen earlier, and returned to the attic. She handed the package to Brooke while she caught her breath.

"Thanks." Brooke switched the light on. The glow lit the space adequately so that the details of the trunk came fully into focus.

She ran her fingers along the wood grain. By her estimate, the trunk could have dated back as far as World War II. Did Aunt Nora have this trunk in Oak Ridge? Had it traveled with her ever since? Had it been with her overseas? Or was the trunk something she picked up when she returned to the states to live?

The wood was a green hue, as though it had once been painted but the finish had faded. Its sides and seams were reinforced with metal strips and hinges, and the clasps on the front latched like buckles. In the center was a key inserted into a keyhole lock. With trepidation, she turned and removed the key, opened the lock, and unclipped the buckles.

"Are you ready for this?" Brooke asked. She held the lamp aloft so that Diana could see what she was doing.

She sucked in a deep breath. Was she? Once she opened this lid and discovered the contents within, there was no going back. Whatever was inside, Aunt Nora harbored shame about it. Maybe they should simply walk away. Some things were better left undiscovered.

As if reading her thoughts, Brooke said softly, "Nora instructed us to investigate. It was one of her dying wishes. We have to honor that, even if we're afraid of what we might find."

"I know." Diana sighed. "I just... What if what we find makes us think less of Aunt Nora? What if it tarnishes her memory?"

"I guess that's a bridge we'll have to cross when we get to it. I worked with Nora for years. Her stellar reputation is ironclad and well deserved. Besides, we owe it to her to follow through, don't you think?"

"Okay. Here goes nothing." Cautiously, Diana lifted the lid. It was heavier than she anticipated and took both hands to heft. She crinkled her nose at the musty odor. "No one could say Aunt Nora wasn't organized."

"Not surprising, when you consider how carefully she's planned every step of this process."

"True." Diana peered inside. The left side was filled with a series of ledgers and manila file folders, all neatly stacked and labeled in the courier font typical of old typewriters.

The main compartment of the right-hand side was obscured by a large tray that fit into a wooden ledge. She tilted her head to see the embossed lettering on the bottom left corner of a leather-bound journal that took up the entire tray. *N.L.*

Goosebumps broke out on her arms. This was Aunt Nora's personal journal—her most private thoughts. Gently, reverently, she lifted the book out and held it in her hands. Gold metal guards protected the corners of the leather, and the journal itself was clasped closed by a leather strap fitted through another vertical strip of leather. She turned it over and examined it from every angle. The pages appeared to be linen paper, saddle-stitched into the binding.

"That's in remarkably good condition," Brooke noted. "It's hardly even got any dust on it."

She nodded. She knew she should open it, but she couldn't bring herself to do it yet. Aunt Nora deserved her privacy, didn't she?

How would Diana feel if someone read through her journal? She'd never kept a journal, but that was beside the point, wasn't it?

"How about if we set that aside for right now and decide whether to read it or not later?" Brooke asked.

Diana faced her. "How is it you always seem to know what's on my mind without my ever saying a word? You're freaking me out." Brooke smiled and winked. "It's a gift. Plus, your thoughts are loud and generally written all over your face."

"Good to know."

She set the journal down carefully on the canvas chair and removed the tray from the trunk. Underneath, she discovered bunches of letters bundled into several groups, a colorful, intricately patterned Japanese silk kimono, and a reddish-gray fossilized piece of stone the size of her palm. "What do you suppose this is?" She handed the stone to Brooke.

Brooke rotated it in the light of the lamp and rubbed her thumb and forefinger over the surface. "I'm not sure. We need better lighting."

"Agreed."

"How heavy do you think the whole trunk is? Maybe we should carry it downstairs with everything in it?"

Diana shook her head. Moving Aunt Nora's trunk from its resting place simply didn't feel right to her—like it would be a desecration of her private space. "No. I think we need to look at everything here. That's what Aunt Nora would want."

"In that case, we're going to need a second chair, warmer clothes, and more lighting. It's dark and freezing up here."

Two hours later, they returned to the attic with full stomachs, a new canvas chair purchased at Target, fleece throws to cover their legs, and three additional battery-operated lamps.

"I can't imagine why, but wearing long johns, a turtleneck, a sweatshirt, a micro-down vest, and fingerless gloves makes it hard to maneuver."

"You look like an astronaut ready for a spacewalk," Diana said.

"Great visual. Thanks. Good thing I wasn't feeling self-conscious or anything."

"What was it you told me? 'It isn't about style; it's about comfort.' Want to take that back now?"

"No. I offered to buy you gloves too. Remember that when your little hands fall off later." Brooke stuck her tongue out at Diana for good measure. The more time they spent together, the more she saw the relaxed, genuine Diana she'd imagined existed underneath all that emotional scar tissue she carried. *I so easily could fall in love with you, Diana Lindstrom.*

But Brooke hadn't planned to fall in love. In fact, she hadn't planned at all. *I need more time. I haven't figured out if I want to go back to Dana-Farber or even if I want to stay in nursing. How am I supposed to factor dating into that chaos?*

"Did you hear me?"

She shook her head to clear it. "I'm sorry. What did you say?"

"Where were you just now?"

"Post-lunch brain fog. It's a thing."

"Uh-huh."

"What did I miss?"

"I said, do you think we should start with the professional stuff or the personal stuff?"

"Oh." She bit her lip and weighed the options.

"Don't do that."

"Do what?"

"Chew on your lip."

"Why not?"

"Because I find it incredibly erotic and I'm trying to focus here."

"Reprobate."

Diana made a face. "What the heck does that mean?"

"I assume you have a dictionary app on your phone. I suggest you use it."

"As if."

"You have a doctorate, for Heaven's sake."

"In neuroscience, not English."

"You need to broaden your horizons, Dr. Lindstrom."

"And you need to use fewer syllables, Nurse Sheldon."

"Your Aunt Nora had an extensive vocabulary. It's why she was such a whiz at crossword puzzles. Maybe you should strive to be more like her." Brooke realized her mistake too late. "Diana, I'm sorry. I was joking."

"I know you were." Diana's face, so open and relaxed moments ago, was closed and unreadable now. She sat down heavily and hunched forward, her hands clasped loosely between her knees. "I miss her, and I'm so conflicted about all of this."

Brooke sat in the other chair. "Let's talk through it."

"Some of this stuff is so personal. I feel like a voyeur. That's not who I am."

"That's not who or what either of us is," Brooke said softly. "The way I see it, Nora wanted to get these things off her chest. It's almost as though she wanted to confess… No, confess is too strong a word. She wanted us to know all of her—all of what she'd been and done. How did she put it? 'Use my life as a cautionary tale. Don't make the same mistakes I did and live your life with regret.' Do you remember her saying that?"

Diana nodded slowly. "I do. She also wrote it in her letter. Still…"

"We won't be able to understand what she was trying to share unless and until we know more. That's why she left all this here for us to find. She could've destroyed the trunk and its contents, just like she discarded the clothes in her closet. But she didn't do that. Instead, she told us right where to find it. I don't think she was hiding who she was and what she did from us. I just think she didn't want us to discover all of it until after she was gone."

"Why do you suppose she was so adamant that we only explore the contents of the trunk in each other's presence?"

Brooke smiled. "Well, for one thing, I think that was one way she could guarantee you and I would have to continue to see each other."

"That's Machiavellian."

"It certainly is."

"I like the way she thinks."

"Honestly, while I appreciate that Nora wanted love for both of us," Brooke said, "I almost wish she'd stayed out of it. I don't want to wonder for the rest of my life if you want to date me because it was what Nora desired for you, or because it was what Nora thought you should do."

Diana looked genuinely stung. "I'm a big girl. I can make up my own mind. Yes, I loved Aunt Nora, but that doesn't mean I'd choose to spend the rest of my life with someone because she hand-picked her for me."

Brooke raised both eyebrows. Did Diana really say she wanted to spend the rest of her life with her? Surely that wasn't what she meant.

"Now I've scared the living daylights out of you." She started to get up.

"No." Brooke restrained her with a hand on her arm. "Don't run. Please?"

Diana sat back down. Her expression was glum.

"Listen, I…" If Diana was going to be honest, Brooke needed to be forthright too. "I've had three relationships in my life with three really terrific women. I screwed up every one of them because I was so focused on work that I didn't pay enough attention at home. Right now, I have no idea where I'm going professionally or what I want to do next with my life. How can I possibly enter into a relationship under those circumstances and expect it to succeed?"

"All right," Diana said. "True confessions time. I lost a twelve-year relationship because my partner thought I was too boring. She left me because she wanted to have more fun, and I've felt like a miserable failure at love ever since." She took a deep breath in and released it. "So, here's what I think. I think when you find the right person, you compromise. You work through it together and find ways to help it succeed."

"Are you saying you think I might be that person for you?" Brooke asked.

"I do." Diana sat up straighter. "I really, really do."

She appeared so vulnerable then, so fragile. "I think you might be that for me too," Brooke answered. The admission surprised her. "And it scares me that I might screw it up again."

"I'm afraid too, but I think we could have something incredible together, and I'm willing to take a risk. How about you?"

This time Brooke took a deep breath in and let it out slowly. Could she? Could she risk her heart again? "Me too."

Diana sat back. "Okay, then. Let's see what Nora was up to, shall we?"

CHAPTER EIGHTEEN

D iana and Brooke stared at the piles on the attic floor. They'd separated the contents of the trunk into categories. Professional records, reports, and formal letters and correspondence comprised the first set of materials. Personal letters and the journal formed the other stack. They left the kimono and the fossilized stone in the trunk for the time being.

"Now what?" Brooke asked.

"My inclination would be to start with the work-related materials. That would give us context for Aunt Nora's personal life and interactions, don't you think?"

"Agreed. Although I have to say I'm intrigued as hell about her private life."

"Me too. But I think one feeds off the other." Diana lowered herself to the floor and sat cross-legged in front of the professional records, reports, and correspondence. "You remember I told you about Aunt Nora and the Manhattan Project and how she sounded so disappointed in herself about the whole thing?"

"I do."

"I'm hoping that whatever's in this pile gives us a lot more detail and helps us understand the extent of her role and why she felt so ashamed of it all."

"I wonder how much historical background we'll need to understand what she was doing?" Brooke asked. "I read about World War II in history classes. I know about the Nazis and Hitler and the Japanese attack on Pearl Harbor, but I'm no expert."

Diana searched her memory banks. History never had been her strong suit. "I know that Germany fell and surrendered first, but it wasn't until we dropped the atomic bombs on Hiroshima and Nagasaki that the Japanese finally waved the white flag."

"Right. I know that the Manhattan Project and the making of the atomic bomb were super-secret and compartmentalized. Only a handful of people knew the scope of the whole thing."

Diana pulled out her phone and clicked on the Google app.

"What are you doing?"

"When in doubt, ask Google. We don't have years to study everything about World War II, so let's narrow it down to what's pertinent to us right now."

Diana plugged in, "Women scientists who worked on the atomic bomb," and scrolled through the results. She selected what seemed like a promising website. "Holy mother..." She uncrossed her legs and shot to her feet. "Look at this."

Brooke squinted to see. "Can you enlarge that?"

"We really need to get Wi-Fi in here. This would be a lot easier to read on an iPad or a laptop. I love Aunt Nora, but the lack of technology thing gets old fast." Diana expanded the image on the screen so that Brooke could read it.

"Razmmfrazzm fifty-year-old eyes. I still can't see it."

Diana laughed and pulled the phone back. "It's hell to get old, just ask me."

"Ha. I'll always be older than you."

"Four years is nothing. Just the same, I'll read it to you, Granny. 'Although the history books credit several prominent male scientists with the advancements and achievements that led to the successful creation of the two atomic bombs that ended the war, several accomplished women physicists and chemists played vital roles in bringing the Manhattan Project to a favorable conclusion.

'Perhaps most influential among these women were a pair of young, recently graduated doctorate students, Leona Woods Marshall Libby and Nora Lindstrom, both twenty-five.'"

"Wow!" Brooke exclaimed.

Diana continued reading. "'At twenty-three, Libby was the youngest physicist to work on the Project. Her work at the Chicago Met Lab with Enrico Fermi, and later at Hanford, Washington, where she worked on reactor development, was critical to the successful creation of Fat Man, the plutonium bomb dropped on Nagasaki.'"

"Get to the part about Nora already."

"I'm getting there." Diana scrolled down the page to find the relevant section. "'Nora Lindstrom, who graduated with a Ph.D. in Physics in 1943 from Columbia University, birthplace of the Manhattan Project, was a central figure in the separation and production of uranium isotopes at Oak Ridge, Tennessee. This endeavor allowed for the production of sufficient quantities of enriched Uranium-235 to fuel Little Boy, the first atomic bomb, dropped on Hiroshima, Japan on August 6, 1945.'"

"Oh, my God. Our Nora was a superstar."

Diana absorbed the information and tried to square it with the woman she remembered from childhood, and the great-aunt she'd seen at the twilight of her life. "I don't think she saw it that way."

Brooke sat down in front of the first pile and patted the floor next to her. "I guess we'll find out."

Diana sat so that her thigh brushed against Brooke's leg. That little bit of contact was at once comforting and enticing. She sifted through the records. Aunt Nora had ordered them chronologically from earliest on the bottom, to latest on the top. "I wish I was half as meticulous as she was," Diana muttered.

"I wish all of the doctors I worked with were as conscientious as Nora. She was one-of-a-kind and a joy to work with."

Brooke's voice cracked on the last word, and Diana cupped her jaw. "We both lost so much when we lost her."

"The world lost so much when we lost her."

Diana temporarily got lost in Brooke's eyes. They were bright with sadness and unshed tears. "You're really very beautiful, you know."

Brooke glanced down as a blush crept up her neck and settled in her cheeks. "Nobody's ever said that to me before. Nobody I cared about, anyway."

"Is that right? Well, they were all fools." Diana leaned in and kissed Brooke softly. She didn't intend for the kiss to linger. Now wasn't the time or place for that. But neither could she help herself. Reluctantly, she broke the kiss. "All righty, then, let's have a look at that first envelope."

Brooke picked up the envelope and opened it. The letter, dated March 23, 1943, was on official University of California, Berkeley, stationery, from Ernest Lawrence, Director of the Radiation Laboratory.

"Who is that guy?" Diana asked.

"You're the one with the Google app at your fingertips. Look him up."

She once again pulled out her phone. The locked screen indicated she'd missed a call. "Oh."

"What is it?"

"The mortuary called." With a heavy heart, she unlocked the phone and replayed the voicemail.

"What did they want?"

"Aunt Nora's ashes will be ready day after tomorrow. That was quick, wasn't it?"

"Three or four days is about normal." Brooke slid her arm around Diana's waist. "Do you want me to go with you?"

She nodded. "If you don't mind." She sighed. "I haven't even made any funeral arrangements for her."

"It's okay. You've had a lot going on. You can't be expected to do everything at once. How about if we talk through that and strategize over dinner tonight?"

"Yeah. You're right," she agreed. "One hard task at a time. We should keep going here." She stared at the phone. She knew she'd taken it out for a reason that wasn't the missed call, but for the life of her, she couldn't remember what the reason was.

"Want me to do that?"

"No. I'll do it, if only I could remember what 'it' was."

"You were about to look up Ernest Lawrence."

"Right." Diana plugged in the search parameters. "Here goes. 'Ernest Lawrence won the Nobel Prize in Physics in 1938 for the invention and development of something called a cyclotron. When World War II began, Lawrence turned his attention to converting his cyclotron into a mass spectrometer called a Calutron that could separate uranium isotopes. He and his friend and colleague, J. Robert Oppenheimer, were instrumental in building the atomic bombs that ended the war.'"

"It would seem that the Calutrons are where Dr. Lawrence and your Aunt Nora's paths intersected."

"It would seem so. What does the letter say?"

Brooke again picked up the faded sheets. The courier typeface made it easier to see the words on the page, and for that she was grateful.

Dear Doctor Lindstrom (please excuse the presumption of title, as I know you will not officially receive your doctorate until May):

My colleague and friend, Bob Oppenheimer, says he met you recently at Columbia and he has apprised me of your work in Puppin Hall. He tells me you have some interesting theories and a keen understanding with regard to uranium-isotope separation using electromagnetic fields. Bob also tells me you are a scientist of the highest integrity.

As it happens, I have need of someone meeting your description, especially a female. While I cannot relate more details, I wonder if I might entice you, upon your graduation, to embark upon an important scientific assignment that will be of utmost importance in the war effort?

I assure you that the pay will be more than you can imagine, and that the work will be tremendously satisfying. The assignment will require your relocation to a new, secret environment. All of that will be disclosed at a later date should you choose to accept this offer of employment.

Time is of the essence, so if you could please respond to this letter as soon as practicable, I would be most appreciative.

Thank you for your consideration, and congratulations on your upcoming graduation.

Sincerely,
Ernest O. Lawrence

Brooke lowered the letter to her lap. "A Nobel-Prize-winning scientist, a man responsible for one of the greatest advancements in nuclear physics, personally recruited Nora. That's amazing. Obviously, she said yes."

Diana nodded. "The secret location must've been Oak Ridge, which then was called the Clinton Engineer Works, or CEW."

"Should we read the next piece of correspondence? It's what's next in the pile."

"Sure."

Brooke returned the Lawrence letter to its envelope and carefully placed it back at the bottom of the stack. "We're handling pieces of history here. Do you think we should put them in a protective case or something to preserve them?"

"I think we should finish going through all of it and catalog what we have. Then we can decide what to do next."

"Okay." Brooke gently teased open the next envelope. "It's from The War Department—General Leslie Groves, Office of the Chief of Engineers in Washington."

"What in the world would the Army want with Aunt Nora?" Again, Diana pulled out her phone and tapped on the icon for the Google app.

"You probably should just keep it out," Brooke advised.

"'General Leslie Groves, Jr. was appointed to direct the Manhattan Project in September 1942, after successfully spearheading the construction of the nation's largest office building, the Pentagon. Groves was in charge of every facet of the Project, including the three major atomic bomb sites, Los Alamos, New Mexico, Hanford, Washington, and Oak Ridge, Tennessee.'"

"So, this General Groves was the big boss. Let's see what he had to say to Nora," Brooke said.

"When is the letter dated?"

"May 1, 1943."

"So, less than two months after the letter from Lawrence."

"Exactly." Brooke angled the letter to catch the light from the lamp.

Dear Dr. Lindstrom:

E.O. Lawrence informs me that he wishes to add you to the team, and that you have agreed.

Please present yourself at Pennsylvania Station in New York City on May 7, 1943. You will be met at the station, provided with a train ticket, and escorted to the train by my representative. A hired, private car will meet you at your designated stop and transport you the rest of the way to your final destination.

This assignment carries with it the burden of absolute secrecy. You must tell no one of these instructions, nor convey any information whatsoever to anyone, including your parents and family members, for the duration. Your country is counting on you.

Sincerely,
General Leslie R. Groves

"Wow. Kind of spooky, don't you think?" Diana asked. "I mean, Aunt Nora has no idea where she's going, can't even tell her family she's getting on a train, doesn't know exactly what the job is she's being asked to do..."

"And, most amazing of all, she agrees to it!" Brooke finished. She returned the letter to its envelope and selected the next item.

"What's that?"

"It's a laminated ID badge. Nora's picture is on the front, and a number, her name, signature, personal statistics, and issue date are on the back."

"Let me see." She leaned over to get a better look. The maneuver unbalanced her and sent her head-first into Brooke's lap. Warmth, borne of equal parts embarrassment and desire, coursed through her. If she put her hands down to right herself...

Before she could decide on an appropriate escape, Brooke's fingers were tangled in her hair.

"This might be the single most unique approach anyone's ever taken to get into my pants."

Brooke's silken voice was so close to her ear that it vibrated with the sound.

"Is it working?" Diana put her hands on Brooke's thighs and hoisted herself up enough so that she could see her expression. Her eyes were heavy-lidded and intensely focused on Diana's face. "If it isn't working, please stop looking at me like that because I won't be responsible for my next actions."

"It's definitely working," Brooke answered. She threaded a hand underneath Diana's head and lowered herself so that their mouths met.

Diana groaned and slipped her hand in between Brooke's legs, cupping her over her jeans. "Can we..."

"Do you want to..."

They spoke at once.

Brooke stilled Diana's hand. "I think we've done enough research for now, don't you?"

"You want me to stop?"

"What? No. No," Brooke said, more softly. "Not in the way you mean. I'm suggesting that we set Nora's stuff aside and adjourn to a more…conducive…setting."

"Oh. Um, absolutely."

"Diana?"

"Yes?"

"You're going to have to take your hand out of my crotch if you expect me to be able to think and function long enough to close up shop here."

"Right."

"But don't forget where you left off."

"Not a chance."

It didn't take long for them to tidy up and return everything to the trunk and turn off the lamps. But it was long enough for Diana to develop a severe case of performance anxiety. What if Brooke found her wanting as a lover? What if they were incompatible in bed? What if…? They were at the bottom of the attic stairs.

"Hey." Brooke pulled her close so they were touching all along their lengths. "I'm scared too."

Diana's jaw dropped open. "How did you…?"

"Know you were frightened?" Brooke smiled and it crinkled the skin at the sides of her eyes.

"Yeah."

"It's written all over your pretty little face. We'll be fine." She leaned in and ran her tongue along Diana's lips, teasing open her mouth.

The combination of her tongue and their bodies fused together set Diana's body on fire. At that moment, she would've followed Brooke anywhere.

Brooke tugged on her hand and led them to the room Diana had chosen for herself. She backed Diana toward the bed.

What had happened? Up until this point, Diana always had been the aggressor. She fought for control now but found that her body had other ideas.

"I should… Oh. Oh." She arched back as Brooke undid the button on her jeans and relieved her of her turtleneck and hoodie.

"Is this okay?"

"Yes," she breathed. Brooke unclasped her bra and cupped her breasts. "Can I...? Will you...?" Diana quickly lost the ability to articulate.

"Yes," Brooke answered the unfinished question, releasing her long enough to strip to the waist.

You're gorgeous. It was the last coherent thought she had as she felt the cold air buffet her now naked body. The frigid air instantly was replaced with liquid heat as Brooke's body covered hers and the softness of the mattress rose up to meet her back. "Brooke..."

∽᷂᷂᷂

Brooke stretched languorously and opened her eyes. Diana was lying on her side, an arm carelessly thrown over Brooke's midsection, her head pillowed against Brooke's breast. The streetlights were on outside, and although she couldn't be sure, Brooke estimated they'd been in bed for at least a couple of hours.

She smiled, quite pleased with herself. *You haven't forgotten how to make love, after all. Thank God.*

"What are you smiling about?" Diana's voice was husky from sleep.

"Us. I'm smiling about us."

"You are, are you?" Diana lifted herself up onto an elbow.

"I am."

"Well, you have plenty of reasons to congratulate yourself, I'll give you that." Diana grazed the fingers of her free hand over Brooke's breast.

"Stop that or we'll never get out of bed."

"You say that like it's a bad thing."

"It is if you're starving like I am." As if to punctuate the point, her stomach growled.

"I'll stop under one condition."

"What's that?"

"You promise me you'll sleep naked with me tonight."

She made an exaggerated show of looking first at herself, and then at Diana. "I'm pretty sure that was implied by our current position. Or was that inferred? I always get those confused."

"So, that's a yes?"

"That's an affirmative."

"Okay, then." Diana dropped her hand and Brooke immediately missed the contact.

"Diana?"

"Mm?"

"You were amazing."

"You too." Diana leaned down and kissed her on the mouth. "Are you okay?" she asked.

"We make mad, passionate love, and you want to know if I'm okay?" Brooke sat up and pulled the covers up with her. "Yeah."

"I'm perfect."

"Me too." She kissed Diana briefly and slid out of bed. "How about if we get cleaned up and I'll make us some dinner?"

"Capital idea." Diana paused.

"What is it?"

"One shower or two?"

She laughed easily. "Two. One shower means it'll be another three hours before we have dinner."

CHAPTER NINETEEN

Diana stared openly at Brooke's backside. From her current vantage point, sitting at the kitchen table, she had an unobstructed view while Brooke bent over and peered into the oven. "Whatever that is, it smells incredible."

"Garlic roasted new potatoes, marinated boneless, skinless chicken breasts, and sautéed green beans. Dinner should be ready in about ten minutes."

"That's good because I don't know about you, but I worked up an appetite."

Brooke spun around, her smile radiant and relaxed, and Diana's heart tripped. She rose, closed the distance between them, and swept Brooke into her arms.

"I know the situation is ridiculously complicated, the timing is unfortunate, and the logistics are the proverbial elephant in the living room, but I'm falling in love with you, Brooke Sheldon, and I feel powerless to stop that."

"Do you want to stop it?" Brooke's voice was small and uncertain.

She breathed in Brooke's scent, felt the warmth of her body, and basked in the gentleness of her spirit. Something deep inside her shifted, as though her heart had cracked wide open. "No."

"No?" Brooke's eyes searched her face, as if assessing the truth of the statement.

"No," she said emphatically. "I don't know what it is about you, but you're different than anyone I've ever known. With you, I feel so safe and free to be myself. With you, I feel valued and trusted in a way I don't remember feeling before. But most of all, with you, I see a future I couldn't imagine before."

She held her breath. She hadn't intended to say so much. After all, they'd only known each other for less than a month, and they'd slept together exactly once. This wasn't some romance novel. This was real life, and in real life, saying too much too soon left you open to getting your heart crushed.

"Don't." Brooke's voice cut through her thoughts.

"What?"

"Don't pull back into your shell. Don't let fear get in the way of what your heart wants."

She hated being so transparent. She felt so exposed. Her instinct was to run. She started to withdraw from their embrace, but Brooke held her fast.

"I'm falling for you too, Diana. You're not in this alone. You don't have a corner on the market for self-doubt and the fear of your heart getting ripped out." Brooke traced her cheekbone with her fingers. "We're not kids in love for the first time. We're at the midpoint of our lives. We've both experienced heartache and loss, and we carry those scars with us always. Those truths don't magically disappear simply because the right person walks into our lives one day out of the blue."

She started to say something, but Brooke gently placed her fingers over her mouth. "I'm not done yet."

She kissed Brooke's fingers and sucked her forefinger into her mouth.

"Not helping." Brooke stepped back and intertwined their hands. "My point is, we both have something to lose if we let ourselves follow our hearts. But we have so much more to gain, that I, for my part, think it's absolutely worth the risk. There always will be reasons not to open our hearts and lives to someone new. But now that I've found you, I realize I don't want to live the rest of my life playing it safe and being solo."

Diana swallowed hard. "Me, either. I can see now that I've been existing for too long, not living. I want to live."

"Exactly. What do you say we take a leap of faith together and see what happens next?"

"I'm with you. Wherever you're going, that's where I want to be," Diana said. As if to seal the pact, she leaned in and claimed Brooke's lips in a searing kiss.

The piercing sound of the oven timer startled them apart, and Diana clutched at her heart. "Dear God."

"Timing is everything." Brooke kissed her once more and donned the oven mitts. "Why don't you grab the file with Nora's burial instructions and we'll talk through it while we eat?"

∽᥎

As Diana went upstairs to retrieve the file, Brooke plated their dinner and willed her heart to settle. What she'd told Diana was the truth, but knowing the truth and living it were two different things. Was she ready to make room in her life for someone like Diana, someone to whom she wanted to give everything?

In the past, she'd always known her career was the priority. Now? Now she could see herself putting a relationship first. Correction, not *a* relationship, *this* relationship—the partnership for which she'd waited a lifetime.

Diana was so different from her previous partners. Yes, she carried emotional scars, but who didn't at this age? Diana was accomplished and stable in her professional life. She knew who she was and didn't feel the need to prove herself or compete with her. She'd lived long enough to recognize what was important to her and how to manifest that in her life.

Would Diana make time for her? Would she make time for love? There was only one way to find out. Brooke imagined that if they could keep the lines of communication open and be compassionately honest with each other, they could overcome any obstacle they faced.

"You're deep in thought."

Brooke straightened. "Sorry. I didn't hear you come back down."

"What were you thinking? Care to share?"

"Honestly? I was thinking I'm glad we met at this stage of our lives instead of years ago." She set the plates on the table and sat.

"Why is that?" Diana sniffed appreciatively. "Oh, my God. This smells heavenly. Thanks for making dinner."

"You're welcome." She speared a potato and popped it into her mouth in order to give herself time to formulate her reply. "Earlier in my career, I was so driven, so focused on trying to prove myself, that I prioritized my work over everything else in my life. I would guess you were much the same. The world of academia is brutal. Publish or perish, fight for tenure, battle for respect, standing, and recognition..."

Diana chewed and swallowed. "This tastes every bit as good as it looks. Yum. And yes, you're right on target. I was a woman in a field dominated by men who didn't think I belonged. I worked twice as hard as they did to receive the same consideration."

"That's my point. We wouldn't have had the time or space to put our relationship first."

"You think it will be different now?"

"I think it can be different now, if we choose to make it so." Diana stayed silent so long Brooke wondered if she had miscalculated. "Say something."

"I want it to be different this time. I do. And, I think it really helps that you're in the medical field and can understand and appreciate what I do, just as I can understand and appreciate what you do."

Her heart skipped a beat. "It sounds like there's a 'but' in there."

Diana put down her fork. "But the reality is that I'm based in New York, and your life is here in Massachusetts, especially now that you own a home on the Cape. Also, I'm about to embark on the dream project of a lifetime, backed by a brand-new NIH grant, based on work I've been doing at Columbia."

"I see." She lowered her fork as well, her appetite suddenly gone.

"I'm not saying these are obstacles we can't overcome."

She closed her eyes. Maybe she was being naïve to think this time could be different. She opened her eyes and stared down at her plate. "Aren't you?"

"No." Diana lifted her chin with two fingers so they were eye to eye. "No, I'm not. I'm trying to be realistic. I wasn't kidding earlier when I said logistics and timing make this exceedingly complicated. I'm acknowledging that up front, because I care too much about you, and us, not to address it."

"You don't think we can make this work."

"I'm not saying that. I'm saying we have to take all of these factors into consideration."

Her heart hurt. If Diana didn't have faith in the relationship at the outset, what was the point in moving forward?

"Brooke..."

"I heard you, Diana. Let's focus on Nora's wishes and the funeral, okay?" She stacked their plates and carried them to the sink.

"Brooke..."

She couldn't have this conversation right now. She needed time alone to think and to sort through her emotions. "I know we're not done talking about this. But, I need time to process before either one of us says something she'll regret."

She squeezed a dollop of dish soap into a large, round Tupperware container, added soap to the sponge, and buried her hands and the dishes in the soapy water. She could feel Diana's eyes on her back. "What does Nora say about a burial plot? Anything?"

Diana sighed heavily. "She doesn't want to be buried."

"Does she want her ashes sprinkled somewhere? Or does she want you to hold onto them?"

"Huh. I didn't see that coming."

"What is it?"

"I'm reading her internment wishes. Aunt Nora wants her ashes buried near the Chapel-on-the-Hill at Oak Ridge."

"Why? Does she say?" Brooke dropped any pretense of doing the dishes now. She dried her hands and returned to the table. "As far as I know, your great-aunt didn't have a religious bone in her body."

"She says that's where her life really began and ended, so that's where she should be."

"Oh, my goodness, that's a loaded statement."

Diana's gaze was filled with sadness. "I suppose we'll understand it better when we read her journal."

"I sure hope so. What about a funeral? I know many of her colleagues and friends at Dana-Farber will want to be there. Probably some of the Harvard faculty too. She stayed close to those folks."

"Would you know who to invite or how to get in touch with them?"

"I can take care of Dana-Farber, and they can take care of Harvard. Also, we probably should place an obituary in the *Boston Globe* and the *Herald*."

Diana removed a piece of paper from the folder and handed it to her. "Looks like Aunt Nora's done the work for us."

Brooke shook her head in admiration. "Leave it to Nora to pen her own obituary."

Lindstrom, Nora – Dr. Nora Lindstrom of Cambridge, MA passed away on the _____ of _____, 20__, at age _____. Dr. Lindstrom retired from the Dana-Farber Cancer Institute in 2000 following a lengthy career dedicated to bettering the lives of children with leukemia. In lieu of flowers, please donate to the Dana-Farber Cancer Institute.

"Short and to the point," Diana said.

"And lacking in any detail, which I gather was the point of her writing it, rather than leaving it to someone else."

"Speaking of the details of Aunt Nora's life—"

"Yes, we should."

"I didn't even finish my sentence," Diana complained. "How do you know what I was going to say?"

"You were going to suggest that we resume our attic adventure."

"I hate that you're right, you know that?"

"It's a gift. Let's go."

Brooke led the way back upstairs and into the attic. Was sleeping with Diana a mistake? Should they have hashed out their feelings and plans more fully before becoming intimate?

Diana was a tenured professor at the height of her career, and that career was based in New York City. *Duh, Brooke. Of course she's not going to walk away from that or place a relationship highest on her list of priorities. How did you miss that red flag?*

Sure, her own career was in flux, but the idea of moving to New York held absolutely no appeal for her. She wondered if Diana remembered that one of the first times they'd spent time together she shared that she preferred the quiet of nature to the bustle of a big city.

"Earth to Brooke, come in, please?"

"Huh?"

"If you don't want to go through more of Aunt Nora's stuff right now—"

"No. I want to do this." The sorrow and uncertainty in Diana's gaze pierced her heart. "Where did we leave off?"

"Nora's ID badge."

"Right."

She handed the badge to Diana. As she did so, she noticed another ID card hiding underneath. This one said *Townsite Resident's Pass.* The pass certified that Nora was a resident of Oak Ridge, gave her particulars, was signed by her and a security guard, and authorized her to enter and leave the premises without search only through the gates on Highway 61. "You'll want to see this one too. Looks like they go together." She handed it to Diana, along with a pay stub.

"This is so cool. This stuff brings history to life."

"If Nora was ashamed of this part of her career as you seem to believe she was, why do you suppose she saved all of these mementos?"

"I haven't figured that out. Maybe because she knew they had historic value?"

Brooke considered what she knew of Nora. "I don't think that would motivate her."

"Well, she's not here to tell us, so unless there's an explanation in her personal letters or the journal, we may never know."

"There's one more letter in this stack." She slid the contents out of its envelope. "It's from Ernest Lawrence, again."

Dear Dr. Lindstrom,

I understand congratulations are in order. I don't know how you did it, but you have managed to train high school-educated girls to operate my highly sophisticated Calutron machines and achieve better results and more product than my doctoral students.

Keep up the good work.

With admiration,

Ernest O. Lawrence

She passed the letter to Diana. "That tells us a little more about what Nora's function was in Oak Ridge, doesn't it?"

"That corroborates what Aunt Nora said to me in that last conversation. She told me she supervised the girls who operated the machines that created the enriched uranium."

"Now you have proof."

"Now we have proof."

She accepted the letter back from Diana and put it at the bottom of the stack. "That's the end of the professional materials."

Diana checked her watch. "It's getting late. Maybe we should call it a night and start fresh in the morning with the journal."

"Okay." She stood. She'd promised Diana they would sleep together tonight. In light of their earlier conversation, she wondered if that was the best plan. Well, a promise was a promise, wasn't it?

❦

Diana's eyes had long since become accustomed to the room's darkness. She could easily make out Brooke's silhouette, scant inches away from her. Brooke's back was to her and she was curled on her side, one arm thrown over the covers, the other tucked underneath her pillow.

When Diana had made her promise they'd sleep together naked tonight, this was not what she had envisioned. Then again, she imagined it wasn't what Brooke had pictured, either.

She rolled carefully onto her back so as not to wake Brooke. She put her hands underneath her head. Why was it that every time she made progress with Brooke, she stuck her foot in her mouth and wrecked everything? Self-sabotage? A latent desire to fail? Fear of success? All of the above?

All you did was tell the truth as you see it. You were being practical and realistic, not to mention the fact that this research project has the potential to drastically alter and save lives. Surely that was something Brooke could understand and appreciate?

She had told herself the same thing ten other times tonight, but it still sounded contrived. Other people made these kinds of situations work all the time. Was she a commitment-phobe? Selfish? Uncompromising? What would a reasonable compromise be? Meet on the weekends out at the Cape? Making that commute from New York every week would be pure hell. It was one thing to do it while Aunt Nora was dying, it would be quite another to undertake that drive on a regular basis.

Besides, she didn't want to be a weekend warrior who showed up, made love to her girlfriend for three days straight, and then returned to her "normal" life. She was too old for that crap, and she couldn't imagine treating Brooke as a part-time playmate. Brooke simply wasn't that kind of girl.

Therein lay the crux of the problem. She meant every word she said before things went south. She truly was falling head over heels for Brooke—not the kind of infatuation she experienced when she first met Bethany—no, this was something so much deeper and more profound. It was the kind of connection she wanted to nurture, protect, and spend a lifetime exploring.

Tell her that. She's right there. Go on, tell her. She turned toward Brooke and reached out to stroke her bare shoulder.

They're empty words until you back them up with concrete actions that prove you intend to put the relationship, and her, at the center of your universe.

She pulled back without making contact and glanced at the clock on the bedside table: 4:35 a.m. One thing was for certain, none of this ruminating was getting her closer to a solution, and the lack of sleep meant that she was going to be a zombie for the day.

CHAPTER TWENTY

The first thing Brooke noticed when they met in the
kitchen after their morning showers were the deep purple
circles underneath Diana's eyes. Brooke didn't need to
be a detective to know Diana had slept poorly. In addition to the
dark circles, Diana had risen before her and disappeared into Nora's
bathroom, and she barely mussed the covers on her side of the bed.

Brooke tossed and turned a fair amount too, prior to giving in to
emotional exhaustion. Still, she was in better shape than Diana. "I'd
ask how you slept, but I'm pretty sure I know the answer."

Diana poured herself a cup of coffee and stood at the kitchen
island. "Is it that obvious?"

"Mm-hmm. Are you hungry?"

"I can get it, thanks. I'm going to have one of those bagels. Do
you want one?" Diana asked.

"No, thanks. Yogurt and fruit for me. Too many carbs and I
won't be able to climb those attic stairs."

She was painfully aware of the awkward silence that ensued as
the two of them went about putting together their own breakfasts.
Since she'd been the one to postpone the conversation about the
parameters of their relationship, she supposed it was up to her to
broach the subject again.

What was she going to say? It didn't matter that Diana believed
her career was the most important thing? It did matter. In fact, it
mattered a great deal.

But was that really what Diana said? What she said was that she
was in the prime of her career and was about to embark on a
critically important research project backed and bankrolled by the
NIH.

Whatever the words, the bottom line was that Diana's heart was in her work, and that work was based at Columbia. There was no way to put a pretty face on it.

She got up, rinsed her dishes in the sink, and put them in the dishwasher. "If we're headed back up to the attic, I'd better put on a few extra layers."

As she navigated the space between the sink and the eat-in nook, Diana latched onto her forearm. "Please, don't go yet. Can't we talk about it?"

She paused. "Honestly, I don't know what to say. If I did, I'd say it. You were kind enough to make your priorities plain before we got ahead of ourselves, and I appreciate your candor. You no doubt saved me a lot of heartache."

"That's it?" Diana pushed her chair back and stood up so they were eye to eye. "You're just going to give up without a fight?"

"I detest confrontation, so let me be clear that I don't want to fight with you...now or ever."

"I didn't mean fight in the literal sense, Brooke. I meant you don't think what we have is worth trying to salvage?"

Salvage? The word stung. Salvage was like dumpster diving to find an item that might be of use. *Step back. Take a deep breath. You're tired, you're cranky, and it's an emotionally charged time. Don't react.* "There's nothing to salvage. We kissed a few times and slept together once." As soon as the words were out, she regretted them. Diana looked crestfallen.

"What happened to the heartfelt things we said to each other yesterday? Was that post-coitus bullshit on your part, then?"

She recoiled as though she'd been slapped in the face. Whatever guilt she might've felt for her injudicious choice of words evaporated in an explosion of pain and anger. "That right there? That's why I didn't want to have this conversation." She was mortified that tears threatened. "If you only learn one thing about me, Diana, it should be that I never lie or 'bullshit,' as you put it. If I say it, I mean it." *Except for making it sound as though what we shared meant nothing to me. That I said in self-defense to protect my heart. The truth is, I'm in love with you, Diana.*

"I-I'm sorry. That was an unfortunate turn of phrase. That was my hurt talking. I apologize."

Diana attempted to take her hands, but she stepped back. "I think we both need some time. Emotions are running high. We're mourning Nora, and you've got a lot on your plate and a short timeframe in which to accomplish it before your bereavement leave is up."

She strode out of the kitchen and up the stairs to the third-floor bedroom where she'd left her suitcase. Her heart hammered in her chest and her legs felt like Jell-O. How had it come to this? How had the situation spiraled so far out of control?

She hoisted the suitcase onto the bed and threw in the few things she'd unpacked. Then she snatched up her toiletry kit from the bathroom and tossed that in the bag, as well.

She'd noticed a T stop at Harvard Square. She could take that...

"Wait." Diana stood in the doorway. "Wait. Where are you going?"

"I don't know yet."

"Don't go. Please, let's talk through this."

"Talking hasn't gone all that well for us."

"Aren't you the one who told me not to run? That's exactly what you're doing."

She zipped the suitcase. "No. What I'm doing is trying to keep us from saying anything more damaging than already has been said. I'm trying to salvage—since you seem to like that word—any chance of a relationship of any kind between us." She raised the handle and rolled the suitcase toward the door. "Please, get out of the way."

"What about Aunt Nora's journal and her requirement that we go through the items in the trunk together? What about the details of her funeral and burial?"

Brooke's temper flared. "That's what's foremost in your mind? Very well. Let me know when you've selected a date for the service and I'll take care of securing a venue. I'd recommend that it be somewhere here in the metro-Boston area, since that's where she lived for most of her career."

"That makes sense."

"I'll see to it today that Nora's colleagues and professional friends are informed of her passing and talk to them about who should speak at the service, if you want any of her work associates to deliver a eulogy. You take care of getting the obit placed in the newspapers."

Diana continued to block the way. Her arms were crossed and her chin quivered. Brooke knew that if she was going to find the strength within to go, she needed to do it now.

"As for the journal, Nora's just going to have to forgive me." She choked on the words. It was unthinkable to let Nora down, not to mention Diana, but to stay would only make things worse.

"You don't mean that."

She swallowed hard. "Right now, all I know is that staying here with you is not an option. I'm sorry. I'm sorrier for that than you can imagine. Now please, let me go."

Reluctantly, Diana stepped aside and allowed her to pass.

Brooke hustled down the stairway, exited out the front door, and didn't stop walking until she was several blocks away. She spotted an empty bench in a green space and sat down. Her whole body vibrated with a mixture of anger, hurt, and despair.

Diana's question echoed in her mind. "Where are you going?"

"Excellent question," she muttered aloud. She had no car, since they'd driven Diana's car to Cambridge. *But you have a best friend who works a few miles away.* She pulled out her phone and called Daniel.

"Hello?"

"Are you at DFCI right now?"

"Hello to you too, BFF."

"I'm sorry. My manners are sorely lacking today. Hi, Daniel. Do you happen to be in your office today and would you have lunch with me?"

"Yes, and yes. I'll have my scheduler make a hole. If you don't mind my saying so, you sound rough."

"Let's just say I could use my favorite sounding board and some sage advice. Also, a comforting hug would be most welcome."

"You've got it. Where are you?"

"I'm going to take the T from Harvard Square."

"Okay. Come on up when you get here."

"Daniel?"

"Yes?"

"I don't ever think I say thank you often enough to you. So, thank you."

"You're welcome. Now get your butt over here."

⋖⋗

Brooke pushed the beet salad around on her plate.

"I bring you to my favorite lunch joint, offer to pay for your meal, and you can't even pretend to enjoy it?" Daniel asked.

Brooke smiled grimly. "I'm sorry. The salad is excellent, as always. I'm crappy company."

"What you are is a mess. Let's hear it. Is this about Nora's death, and what are you doing in town? Should I be offended that you didn't let me know you were coming?"

"Which of those questions would you like me to answer first? You know that at my age I can only remember one thing at a time."

"Very funny."

"Sorry. I'm all out of witty banter."

"Stop apologizing, for God's sake. What the heck is going on with you?"

She filled him in on everything that had happened since she'd called him to sign the death certificate. She hesitated about telling him that she and Diana made love, but since that was central to the reason she was sitting here with suitcase in hand instead of in the attic at Nora's house, she included that tidbit too, albeit leaving out the intimate details.

"Wow. Leave you alone for a second, and you find all kinds of trouble." He smiled kindly. "First, bravo for recognizing Diana might be the perfect love match for you. I thought as much, but I didn't want to influence you."

"You did?"

"Duh. She's intelligent, caring, not a serial killer, at least not that we know of..."

"You're a laugh a minute."

"Come on, Brooke. Anyone with eyes could see you two had chemistry."

"That's part of the problem. *Chemistry* isn't enough. You were by my side through three breakups, each one a result of me not

215

putting the relationship first. Now I'm finally ready to make that the top priority, and she's the one focused squarely on her career."

He sat back. A self-satisfied grin split his face.

"What?"

"Now we're getting somewhere."

"You look like a shrink who's led the patient right where he wants her to go."

"I am pretty proud of myself."

"Because...?"

"Did you hear what you said? She's in the exact position you were in, and you're accusing her of the very same thing those three-who-shall-not-be-named accused you of."

"This is not the same..." Her jaw clicked shut. He was right.

"Uh-huh. So, how did it feel when you sat on the other side of that conversation?"

Misery roiled her stomach. "Like hell. Like I was stuck between a rock and a hard place. Like I was being asked to make impossible choices."

"And how do you think Diana felt in that moment?"

Her shoulders sagged. "About the same."

"Remind me what it was you said to her? Right before the part where she lashed out at you about what the intimacy did or didn't mean to you?"

She hung her head. She wasn't proud of what she'd said; it was so far removed from her usual measured, calm self. To repeat it now? That made her feel sick inside.

"I said, 'There's nothing to salvage. We kissed a few times and slept together once.'"

"Ouch. That was cold."

What could she say? He was right. It wasn't cold—it was heartless.

"Brooke?" Daniel briefly laid his hand on top of hers. "Don't beat yourself up too badly. You felt exposed and raw, and Diana triggered you."

"I knew better. In my head I kept telling myself to walk away from the conversation without saying a word."

"You're human, my friend. Congratulations. We all say things at one point or another that we wish we could take back."

"Not me," she said quietly.

"Excuse me? Not you? What? You're perfect?"

"I'm better than I showed in that moment."

"Yes, you are. I'm willing to bet she is too. Your initial instinct to let emotions cool before having the conversation was correct. You ignored your gut because she pushed you to talk. Next time, I'm confident you won't make the same mistake."

"You're assuming there'll be a next time," she mumbled.

"I know there'll be a next time, as surely as I know my assistant is going to kill me if I don't show up soon for the next patient's appointment." He pulled out his wallet and caught the server's eye. He motioned for the check.

"I'm sor—"

"No more apologies, do you hear me?" He glanced at the check and gave the server his credit card. "Now, what's your plan of action?"

She sighed. "I haven't gotten that far."

"You said you'd help with the notifications of Nora's colleagues, correct?"

"I did, and a venue."

"The venue is easy. Book the Dana-Farber Chapel, and the Director of the Center for Spiritual Care can conduct the service."

"Wow, that would be perfect. Easy for the staff and the folks at Harvard to get there."

"I would pick a Friday or Saturday. I'm sure the chapel is busy on Sundays."

"Of course. I'll call them and see what dates they have available." She pulled out her phone and wrote herself a note. "This is one of those moments when I wish I still had an internal e-mail address. Then I could send out an all-departments e-mail about Nora's death and the details of the service and capture everyone at DFCI who might be interested all at once."

"Brooke, Brooke, Brooke. You really aren't thinking clearly, are you? We can use my e-mail."

"I couldn't ask—"

"Then it's a good thing you didn't. I'll take care of it, unless my assistant volunteers to do it, in which case, she's far more adept at this sort of thing than I am."

"Don't you dare ask her. She's not your personal assistant, she's your employ—"

"Are you done yet? Good Lord. What kind of boss do you think I am? Worse yet, what kind of human being do you think I am? You should know better."

"I'm sor—" He gave her a murderous glare, and she left the apology unfinished. "I snapped a photo of the handwritten obit Nora left. I'll include the details of that along with the particulars of her service and e-mail it to you for dissemination as soon as Diana and I nail down the date and time."

Her heart ached even as she said Diana's name, and she rubbed the sore spot in the middle of her chest.

"What are you going to do about Diana?"

She heaved a heavy sigh and slowly shook her head. "I don't know. I can't ask her to choose me over the job and the grant. That's not fair. And if she did choose me, she'd always wonder 'what if' and resent me because she'll never know what would've happened if she'd chosen differently."

"A reasonable hypothesis."

"But I also won't sit around and twiddle my thumbs waiting for her to show up for a quick stolen weekend together here or there while her world otherwise stays unchanged." She held up a hand even though Daniel hadn't indicated he was about to interrupt. "And don't even talk to me about relocating to New York. I would never be happy in the city, or even in the suburbs. Heck, Boston is bad enough."

He folded his arms.

"What?"

"I'm just waiting for you to run out of steam."

"I'm done, I guess."

"The short answer is, you don't have any idea. That's okay. Take your time. Let things settle down a bit. Get quiet. Go within. Sit in stillness with your heart and your head and find out how you really feel, what you ultimately want, and what you're willing to do to make that happen."

She raised an eyebrow. "How very spiritually enlightened of you."

"I've been listening to you all these years. You're surprised that I paid attention?"

"I love you, Daniel."

"I love you, Brooke."

He checked his watch. "My advice? Catch the T to Logan and hop on a Cape Air flight to Provincetown. Go home. Heal. Breathe. It'll do you a world of good."

"You're pretty smart, you know that? Wise too."

"You should listen to me. Doctor's orders. Now I've really got to get back. Keep me posted and I'll await your e-mail with the Nora verbiage."

She leaned in and kissed him on the cheek. "Thanks. For lunch, and everything else. You're the best BFF a girl could have."

"You're not too bad yourself. Take care, Brooke. I'm here if you need me." He waved and disappeared into the post-lunch crowd on the sidewalk.

She watched after him for a moment and then dragged her suitcase in the direction of the T stop. The fresh ocean air might be exactly what she needed to clear her head.

While waiting for the T, she would buy her ticket for the 5:25 p.m. flight to Provincetown.

Briefly she wondered if she should text Diana, tell her she was all right, and let her know where she was going. Brooke opened the messenger app and started typing. *No. That's co-dependent. Take the space you need and give her some room as well. Get your head on straight so that you don't get sucked back in.*

She deleted what she'd written, closed the app, and opened her web browser. Several clicks later, she had a seat on the flight.

Diana stared unseeing out the sunroom window. She checked her watch...again. Brooke had been gone for two hours. At first she convinced herself Brooke would turn around and come back. When that didn't happen, she told herself Brooke would call or text any second.

Two hours later, she had to admit Brooke was gone. She leaned her forehead against the cool glass. The place seemed so empty now. She couldn't even bring herself to walk into the bedroom they'd shared. The bed remained mussed where Brooke had thrown off the covers this morning.

Snippets of their lovemaking played like a romance movie in her head. It all had seemed so perfect. Somehow, Brooke knew exactly how to please her and vice versa. It was as if they'd been waiting for each other their entire lives.

She groaned. This line of thinking wasn't going to bring Brooke back. Maybe nothing would. Maybe they'd see each other once more at Aunt Nora's funeral and go their separate ways with nothing but the memory of a brief moment in time tying them together.

The thought of things playing out that way made her want to throw up. She strode out of the sunroom. Aunt Nora had given them an assignment. If Brooke reneged, so be it, but Diana was going to bear witness to Aunt Nora's truths with or without her.

She climbed to the attic, plopped into her chair, and pulled the pile of personal correspondence and the journal in front of her. Her fingers caressed the smooth leather cover. She tugged on the strap to release it from the leather clasp. Her fingers shook. This felt so wrong.

She revisited the conversations between her and Aunt Nora about Brooke. How disappointed would Aunt Nora be to see how all of this was unfolding?

"I can't. I can't do this to her. I won't." Diana threaded the strap back through the clasp, gathered up the entire stack of personal materials, and headed back downstairs.

Carefully, she stowed them in her computer bag. She couldn't stay here. Not now. Not with things the way they were. She pulled out her phone and crafted an e-mail to the head of department telling him she would be returning to work early—day-after-tomorrow, in fact, although she still might need a few days leave in the next couple of weeks to tie up loose ends.

Next, she stripped the bed and threw the sheets into the washing machine. By the time everything was dry, she could be fully packed and have the house closed up.

She texted Trent. *"I'll be leaving for New York in a couple of hours. Can you please resume your duties? I'll be in touch before I come back. How much notice do you need?"*

The telltale three dots popped up almost immediately. *"I'll take care of everything, I promise. I don't need more than a few hours' notice, though a day in advance would give me a chance to really get the place set up nice and cozy for you. Safe travels."*

She replied. *"Thanks. I'll be in touch. Let me know if anything comes up that requires my attention. Take care."*

She stashed the phone back in her pocket and set about the task of packing. If she didn't think too much, surely she could do this.

CHAPTER TWENTY-ONE

Diana collected her notes from the lectern and packed them in her computer bag, along with her iPad. It felt weird to be back here, as though nothing in her life had changed. In truth, in the span of less than a month, her entire world had been turned on its ear.

Before, every aspect of her life had been predictable and orderly. She knew who she was; she had a purpose in her teaching and her research. While part of her longed for companionship and love, she'd resigned herself to a solo existence. She'd convinced herself that, in many ways, this was better. There was no one to answer to and her time and space were her own.

One phone call from Charles Fitzgerald changed all of it. If she'd ignored the call, if she hadn't agreed to go to Truro and see Aunt Nora... "If, if, if," she muttered to herself as she headed toward her office. "You went. You fell under Aunt Nora's thrall all over again, and on top of everything else, you met the woman you know you should spend your whole life with and promptly lost her. All in the span of one month. Way to go."

"Well, well. Are you talking to yourself? Because you know what they say. Talking to yourself is the first sign of..." Rosemary Neufeld rotated her forefinger in a clockwise motion next to her temple as she fell into step alongside Diana.

Of all the people in the world she might have wanted to run into, Rosemary never would've made the list. If Diana had known Brooke four years ago, she never would've made the mistake of the Rosemary-one-night-stand debacle. Whatever had possessed her to think Rosemary was an appropriate or desirable choice for her?

"Hey, did you hear the scuttlebutt? Roger Deacon is moving his research here to Columbia from Penn."

"No, I hadn't heard. My great-aunt just died and I've been tied up with her affairs."

"Oh, sorry to hear that. Anyway, apparently Columbia enticed him away, NIH grant and all, with the promise of a dedicated lab and a tenured position. Deacon is a superstar. This will bring the department a ton of prestige. I'm going to ask him if I can join his team."

"Good for you. I hope you get in." She meant it because if Rosemary managed to wheedle her way onto Deacon's research staff, it would mean she would stop hounding Diana about joining her team.

"Well, I've got to run. It's been fun." As she jogged on, Rosemary turned to glance over her shoulder. "Oh, and for God's sake, stop talking to yourself in public. People are going to think you've lost your mind."

❧❧

The ocean roiled, swelled, receded, and crashed against the boulders again. Brooke perched on a rock far enough away from the action to avoid getting soaked. Idly, she observed that Mother Nature seemed as unsettled today as she felt. The low-hanging, charcoal-gray clouds perfectly matched her mood.

Was Diana as miserable as she was? Brooke started to pull out her phone to check for text messages. She paused with it halfway out of her pocket and pushed it back down.

"Like the answer's going to be any different than it was five minutes ago when you last checked. If she'd texted, you'd have felt the phone vibrate."

She pushed off the rock and carefully picked her way across the slick boulders of the breakwater and back to the safety of the sandy beach. She zipped her jacket higher to fight the buffeting wind and stuffed her hands in her pockets.

She felt like a woman without a home. She couldn't bring herself to stay at the cottage, despite what Nora's letter said. It was too soon and Brooke had yet to reconcile herself to the new reality that she owned the place. Being in the rented house in P-town—the house that still carried faint hints of Diana's perfume—was practically intolerable, but the better of the two options.

When she was halfway back to her rental, she felt the phone vibrate and snatched it up.

"Hi. Hope this text finds you well. Sorry it took me a few days to figure out the timing. If the offer still stands, do you think you could secure a venue for two weeks from now? I'm thinking maybe a Friday night or a Saturday afternoon service. FYI, I placed the obits as discussed. The newspapers are waiting for the funeral details before finalizing the copy. The announcements will run this coming Sunday. I guess that's all for now. Be safe, sweet Brooke."

Brooke cradled the phone and stared at the words. She particularly focused on the last line. It wasn't much, but it was at least something—a modicum of affection to offset the sadness and uncertainty that permeated the remainder of the text.

"Hi yourself. I have a venue—The Dana-Farber Chapel. I already checked open dates. That Saturday afternoon is available. How about 2 p.m.? I will nail down the details ASAP so that you'll have them in time to meet the newspaper deadlines. The Director for the Center for Spiritual Care there can officiate, if that is something you want. I have an e-mail ready to go for Dana-Farber and Harvard as soon as the date and time are confirmed. I'll cc you on the letter. Once we know who can attend, maybe we can select a few speakers? This is your show, so you let me know what you want and I will help make it happen, if you so desire."

She reread the note and hit send. After a beat, she sent a follow up. *"I hope you are practicing excellent self-care, sweet Diana."*

She gripped the phone tightly. Had she said too much? Overstepped? Should she not have added the postscript? She hated having to weigh every word. The phone buzzed again.

"That all sounds great. Thank you."

She breathed a sigh of relief. *"You're welcome. I'll be in touch as soon as I know more."*

"Okay. Thanks."

She waited as the three blinking dots remained on her screen for several moments. When they disappeared without another word, she trudged wearily toward the house.

225

Diana hadn't indicated where she was, how she was doing, or what she was feeling. But then again, Brooke hadn't said anything personal beyond telling Diana to take care of herself.

She envisioned Diana alone in the attic hunched over Nora's diary. Her heart stuttered. Nora would be most disappointed in her right now for abandoning Diana to handle the task without her.

Brooke unlocked the front door, hung up her jacket, and dropped onto the couch. Something niggled at her. Nora clearly put a lot of thought into every detail of what would happen after her death. From the disposition of her property, to the reading of the will and the letters, to the discovery of the trunk and its contents, each and every aspect of this process had been expertly choreographed and orchestrated.

What really had possessed Nora to leave the cottage to her? Seeking clues, she reread Nora's letter to her. Somehow the words on the page seemed inadequate to explain this choice. She was missing something, but reading between the lines was getting her nowhere.

Frustrated, she set the letter aside. It was late in the day. She should call and finalize the funeral arrangements with the chapel. That would give her one last excuse to have a text exchange with Diana. Then she could get the letter off to Daniel for dissemination. After that, the next move would be up to Diana.

Diana stared at Brooke's e-mail on her computer screen. The letter to Aunt Nora's Dana-Farber and Harvard colleagues was pitch perfect. She'd been good for her word and taken care of everything. The venue was ideal, and she'd secured the desired time and officiant.

So, what was the problem? "Now you have no reason to interact with her again until it's time to choose speakers." She sat back and crossed her arms. The bigger problem was that she felt like she needed a pretense to talk to Brooke.

Just once, why couldn't she have everything she wanted? Why couldn't everything fall into place and go smoothly? *You're brooding.*

Why shouldn't she brood? She mentally counted off the many ways in which the fates conspired against her.

One. Aunt Nora came back into her life, but for such a brief moment that Diana might've imagined it. Two. After years alone, she found the woman who could be "the" one, only to be thwarted by geographic challenges. Finally, three. The NIH selected and agreed to fund her project, something she'd been working toward for a decade, and she was finding it hard to muster any enthusiasm for it in light of the situation with Brooke.

Yes, the fates indeed were cruel. She balled her hands into fists and banged them on the desk. Several precariously perched books slid off the corner and landed with a thud on the floor at her feet. "Perfect."

As she bent over to clean up the mess, her eyes alit on a self-help book she'd bought in a low moment after the breakup with Bethany. She stuffed the other books in a drawer.

She had ignored most of the guidance contained in the self-help book, which she'd felt foolish for buying in the first place, but two pearls of wisdom had proven useful.

How had the author put it? Diana closed her eyes and tried to recall the sentiment. In the early days after the breakup, she'd repeated the mantra often as she endeavored to put the pieces of her shattered life back together again.

"All the help you need is supplied to you as soon as you ask for it. The answer may not look the way you expect it to look and/or may come to you in an unexpected way, but if you are open to it, you will see the path forward."

The second piece of guidance was more complicated. Diana palmed the self-help primer and thumbed through only the dog-eared pages until she found what she was looking for.

"You attract to yourself that upon which you focus. You have two choices. You can continue to dwell on negative thoughts and manifest those in your life. Or, you can envision the outcome you truly desire and point your energy in that direction. When you shift your mindset, you realign your energy and attract everything positive you can imagine. Your life. Your choice."

She flipped to the back of the book where the author included action items to facilitate the shift.

"Start by making two columns. In the first column, list what is true right now. In the second, posit what you wish was true."

She fished around in the drawer and pulled out a notepad. This was crazy and foolish, wasn't it? She was wasting her time. *But what if it works?* She sighed. It wasn't as though she had anything better to be doing tonight.

"Let's see, Column One, *What is True*... One. I'm a tenured professor at Columbia, which is located in New York City. Two. I recently received a major grant to conduct research that, if successful, could change hundreds of thousands of lives for the better."

She paused with her pen over the page. *Honesty is the best policy.* "Three. I am in love with a woman who prefers to avoid New York City and really, all big cities. Four. I recently inherited a house in Cambridge, Massachusetts." She cocked her head to the side. In the margin she wrote as she mumbled, "Does Cambridge count as a big city? The house is in a bucolic, sleepy neighborhood."

Again, she hesitated. Oh, what the hell. In the column directly across the way, under the heading, *What I Wish was True*, she jotted, "I am happily sharing my life with Brooke, living under the same roof, and conducting my research at the same time."

She exhaled and tapped the pen against the page. She liked the sound of the right-hand column. She returned to the exercise in the book. "Now, ask yourself this question: What would it take to transform the item in Column One into the item in Column Two? What is holding you back? Are there action steps you can take right now to facilitate this shift?"

What was standing in the way was the immutable fact that her research and job were in New York City. If she were going to put her relationship with Brooke first, as she should do and as Brooke required of her, that would never work. Brooke didn't want any part of living in New York.

What was the second question? "What action steps could you take to shift that dynamic?"

She scoffed, "For starters, I could relocate to a place that's acceptable to Brooke so that my two priorities aren't mutually exclusive." Slowly, she repeated, "I could relocate to a place that's acceptable to Brooke so that my two priorities aren't mutually exclusive."

She dropped the pen on the page and mumbled, "The path forward may present itself in an unexpected way and from an unusual source." Rosemary Neufeld certainly counted on that front. What was it she'd prattled on about this afternoon? Columbia had enticed Roger Deacon to pack up his grant and move it from the University of Pennsylvania to Columbia.

She rocked back in the chair. Deacon kept his grant and shifted it from one university to another. Of course he did. That sort of thing happened all the time. What if she could interest Harvard or MIT in her and her research?

You'd have to negotiate tenure and course load, and... Panic bubbled up in her chest. *Breathe.* She reread the worksheet guide. "Are there action steps you can take right now to facilitate this shift?"

She opened her web browser and typed in, *NIH grant, change of recipient organizations.* A plan of action began to take shape.

"Thank you for agreeing to see me, Dean Montrose." Diana sat ramrod straight in the visitor's chair. Her hand rested on the handle of her computer bag, in which she'd placed a manila folder with her notes and forms she'd downloaded from the NIH website.

"You're welcome. I have to say, Diana, I was surprised to hear you were back at work so soon. And again, let me extend my deepest condolences on the loss of Dr. Lindstrom. I hope you take solace in knowing that her legacy endures in all of us whom she trained or mentored."

Diana wanted to tell the dean she hadn't intended to be back at work so soon—that she wouldn't have been had it not been for the falling out with Brooke—and that losing Aunt Nora so soon after finding her again was unbearable. Instead, she said, "It's both overwhelming and comforting to know Aunt Nora was so much larger-than-life, and she left such a lasting impact and impression on so many."

She shifted and crossed her left leg over her right in an effort to appear more relaxed than she felt. "Honoring that legacy is why I'm here, sir."

"Oh?" He raised an eyebrow.

Say it exactly the way you practiced it. "You said you assumed I'd chosen Columbia because it was where Aunt Nora got her start with the Manhattan Project."

"Yes."

"The truth is, she was really conflicted about her role with the project and the moral and ethical dilemmas it posed."

He stroked his chin with his thumb and forefinger. "I can see that. She hinted as much even back when I first knew her."

"The work of which Aunt Nora was proudest was the research and teaching she conducted at Dana-Farber and Harvard."

"There's no question that her research and teaching did more to advance a cure for childhood leukemia than perhaps anyone other than Sid Farber himself. I often told my friend and counterpart at Harvard, Henry Ballinger, that Dr. Lindstrom was the reason so many top-notch scientists chose his school instead of mine."

She resisted the urge to smile. She couldn't have scripted this any better. Dean Montrose had given her the perfect opening. Maybe that self-help stuff really did work. "I'm sure that's true, although Columbia is an amazing environment and you do so much to nurture our work. It's why I came here in the first place."

"Why does it sound like there's a 'but,' coming?"

She took a deep breath. *Stick to the script.* "In her last few days, Aunt Nora and I spoke a great deal about her legacy, the lessons she learned in her career, and her wishes for me. She left me several letters and documents, along with her house in Cambridge. Everything she did, she did with forethought and intent."

Diana chanced a glance at Dean Montrose. His hands were steepled in front of him, his gaze firmly on her. *Right. On with it.*

"Sir, I feel a strong responsibility to continue Aunt Nora's legacy. Her area of expertise was leukemia. As you know, my field of study is seizure foci in patients with epilepsy. If I succeed in my research, I hope to facilitate a cure for epilepsy by identifying, and making it possible to surgically remove, the seizure foci that cause the condition. I hope to do for focal epilepsy what Aunt Nora and Sid Farber did for childhood leukemia."

"An admirable and laudable pursuit. We here at Columbia are very proud of your work and the grant you secured to further that goal."

"Thank you, sir. The thing is, I believe Aunt Nora intended for me to do the work at Harvard. All indications lead to that conclusion." She forced herself to make direct eye contact.

Apart from a minute facial tick, his expression never changed. Finally, he said, "I see."

Her throat was dry. Maybe she should've done what others she'd researched last night had done. She should've secured a deal with the new institution and then simply given notice to Columbia. But that didn't feel right or honorable. It wasn't what Aunt Nora would've done in her place.

"I chose to speak with you directly, sir, before I contacted Harvard. That felt like the right thing to do. You've been a great mentor, and I love it here at Columbia. Honestly, I thought I would finish out my career here and had every intention of doing so. Like you, Aunt Nora was my hero, and that was before I knew anything about her work. Now I feel strongly that I need to carry out her wishes."

She sat back in the chair and released a breath she didn't realize she was holding. There it was. All the cards were on the table now and there could be no turning back. It was the biggest gamble she'd ever taken with her livelihood. What would Brooke think of the gambit?

Her heart quickened. What if she went through all this, risked her standing at Columbia, and things didn't work out with Brooke? What if Harvard didn't want her? What if...

"I appreciate your candor, Diana. Not many people in your position would have approached their current institution without the security net of a new deal in their pocket."

She bore his scrutiny and did her best not to squirm. She recrossed her legs and tried to appear nonchalant. "I've never been most people, sir."

"That's the truth." Finally, he offered a ghost of a smile. "You know that Harvard would be under no obligation to honor your tenure. You might have to start from scratch."

"I do."

"And you know they might turn you down altogether, which would leave you in a precarious position here. How do I know you won't try to shop your research to another school and another until you find the deal you want?"

She bristled. "I'm not some mercenary looking for a sweet deal. I'm simply trying to honor my great-aunt's wishes." *And to find my life.* She clicked her jaw shut. Her personal life was none of his business.

He sat silent for a long time. She resisted the urge to fill the empty space. She'd said what she came here to say. The rest was up to him.

"I could offer you a larger stipend, reduce your class hours for the remainder of the semester until your scheduled research sabbatical, and create a dedicated lab for your research."

She squared her shoulders. "I'm flattered that you would consider those enhancements, sir, but I didn't come here to work out a better deal for myself. This wasn't a negotiating ploy. This is my sincere desire to take what I feel in my heart is the right step to honor Aunt Nora and her legacy."

"It's an emotional time for you, Diana, as it would be for anyone in your position. The death of someone so significant is bound to rock your world. Perhaps you should let this sit for a while before acting. Later, if you still feel as you do now, you could approach Harvard."

"No, sir. I know exactly what I'm doing, and I'm positive that this would be the right move for me."

Dean Montrose pushed back in his chair. He glanced out the window and then down at a metal item on his desk. He picked it up and handed it to her.

"What's this?"

"It's a spare part from a Calutron machine. Your great-aunt gave it to me as a present when I successfully defended my dissertation. With it was a note that read: 'Congratulations, Dr. Montrose. Always remember that the individual components of your work mean nothing without consideration of the totality. Never one without the other. Be mindful, and let your conscience be your North Star.' I've never forgotten that advice."

She examined the piece and handed it back, as yet another wave of sadness and regret washed over her. If Grandpa Bill and her parents hadn't driven Aunt Nora out of her life, she no doubt would've been the recipient of such sage counsel on a regular basis.

"Your Aunt Nora answered my questions and gave of her time and expertise to me when she didn't need to do so. She led by example and taught others to do the same. She was more than a great scientist. She was a remarkable human being."

Diana felt a surge of pride. "I wish I'd had more time with her. But somehow, I feel like she's still here with me, guiding me. I'm sure that sounds crazy."

"Actually, that sounds exactly right." He nodded to himself. "I can't believe I'm going to say what I'm about to say. I told you that Dean Ballinger at Harvard is a friend of mine. He too was mentored by Dr. Lindstrom as a young professor, before he ascended up the career ladder. I know they had a special relationship. If you're serious about this move and committed to see it through, I will talk to Dr. Ballinger on your behalf."

"You'll..." She couldn't speak around the lump in her throat. She swallowed and paused to regain her composure.

"I told you. Your great-aunt changed and guided my professional life. It's only right that I pay her back in the most meaningful way possible. To the extent that I'm able, I will help you transfer your grant to Harvard and make sure that the terms of your employment there are equal to—or better—than they are here."

"You'd do that for me, sir?"

"Sid Farber believed in your Aunt Nora and gave her a chance to thrive at a time when few women were taken seriously in the field of science. As a result, her work changed the world for the better. I have that same confidence in you and your work. You're a gifted teacher, Diana, and I believe your research project has the potential to change the outcome for thousands of patients. It's an honor to be in a position to facilitate your success, even if that success won't happen here at Columbia."

"I-I don't know what to say, sir. Thank you."

"You're welcome. That was a bold and brave move, coming to me first. I appreciate your integrity. Looks like you inherited your great-aunt's strong moral sense. I do believe she'd be proud."

"I certainly hope so, sir. I hope so."

CHAPTER TWENTY-TWO

B
rooke stood up and waved as Daniel entered the restaurant. He was a half hour late for their dinner at Moby Dick's in Wellfleet, but that was to be expected given his patient load and the fact that he drove from Boston. She caught his attention and sat back down.

At the table, he pulled her up, hugged her hello, and then held her at arm's length. "You look like hell."

"Good to see you too."

"I mean it, Brooke. Have you slept at all?"

"It's Wednesday. It's not my day to sleep."

"Don't be glib."

"Don't be over-protective. I'm fine."

He shed his coat and they sat. "I'm sorry I'm late."

She shrugged. "It's not as if I had anyplace urgent to be."

"What can I get you to drink?" The server fished his pen out of his apron and held it poised over his pad.

"What are you having?" Daniel asked Brooke.

"Perrier."

"I'll have what she's having."

When the server returned with the sparkling water, they ordered their entrees.

"So, tell me what's going on." Daniel sipped his drink and broke off a piece of sourdough bread from the loaf in the middle of the table. He dipped it in the olive oil and balsamic vinegar and moaned in delight with the first bite.

"Nothing."

"Well then, this is going to be a short conversation." He took another bite. "When's the last time you heard from Diana?"

Brooke fiddled with the salt and pepper shakers.

"Brooke? Talk to me."

"A little over a week ago via e-mail. She thanked me for getting the letter out to Nora's colleagues and asked me to line up one speaker each from Harvard and DFCI. She also asked for the name of the officiant so she could contact him directly. I did as she asked, lined everyone up, and replied to her e-mail. I haven't heard a word since."

"I'd ask how that makes you feel, but it's written all over your face." He reached out and took her hand. "I'm sorry."

"Me too."

"Are you sure you don't want to soften your position? You know, compromise a little?"

She withdrew her hand. "How would you like me to bend? You want me to say that I'm content to take a back seat to Diana's career? That at fifty years old I don't mind being a weekend girlfriend who gets maybe eight days a month with her partner and otherwise is a long-distance text and call buddy? Or would you have me agree to move to a big city that would eat me alive where I can be an afterthought she comes home to when she's done burning the midnight oil in the lab?"

"Tell me how you really feel." He polished off the last of the bread. "Everything you've mentioned was known to you before you got involved. You were aware that she worked at Columbia and you knew about the grant. How did you think this was all going to work out?"

She shook her head in exasperation. "I don't know. I guess I wasn't thinking very clearly, was I? I made a poor decision."

"Or maybe you followed your heart."

"Yeah, well, we can see how that's working out for me." She glanced down as her phone vibrated against the dinner table. "Oh." Her pulse pounded a tattoo against the side of her neck and her heart fluttered.

"What is it?" He half-stood. "Brooke? Are you okay?"

She nodded. It was several seconds before she trusted herself to read Diana's text out loud.

"Hi. I hope I'm not intruding. Is there any chance I could see you tomorrow? If the answer is yes, and I pray that it is, I would have to know where you're going to be tomorrow. Are you back in Provincetown?"

"Well?" he asked. "What's your answer?"

Her fingers tingled, a sure sign she was hyperventilating. She rotated her shoulders back and consciously drew in a deep breath. What did Diana want?

"Brooke? Drink some water. Your pallor is awful and you're having a panic attack." He handed her the glass of water.

She dutifully drank. "I don't have panic attacks."

"Could've fooled me." He smirked.

"This is not funny."

"You're right. It's not. So, what are you going to do?"

"What do you think she wants?"

He raised an eyebrow. "How should I know? I suggest you either ask her what she wants, or be brave, say yes, and find out what it's all about when she gets here."

She rocked her head from side to side to relieve the tension in her neck.

"Whatever you're going to say, I wouldn't keep her waiting too much longer. It took guts for her to reach out. Be compassionate."

She closed her eyes. Be compassionate. What was the worst that could happen? Could things between them be any more broken than they already were?

"Hey," he said softly, "with great risk comes great reward, right?"

"Or, conversely, with great risk comes greater heartache."

"Since when did you become such a pessimist? What happened to my always Zen, always sunny, Brooke?"

She smiled sadly. "She fell in love and got her heart ripped out, all in short order."

"You haven't asked my advice yet, but I think you should let her come and see what she has to say. Give her a chance. If you don't like it, tell her to go pound salt, see her at the funeral on Saturday, and be done with her. You'd be no worse off than you are right now."

She bit her lip. Maybe he was right. What was she afraid of? *You're afraid she'll yank your heart the rest of the way out of your chest and step on it for good measure.* Was that true? Was that really the issue? Or was she afraid Diana would sacrifice things that were important to her, including her self-esteem, to be with the woman she loved? Surely that was a recipe for failure.

Brooke raised trembling fingers and tapped out, *"Yes, you can come. I'm in Provincetown. Staying at the rented house. What time should I expect you?"*

༚ೋ

Diana checked herself in the visor mirror. She ran her fingers through her hair once more to settle it, readjusted her shirt collar, and put her hand in front of her mouth to check her breath. She couldn't remember the last time she'd been this nervous.

Breathe. The worst that can happen is that she tells you it doesn't make a difference and you've turned your life upside down for nothing.

"Please, God, don't let this all have been for nothing." She cracked open the window to counteract the hot flash that threatened to drench her. She was glad she'd freshened her perfume.

With five miles to go, she rehearsed once more what she wanted to say and envisioned a successful outcome. That was the final piece of guidance she'd absorbed from the self-help book.

"Focus on the desired outcome and visualize it as though it already has come to pass."

She was so preoccupied she nearly drove past the address. She parked the car, cut the engine, and got out. When she glanced up at the house, Brooke was standing on the front steps.

She had her hands jammed in the pockets of her jeans. As Diana approached, she idly noted that the forest green sweater set off her hair and eyes. She seemed somehow more fragile than Diana remembered, but also more beautiful.

"Hi."

"Hi, yourself," Diana responded. Her heart pounded so hard she thought it might burst out of her chest. "Thanks for letting me come."

"You're welcome. Want to come inside?"

"Yes, please." She followed Brooke into the living room.

"Sit down. Do you want anything to drink? I can make a pot of coffee if you like."

"No, thank you." They were like polite strangers, warily circling each other, feeling their way, careful not to give away too much.

She sat on the edge of the couch while Brooke chose the chair opposite her.

"So..." They both said at once.

"You go first," Diana said.

"I was just going to ask you how you've been."

I've been a mess without you. "Fine. Okay. You?"

"Fine."

She wanted to tell her that she didn't look fine. She looked vulnerable and scared, and Diana would've done anything right then to change that. "Thanks again for doing all of the leg work for the funeral."

"You're welcome. I had the contacts. It wasn't hard."

"Well, I appreciate it."

"Sure." Brooke stared at a spot over Diana's left shoulder. The seconds ticked on. "I'm confident you didn't come all the way out here to tell me that. You could've called or texted me and done the same."

She licked her lips. "You're right. That's not why I'm here."

Brooke sat back and crossed her arms. Obviously, she wasn't going to make this easy.

"I-I've missed you."

Brooke nodded imperceptibly.

"I've done a lot of soul searching since you walked out. I need you to know I understand why you left. You were right to take care of yourself. You deserve someone who puts you first, and you have every right to expect that. I didn't give you any reason to believe I was that person." Shame stained her cheeks red.

Brooke continued to sit stoically, so she plowed onward. "Instead of focusing only on the ways in which this couldn't work, I should've spent my energy figuring out solutions. That's what I've been doing since you left."

Brooke's scrutiny made her too nervous to sit still any longer. She jumped up and began to pace. "I realize I may be too late. You might not be willing to hit the restart button. Perhaps I've already blown my chance, but I hope not." She came to stand in front of her.

"I'm rambling, I know. That's because I'm scared. It terrifies me to think I might have to walk through the rest of my life without you by my side. So, here goes." She sucked in a deep breath and blew it out.

"Yesterday, I went to Harvard and met with Henry Ballinger, the Dean of the Faculty of Medicine, and Roberta Dubnick, Dean for Faculty and Research Integrity. With the blessing of my dean at Columbia, we agreed in principle on a deal that will transfer my research and my tenure to Harvard and release me from my contract at Columbia."

Brooke gasped and covered her mouth with a trembling hand. Diana knelt in front of her.

"Brooke Sheldon, I know you may not be able to forgive me for my myopia and stupidity, but I want you to know that I would do anything for you, including relocate to a place you call home, just to have a chance..." Her voice cracked and she took a moment to gather herself. "...just to have a chance to call you mine and spend the rest of my life with you. I love you, and I can't imagine my world without you in it."

Brooke shook her head slowly. She opened her mouth to speak, but no words came out.

Diana sat back on her heels and bowed her head. She'd done her best and she had no regrets. She'd known there was no guarantee that Brooke would forgive her and open her heart again. Still, she was proud that she'd tried.

Soft hands caressed her face and raised her chin. "Diana Lindstrom, I can't believe you did that. I-I don't know what to say."

She smiled tentatively. "You could start by saying I have a shot with you."

"Yes. Yes, a thousand times yes." Brooke kissed Diana's eyelids, her nose, and finally her mouth.

Diana pulled Brooke to her as they tumbled to the floor in a heap. She brushed Brooke's hair back. "I couldn't imagine not waking up to this face every day. I had to do what I could."

"You really quit Columbia for Harvard?"

"I did. Well, it's not officially official yet. It will take time to get all the paperwork and details in order. But, yes, I did. Technically, Cambridge isn't Boston, and Aunt Nora's house is on a nice, quiet street with lots of trails and green spaces. I thought maybe it would be on your 'acceptable places to live' list. And we could spend every chance we get in Truro at the cottage."

Brooke laughed. "You've lost your mind." She kissed her again. "Harvard will give you tenure?"

"Yes. And a kick ass research team, an amazing lab, and classes that I'm really jazzed to teach. Also, Massachusetts General Hospital has a tie-in with my research and will contribute to funding my position."

"Wow. Just...wow!"

Diana pulled back so that Brooke's face was in focus. "I know I'd still be working hard on my research and teaching, but I promise those things will never supersede us in importance. You have my solemn word."

"You worked all this out yourself?"

"It helped that both deans were Aunt Nora's mentees."

"I'm sure there's a story there, but right now, I don't want to hear it." Brooke leaned in and claimed her lips again.

Diana ran her fingers underneath Brooke's sweater seeking the soft skin of her abdomen. She was quickly losing any ability to hold herself back. She brushed her thumbs across Brooke's erect nipples and moaned.

"Can I...? Is this okay...? Please...?" She recognized that she wasn't able to complete a coherent thought.

"Yes. Yes. And absolutely." Brooke arched backward to give Diana better access.

"Should we...?"

"Yes."

They separated only long enough to stumble to the bedroom.

"I love you, Brooke."

"I love you, Diana. Make love to me, please."

Brooke stretched and shifted onto her side. She skimmed her fingers over Diana's shoulder, along her collarbone, and dipped downward. Diana groaned and rolled toward her.

"Anyone who says women are washed up after forty-five has never met us."

"Who says that?" she asked as she bent to taste the soft skin at the base of Diana's throat.

"Those 'they' people." Diana squirmed under her ministrations. "Oh, my God. You have to stop now or I won't be able to walk for a week."

"I thought you said…"

"I know what I said. Pace yourself. I'm not going anywhere." She stilled her motion. Her heart paused and resumed its normal rhythm. "Are you sure? Sure you're not going anywhere, I mean? Sure that you made the right choice? Sure that I'm worth that sacrifice?"

Diana scrambled to a sitting position and fluffed a pillow behind her back. "I've never been more certain of anything in my life."

"Diana, you're giving up everything you've worked for. I never would've asked—"

"You didn't. This was my decision and my choice. All you did was insist, rightfully so, that our relationship be the most important thing in our lives. How I chose to honor that requirement was mine to determine. And I'm positive that we're worth this shift."

"What if…" She willed her heart to settle. "What if you hate it at Harvard? What if you regret your choice? What if you gave up everything you worked for and then you figure out that we're not right for each other?"

There, she'd given voice to her greatest fear. If Diana relinquished everything she'd worked toward and it didn't work out, it would be all Brooke's fault. How could she live with that?

Diana leaned over and brushed her fingers along Brooke's cheekbone and caressed her jaw. The pure love in her gaze made Brooke want to weep.

"Brooke Sheldon, I am madly in love with you. You make me better in every way. I am more confident that you're the one for me than I am of anything else in my life. Aunt Nora knew it too."

She nodded.

Diana continued, "Why do you suppose she left me the house in Cambridge and you the place in Truro?"

"I've been asking myself the same question."

"She did everything with such intent and deliberation. You have to know she gave all that careful thought. I believe she already knew how this was going to play out."

"Or at least how she wanted it to play out."

"Exactly. I think she meant to set us up for life together—a place in town for work for me, where I could do my research in an optimal setting and build my own legacy as she built hers."

"And a place at the beach for me, in an environment she knew I'd already chosen as a retreat, for rejuvenating our souls."

"Yep. And because of the locations, you have the option to reboot your career at Dana-Farber or do something different, without the pressure of worrying how you're going to pay the mortgage. These were Aunt Nora's gifts to us."

She shook her head in wonder. "She thought of everything."

Diana nodded. "She thought of everything, God bless her."

"That reminds me..." Brooke sat up and pulled the covers with her. "What was in the journal? And what about those letters?"

Diana smiled. "I went back up to the attic that day, but I couldn't bring myself to read them without you. They're in the trunk of my car outside."

"You brought them with you?"

Diana shrugged. "I was cautiously optimistic."

She kissed her soundly. "Go get them. We have to know."

"Should I put on clothes first?"

"I guess that depends on whether or not you want to scandalize the neighbors."

Diana pulled on her pants and shirt and headed toward the bedroom door. "What do you think about going over to the cottage and reading the materials over there?"

She pursed her lips in thought. "You know, I bet Nora would like that. Let's jump in the shower, get cleaned up, and we can stop for dinner at Napi's along the way."

"I do like the way you think." Diana patted her belly. "I don't know about you, but I'm famished."

"I can't imagine why." Brooke watched admiringly as Diana stripped again and headed toward the shower.

"Coming?" she called over her shoulder.

"Oh, yes."

CHAPTER TWENTY-THREE

Diana hauled the box inside the cottage. Brooke followed behind her with the eggs, bacon, muffins, coffee and orange juice they'd picked up at the grocery store for breakfast tomorrow morning.

"I'm stuffed," she proclaimed.

"Me too. Napi's never disappoints." Brooke unpacked the groceries and stored them in the refrigerator.

"It feels odd to be back here."

"I know." Brooke went to Diana and put her arms around her. "Are you okay?"

Diana glanced around and sighed. "It's going to take some getting used to—being here without Aunt Nora."

"Her strength and essence filled this place."

"I miss her."

"Me too." Brooke rubbed circles on her back. "How about if we spend some time with her now?"

She pulled back. "I think she'd like that." She grabbed the box. "Living room?"

"Living room."

Gently, reverently, Diana slid open the journal clasp. A thin sheet of tissue paper protected the first page. She carefully moved it aside to reveal the first journal entry.

Brooke peered over her shoulder. The entry was written in meticulous script with a fountain pen. "Her handwriting was so beautiful. Nobody writes like that these days."

"Should we read to ourselves or out loud?" Diana asked.

"Hmm. I think it's more impactful to bear witness out loud, don't you?"

"Okay. You read it. I don't want to blotch it with tears."
Brooke slid the journal into her lap.

April 10, 1943
I can't decide whether I'm more nervous or excited. The train is most definitely heading south, but to where I do not know. The meeting with Dr. Oppenheimer, Dr. Lawrence, and that Army General Groves went well, I think. Dr. Oppenheimer and Dr. Lawrence insisted to the general that I was the right person for "the job," whatever that is.

The general argued that I was too young—twenty-five and fresh out of graduate school with a Ph.D. in physics. Both Dr. Oppenheimer and Dr. Lawrence explained that I had the right temperament and that it would be invaluable for a woman scientist to be in charge of a gaggle (their word) of younger girls. I would understand them better, and they would relate more to me than to a man in a similar position.

The general remained reluctant, but my heroes convinced him in the end that if I failed, they would chalk it up to my being a girl, and they would replace me forthwith with a man.

I SHALL NOT FAIL! HA!

The train is pulling into a station, so I shall sign off for now with a solemn promise that I will write as often as time allows.

All my best, dearest diary,
Nora

Brooke took a sip of water and squeezed Diana's hand. "Nora was a feminist way before her time. How cool is that?"

"She didn't know what the assignment was or where she was going, but she packed up her things and went anyway. That's amazing. Would you have done that?"

"No way. I'm way too curious. I would've asked a million questions."

Diana laughed. "Yeah. I could see that."

"Would you have gone?"

"Knowing that two of the greatest scientific minds in my field hand-picked me for a project? Heck, yes, I would. How exciting!"

Brooke smiled. "Like great-aunt, like great-niece. Apple didn't fall far from the tree there."

"Let's keep reading."

They thumbed through entry after entry, most of them describing the muddy conditions, the endless sexism, Nora's fight to have her housing situation upgraded, the construction of the Y-12 plant, and the fits, starts, and stops of the uranium enrichment process.

Brooke stood and stretched. "Want a cup of coffee? This could take a while."

"Sure."

She headed to the kitchen.

"Oh, here's an interesting one," Diana called out.

"Let me see." Brooke returned and sat next to Diana. She pulled the journal into her lap.

July 22, 1943

I am so thrilled I can hardly contain myself. Today, I finally received a response from Leona Woods. As she is one of only a handful of other women scientists I know of, I thought we gals ought to stick together.

Woods presently is stationed in Chicago with Enrico Fermi and says she was the only woman in the room when Fermi's nuclear pile went critical. How exciting it would've been to be present on such an occasion!

We have vowed to keep in touch, though both of us are bound by secrecy not to say much of anything.

Still, dearest diary, this ranks right up there with the response I received from Lise Meitner several weeks ago. She fled those despicable Nazis and is hiding out in Stockholm at present. It was her discovery with Otto Hahn that produced the nuclear fission on which our project is based. Hearing from her is the equivalent of getting a signed baseball card from Joe DiMaggio.

Anyway, I could go on and on, but I simply must get some sleep.

Ever faithfully yours, dearest diary.

Nora

"There were women scientists who were responsible for some of the greatest discoveries of the day? That's amazing. How is it I never learned about them in school?" Brooke asked.

"Was that a serious question?"

"Um…yes?"

"Did you ever learn about the women from the movie, *Hidden Figures?*"

"Not until I saw the movie."

"Did you ever hear of the Women Airforce Service Pilots—the WASPs who flew all the same planes the men did in World War II?"

"Not until I read *Eyes on the Stars.*"

"Exactly my point. History and our history books have ignored the contributions of women from the beginning of time. Witness the fact that even I didn't know about Aunt Nora's role in ending the war with the atomic bomb until a few weeks ago."

"Point taken." Brooke got up and poured two cups of coffee. "It's depressing."

"It is."

"I'm never going to let history forget when you solve the issue of seizure foci-induced epilepsy." Brooke kissed Diana on the side of the head.

"Is that right?"

"Yep. You can take it to the bank. I'm going to shout it from the rooftops and every social media outlet I can find."

"You're adorable, you know that?" She pulled Brooke to her and kissed her thoroughly.

"If you don't stop that, we're never going to get through this."

"We could call it a night?" She waggled her eyebrows suggestively.

"We could. Or we could keep reading and try to find a reference to someone named Mary."

"Ah. The mystery of the missing Mary. That sounds intriguing. Read on."

Several minutes later, Brooke sat bolt upright. "I've got it."

"What?" Diana, who had been dozing lightly on the couch, yawned and stretched.

"Mary."

"You found her?"

"Oh, yes. I most assuredly did." Brooke pointed to the entry.

October 10, 1943
Today I met an angel. I swear she's so beautiful her feet never even touch the ground. Her name is Mary Trask. She arrived on the

reservation yesterday and reported to work at Y-12 under my tutelage this morning.
As with all new recruits, she seems a little shell-shocked. I personally instructed her on the operation of the Calutron machine and kept a close eye on her throughout her first shift.
Oh, dearest diary, how that girl made my heart do somersaults!
Ever faithfully yours, dearest diary.
Nora

"Aha! The plot thickens." Diana rubbed her hands together. "Keep going."

Brooke chuckled. "Well, that little tidbit woke you up, now didn't it?"

She made a shooing motion with her hand. "Never mind that. Keep reading, for God's sake."

Brooke kept turning the pages.

"Why aren't you reading out loud?"

"I will when I get to something worthwhile. So far, all of these are about the plant shutting down because of a malfunction in the design, some handsy guy who made a play for Nora, a bus trip into Knoxville, and a pair of shoes she had to toss out because they got ruined by the mud."

Brooke paged ahead several more entries, and then stopped. "Eureka! I've got it."

December 25, 1943
My hands are still trembling and my lips continue to tingle with the sweet taste of her kiss. When I even think her name, I turn into a quivering puddle of goo.

"That's romantic."
"Shh. Let me read."

*It happened quite by accident, really. I literally bumped into Mary on my way home from services at the Chapel-on-the-Hill. The force of the collision jarred loose the basket of pine cones she was carrying. I apologized profusely, of course, and helped her collect the fallen goodies. Then I offered to make it up to her by taking her to the movies (*Mrs. Miniver *is playing at Center Theatre).*

Oh, dearest diary, she said YES! It was magical. In one particularly gripping scene with Walter Pidgeon and dreamy Greer Garson, Mary actually took my hand and continued to hold it throughout the rest of the movie!

Afterward, we strolled through Townsite looking at the storefronts. I invited her back to my place for coffee. As she was getting ready to leave, I saw her to the front door. After all, that's only polite.

"Polite my pattootie, Aunt Nora, you scoundrel!"

"Shh. Let me finish."

I reached around her to get the door handle, and her hand brushed against my breast. Oh, dearest diary, I have never felt a sensation anything like that. At first, she blushed. But when she saw that I didn't immediately remove myself from the situation... Well, let's just say she got a little bit bolder.

I'm getting all tingly just thinking about it. I swear, I'll never forget this night as long as I live.

It's late, and I'd best try to sleep, although I don't know how I'll manage it.

Ever faithfully yours, dearest diary.

Nora

"Scandal in Oak Ridge!"

"I'll never be able to un-see that image," Diana said.

"I think it's incredibly sweet." Brooke thumbed through more entries. "Oh, this is a good one."

"What?"

March 23, 1944

Today was the day. We moved Mary's things into my Flat Top. I'm so glad I was able to convince the brass that, as a supervisor, I deserved preferential housing. Our bedrooms are adjacent, so no one who visits will be any the wiser. They'll simply think we're conserving housing units by doubling up.

Some of the girls are jealous. They think I treat Mary better than the rest of them. If they only knew! Honestly, we're both relieved

Lynn Ames

that it will be easier for us to be together without being discovered. We've had enough close calls to last us a lifetime!

Well, I hear Mary coming out of the bathroom, so I'd better get ready for bed. For the first time, I'll be able to sleep holding precious Mary all night long.

Dreamy sigh, dearest diary.

Nora

"They lived together. In the 1940s, Aunt Nora lived with another woman right under everyone's noses!"

"That was brazen."

"No kidding!"

Brooke laid the book down. "Is it just me, or does this feel a little..."

"Voyeuristic?"

"Yeah."

Diana nodded. "Kind of. Do you want to stop?"

She shifted so they were face to face. "Yes, and no. I think we need to know what happened to them in the end, you know? Nora's dreams about Mary toward the end seemed so...fraught...so tortured."

"How about if we compromise and skip to the end of the war? Is there an entry for that? Maybe it ends when they have to go their separate ways because the war is over."

"Fair enough." Brooke paged ahead in the journal until she arrived at the entry for August 9, 1945. She pulled out a folded piece of newsprint pressed between two pages. "Wow, this is some piece of history right here."

She held up a yellowed copy of the *Oak Ridge Journal* that bore the headline, "Oak Ridge Attacks Japanese. Workers Thrill As Atomic Bomb Secret Breaks; Press And Radio Stories Describe 'Fantastically Powerful' Weapon; Expected To Save Many Lives."

"Wow. That's in pretty good shape."

"It is."

Together, they read the front page. When they'd finished reading, Diana asked, "What does the journal entry say?"

August 9, 1945

My heart aches with a despair I know I'll never get over. My darling Mary is gone, and I fear nothing I say or do will win her back.

This day, a day that should be filled with joyous celebration, has brought me bitter anguish. I hear the cheers outside the window of our Flat Top, but I cannot bring myself to partake of the celebration.

Mary's accusations are forever burned into my memory and onto my heart. I shall never forget the ugliness of the row and the hatred and disgust in Mary's beautiful eyes as she gazed upon me one last time.

She accused me of knowing what we were doing with the Calutron machines and concealing it from the girls. She said such ugly things, calling me a murderer and insisting I made all the girls accomplices without giving them a chance to decide for themselves whether or not they wanted to be a party to creating a killing machine, which is what she called the bomb.

I tried my best to explain to her that I was sworn to secrecy, that I couldn't tell her or anyone else, just as she agreed not to share with anyone what she was doing here.

She refused to see the parallel, refused to rejoice in the fact that what we did won the war and saved the lives of our boys.

She became fixated on the idea that thousands of Japanese women, mothers, innocent children, and grandparents were killed with an instrument of death we created.

I tried to explain that the world is safe again because of what we did, but she would not hear of it.

In the end, she was inconsolable. She said horrible things. She never wants to see me again. I sicken her. She ordered me to stay away from her. She packed up her things and left. I don't know where she went or whether or not she is safe.

I am worried sick for her safety and well-being, and there isn't a thing I can do about it.

My precious Mary thinks I am a monster. Perhaps she's right.

I cannot write any more through my tears, dearest diary, so I must sign off.

Ever faithfully yours.

Nora

"Oh, my God. That's horrible. Poor Nora. No wonder she was still haunted by that at the end." Brooke wiped away a tear.

"Do you really think they never saw each other again? Never reconciled?"

"I don't know. I guess we could keep reading."

"Are there more entries after the war ends?"

Brooke turned the page. It looks like there's a two-year gap. The next entry is from 1947.

March 27, 1947

It seems only fitting that I should board a plane with my few possessions today, on what would be Mary's twenty-second birthday.

Everything I do now, and most especially the scientific studies I am about to undertake on behalf of the Atomic Bomb Casualty Commission, I do in order to set things right. I cannot undo my role in the historic genocide of thousands of Japanese citizens, but I will dedicate the rest of my life to ameliorating their outcomes.

My job in Hiroshima will be to study and document the effects of the radiation exposure from the bomb blast on residents, their children, and eventually, their children's children. For now, my specific focus is on instances of leukemia, although I am told there are plans underway to institute a life span study of some sort soon and that I might play a larger role once that is established.

Hiroshima seems a world away, and the assignment is daunting. I will have to come face-to-face every day with the destruction I wrought. I will have to live with the reality of that horror and interact with the very individuals whose lives I helped ruin. It seems a just punishment.

Besides, there is nothing for me here in the states. Mother and Dad continue to watch over me like a hawk, concerned for my well-being as I have lost so much weight. I cannot explain to them that my affliction is a hole in my heart that will never heal.

Mary has returned every letter I've sent, unopened. Most recently came the dagger to the heart, a letter from her imploring me never to contact her again. I must honor her wishes, even as doing so irreparably shatters my heart.

So, dearest diary, off to my exile I go. I wonder what Mary would think of my new endeavor and commitment to use my knowledge

and education for good. And I weep with the knowledge that she'll never know.
Ever faithfully yours, dearest diary.
Nora

"That might be the saddest thing I've ever read," Brooke said.
"No kidding." Diana scrolled through the photos on her phone.
"What are you doing?"
"I forgot all about the second document Dean Montrose showed me in the archives."
"What are you talking about?"
"Here it is." She handed the phone to Brooke.
"Dr. Nora Lindstrom will oversee the team conducting the Life Span Study, and will have secondary responsibility for the F1 (Children of the A-Bomb Survivors) Study. She will report directly to the Advisory Committee of the Atomic Bomb Casualty Commission, or ABCC, in Washington, D.C."
"Huh. So, she was right about the longevity study."
"Yep. And she wasn't just part of the team, she ran the team."
"Good for you, Nora." Brooke frowned.
"What's the matter?"
"I'm trying to remember what it was Nora told me about why she came to work for Dana-Farber. I think somehow it's connected to all of this."
"While you puzzle through that, I'll dig out the stack of personal correspondence."
Brooke drummed her fingers on her thigh. Abruptly, she stopped. "I've got it."
"Do tell." Diana moved back to the couch with the stack of correspondence, tied neatly with faded yellow ribbon.
"Nora told me she came back because she lost a patient for whom she cared a great deal. She'd turned down Sid Farber's offers of employment many times, but losing that patient was the last straw, so she returned to the states and came to Boston to work with Sid. That was in 1972, just before you were born."
Diana nodded. "That makes sense. Do you suppose the patient she referred to was one of the bomb survivors?"
"Could be. Or one of their children or grandchildren."

"It would explain why she was so driven to work on a cure for childhood leukemia."

"Should we have a look at that?" Brooke pointed to the letters in Diana's hand.

Carefully, Diana untied the ribbon. The letters cascaded onto the couch, and she picked up the one on top. "Oh." She put a hand to her heart.

"What is it?"

"It's addressed to Miss Mary Trask and marked 'Return to Sender.'" She turned the envelope over. It was sealed shut.

"Oh, Nora." Brooke put her arm around Diana. "That's heartbreaking."

When Diana looked up, there were tears in her eyes. "I can't bring myself to open this."

"I'm with you. That's too private." Brooke pointed to the rest of the letters. "Are they all like that?"

Diana sorted through the envelopes. "Every one of them except for this." She held up an envelope that appeared as though at one time it might've been red. Now it was a pale pink.

Brooke slid the envelope out of Diana's hands. "It's addressed to Nora, but there's no return address. It's already open."

Diana nodded and bit her lip. "Do you think we should read it?"

Brooke furrowed her brow. "Didn't she reference a letter from Mary she received telling her to leave her alone?"

"She did. You think this is it?"

She shrugged. "That would make sense."

"I'd feel like a heel reading it. Like it was a betrayal of her privacy."

"I agree." Brooke picked up one of the unopened letters and examined it more closely.

"What are you looking for?"

"I'm making note of the address." She pursed her lips in thought. "These letters clearly reached Mary since she sent them back."

"How do we know she was the one who sent them back?"

"Hmm. Good question. Let's assume for argument's sake that she did."

"Okay." Diana drew out the word. "Where are you going with this?"

Brooke took Diana's hand and intertwined their fingers. "I want to do something for Nora—something she couldn't do for herself."

"Such as?"

"What if we could find Mary and get Nora closure?"

Diana's eyes opened wide. "Track her down and go see her?"

Brooke sat up straighter. "If possible, yes. What if we could deliver those letters in person?"

"She was twenty-two in 1947, she'd be ninety-three years old now. And that's assuming she's still alive."

"If she's not, no harm, no foul. If she is, and there's any chance she still has feelings for Nora as Nora clearly did for her…"

"It would give us a chance to give them both closure. We could tell her Aunt Nora loved her to the end. We could tell her how Aunt Nora's life turned out—at least the parts of it that we know." Diana sat back. Would Aunt Nora want this?

"These letters were sent to an address in Pennsylvania. That's a start. We could use Google and Ancestry to try to find a Mary Trask in Pennsylvania. If she remained a lesbian, she might not have changed her last name."

"You know this is like looking for a needle in a haystack, right?"

Brooke nodded. "What do you say?"

"What the heck. We've got nothing to lose but time."

"Speaking of time, you do realize it's 3:12 a.m., right? How about if we get some sleep?"

"I thought you'd never ask." Diana rose and took Brooke's hand. "Your bedroom?" She led them down the hall.

"Yes. You know, as much as I hate to change anything so soon, I'm going to have to order a new bed for Nora's room. Sleeping in her bed feels wrong, and my lease on the P-town house runs out at the end of the month."

"We can go bed shopping tomorrow on the way to Cambridge after we pick up Aunt Nora's ashes. I made an appointment to get them at one o'clock. They have the memorial cards and the funeral program ready too."

"It's hard to believe her funeral is the day after tomorrow."

"I know."

They arrived at the bedroom door, and Diana faced Brooke. "You'll come with me to Oak Ridge to bury her ashes, won't you?"

"Of course I will. Did you want to do that right away?"

256

"I'm not sure. I haven't figured all that out yet."

"That's okay. We'll figure it out together."

"I like the sound of that." Diana leaned forward and kissed Brooke. "I'm going to love the sound of my head hitting that pillow even more."

CHAPTER TWENTY-FOUR

Diana stood in the foyer outside the Dana-Farber Chapel, shaking hands with people who knew Aunt Nora far better than she did. It was a surreal experience. If she said, "thank you for coming," one more time, she thought she might shatter into a million pieces.

Most of the service was a blur, except for Brooke's steady, loving presence by her side throughout. Daniel sat with them too, along with Charles and Emily Fitzgerald. Diana appreciated the company, as she'd uncharacteristically found herself missing her parents.

She wondered if word would filter to them of Aunt Nora's death. Then she remembered that it was her grandfather and her parents' lies that had led her to believe that Aunt Nora already was dead, and anger boiled up from within all over again.

"You look like you're about to explode," Brooke whispered in her ear.

"Sorry. I'm going to have to work on my poker face."

"Want to get out of here?"

"Boy, do I. But do you think I should stay until everyone's gone?" She nodded in the direction of the half-dozen or so people congregated several feet away.

"Nah. They're busy talking to each other. I think you've done your duty. Daniel, Charles, and Emily would like to take us out to get something to eat. Are you up for that?"

"Sure." She hadn't been able to eat breakfast or lunch, but a meal sounded good now.

259

"We can walk to the restaurant from here." Brooke looped her arm through Diana's and they joined the group outside on the sidewalk.

"That was a really nice service, Diana. Nora would've been proud," Charles said.

"Although she would've eschewed the platitudes," Daniel countered.

"True. Nora never was one to stand on ceremony. I don't think I ever met a humbler person."

"Or a kinder one," Emily added.

They arrived at the restaurant and settled around a table toward the back.

"I'm so glad you all could make it today. I know Aunt Nora thought the world of you."

"We thought the world of her," Daniel said. "Brooke tells me you're transferring your grant to Harvard. I know Nora would be exceedingly pleased by that. Congratulations and welcome to Beantown."

She felt her blush and nudged Brooke with an elbow. "You didn't waste any time sharing the news, did you?"

"Daniel's my best friend. I have no secrets from him."

"Yes, congratulations, Diana, that's fabulous news. You'll be keeping the Cambridge house, then? Nora would be thrilled." Charles unfolded his napkin and placed it in his lap.

Diana glanced at Brooke. "Yes, we'll be keeping both the Cambridge house and the cottage in Truro."

Charles nodded. "Nora's stroke of genius. When she instructed me to update her bequests and relayed her wishes, I asked if she was sure. She smiled that beatific smile of hers and said, 'Mark my word, those girls'—her term, not mine—'are going to have the happily ever after I never had.' From the looks of it, I'd say she was right."

She felt her blush deepen to the roots of her hair. "Aunt Nora told you that?"

"She did."

"Did you know about...her?"

"You mean did I know she was a lesbian?" Charles asked. "I was her attorney for nearly forty years. I wrote more than one of her wills and created contracts and agreements of all sorts for her. Beyond that, she was my friend. Yes, I knew."

The server took their orders and retreated to the kitchen.

"Since you three knew Nora so well," Brooke started, "is there any chance she shared information with any of you about her time in Oak Ridge during World War II and anyone she might have been connected to back then?"

Daniel shook his head. "She didn't like to talk about it."

Charles chimed in, "She asked me once what would happen if she left a bequest to someone whose whereabouts she didn't know. When I asked her when the last time was she might've had an address for said individual, she said 1947. That's after the war, but I assume she knew the person during that timeframe."

"Do you remember how long ago she asked you that?"

Charles drummed his fingers on the table. "Hmm. I remember that it was around the time I met Emily, so it must've been around 1982 or '83."

Diana gasped and all eyes turned to her. "I'm sorry. That was around the last time I saw Aunt Nora before my grandfather blackmailed her out of my life." She glanced around the table. Apart from Brooke, Charles was the only person who didn't seem shocked by that revelation. So, he had known.

"What did you tell Nora in answer to her question?" Brooke asked. "That would've been long before the internet and Google."

"I told her that an executor would do his or her best to locate anyone named in a will, but that sometimes it simply wasn't possible. It was a hypothetical question, though. She never asked or requested anything more explicit than that."

"Why do you ask, Brooke? That's a pretty specific question." Emily passed Diana the basket of hot rolls and the butter.

"Diana and I have been following Nora's wishes, reading through her papers. There's a...person...who was of special importance to her. We're thinking we'd like to locate her if we can."

Emily leaned forward. "Can you tell us anything about this person? Maybe I can help. I dabble a lot in genealogy. Ancestry is my friend."

"We have her name and a birthdate. We know she would be ninety-three if she's still alive, and we think she lived in Pennsylvania around 1946-47."

"That's a really good start." Emily rubbed her hands together. "Want some help?"

"Seriously?" Diana asked. She glanced to Brooke for confirmation before replying, "We'd love some."

∾৯৶৹

"Did you see that e-mail from Emily?" Brooke asked. She ran her fingers along the new sheets as she waited for Diana to finish getting ready for bed.

"No, what did it say?" Diana came in from the bathroom wearing nothing but a smile, and Brooke's heart fluttered happily.

"What were we talking about?"

"Very funny." Diana climbed under the sheets.

"You know, it's our first night in the new bed. I think we ought to test it out, make sure it's comfortable from all angles."

"Is that right?" Diana rolled on top of Brooke.

"Mm-hmm."

"What about Emily?"

"What about her?"

"You are so easily distracted."

"That's your fault." Brooke trailed her fingers down Diana's back. "Please tell me this isn't a dream, and that I get to sleep with you like this for the rest of my life."

"This isn't a dream, and I promise I'll always be with you."

Diana claimed her mouth and then her body. Emily could wait.

∾৯৶৹

"What was it you were trying to tell me about Emily last night?" Diana snagged the English muffin out of the toaster.

"You mean before you got me off track?"

"That was just as much your fault. You can't look at me like that and expect me to do nothing."

"Noted." Brooke wrapped her arms around Diana from behind and nuzzled her neck. "I was going to tell you what Emily found out about Mary Trask."

"She's got something already? That was quick."

"I e-mailed her Mary's birthdate and a picture of the outside of the envelope from Nora's last letter to her. She said she was able to do a search in Ancestry and found Mary in the 1930 and 1940 censuses. She also came across her senior-year high school yearbook picture from 1943."

"Holy cow! That's amazing. Did she send the picture?"

"She did." Brooke leaned over and took a bite of Diana's English muffin. "I might even share it with you if you're nice to me."

"I can be very nice." Diana held the rest of the muffin out of Brooke's reach. "You said the picture was from her high school yearbook in 1943?"

"I did."

"That means Mary came to Oak Ridge directly after graduating high school. Boy, she was young!"

"Eighteen."

"Let's see it."

Brooke ran to the bedroom and returned with her iPad. "I saved it to my photos." She held it out for Diana to see.

"Gosh, she was pretty."

"She sure was. I think Nora's description of her as an angel was apt."

"She had such delicate features." Diana ran her fingertips along the contours of Mary's face. "I can see why Aunt Nora fell for you, Mary Trask."

Brooke took back the iPad and toggled to Emily's e-mail. "According to Emily, in 1930 Mary was five and living with her mom and dad in Philadelphia. She sent a screen grab of the census report. It has an address for her family."

"Wow. It's amazing what you can find out there. You said the last census information was from 1940, ten years later?"

"Apparently, that's the last one that's available. She still was living with her parents in the same house on Larchwood Avenue."

"Sounds like that was the family home." Diana peered over Brooke's shoulder. "Can you read the house number? That census taker had really crappy handwriting."

"They should test their penmanship before they give them the job. The good news is the 1930 census taker had better penmanship." Brooke scrolled back to the screen grab of the earlier census and held it where Diana could see it.

"What do you suppose the chances are that Mary kept her parents' house?"

"Hard to say. According to these documents, she would appear to have been an only child."

"Did Emily say anything else?"

"She did a blanket search for newspaper articles or anything else related to Mary, including Mary's time in Oak Ridge, any stories about her homecoming, any marriage information..."

"And?"

"She came up blank."

Diana carried her plate to the sink. "You know what's going to happen next, right?"

"We're going to book a trip to Philadelphia?"

Diana nodded. "My geography isn't great, but Pennsylvania is south of here, and Tennessee is south of there..."

"You want to stop in Philly and try to find Mary on our way to bury Nora's ashes?"

"What do you think?"

"I think it's brilliant. We can take the letters with us. They belong to Mary."

"If we can find her."

"I think it's encouraging that Emily didn't find a death certificate for her."

"Can you imagine meeting the great love of Aunt Nora's life?"

"What if she doesn't want to be found, or doesn't want to remember?"

"There's only one way to find out, and I think we have to try."

"For Nora."

"For Aunt Nora," Diana agreed.

⤙⤚

Slight left turn in a quarter of a mile.

"I hate that." Diana said.

"What?"

"That every GPS I've ever used says 'a quarter of a mile,' instead of 'a quarter mile.'"

Brooke laughed. "What are you, the grammar police?"

"In this case I am."

Turn now.
Diana followed the command. "This is the block."
"Are you ready for this?"
"I'm nervous? You?"
"Me too."
"What if she slams the door in our face?"
"What if she's dead?"
"What if we've got the wrong Mary Trask?"
"That would be a huge disappointment."
Your destination is on the left. You have arrived at your destination.
Diana slowed the rental car to a stop and parked in front of a quaint, aging three-story brick-and-wood home. A porch swing, hung in the corner of the front portico, looked as though it hadn't been used in a long time. She cut the engine. "How do I look?"
"Gorgeous."
"I mean it. Do I look presentable?"
"You look amazing and so much like pictures of Nora back in the day that Mary's bound to see the family resemblance."
"Okay, well, here we go." Diana paused halfway out of the car. "Do you think we should take the letters with us?"
"No. I think we should ring the doorbell first and make sure we have the right place and the correct Mary."
"Good call." Diana came around the car and they strolled together up the walkway and the front steps to the door. "Here goes nothing." She took a deep breath to settle her nerves and rang the doorbell.
A moment later, an elderly woman peeked out from around the corner of the door. "Can I help you?"
"We hope so," Brooke said. "We're looking for Mary Trask."
The woman's eyes opened wide in surprise.
"Are you Mary?" Diana asked.
"Heaven's no," the woman answered. "Mary hasn't lived here in, oh, ten years or more."
"Oh, I'm sorry to have bother—"
"Do you know Mary?" Brooke cut Diana off.
"Why yes, of course. She sold me this house. We've been friends for years."

"My name is Brooke Sheldon. This is Dr. Diana Lindstrom. Mary was dear friends with Diana's great-aunt, and we're trying to find her. Can you help us?"

"Is Mary still alive?" Diana asked.

"She is. Still spry and sharp too. Puts me to shame and I'm eight years her junior."

"Do you know where we might find her?"

"Well, she lives in a retirement community now, but most days she volunteers at the Penn Libraries. She retired from there some years ago but likes to keep her hand in and her mind occupied."

"The Penn Libraries?"

"Yes, dear. Mary volunteers at the Biomedical Library."

"I'm sorry. We're from out of town. Where might they be?"

"Johnson Pavilion, 36th and Hamilton Walk."

"Thank you."

Diana and Brooke waved on their way back to the car.

"Tell Mary I said hello!"

"We will."

When they were buckled in and Diana had inputted the address into the GPS, Brooke said, "That was productive. Now we know that not only is Mary alive, but she's still got her mental faculties."

"And, we know where we can find her."

"Assuming she's volunteering today."

"Assuming she's volunteering today. Let's keep our fingers crossed."

"Thank God the day is still young."

CHAPTER TWENTY-FIVE

Three wrong turns and twenty minutes spent parking later, Diana and Brooke entered the Biomedical Library and approached the information desk. A thirty-something balding man behind the counter was assisting a customer.

"I'll be with you in a second, folks."

"Thanks."

"I don't see anyone older than us," Diana mumbled.

"Stop worrying," Brooke whispered. "We'll find her."

"How can I help you?" the man asked.

"We're looking for someone who works here."

"A volunteer, actually."

"Okay."

"Her name is Mary Trask."

The man's face lit up. "Ah, our Mary. I know she was helping one of the students find some obscure medical journal article. Just a second and I'll see if she's available." He started to walk away. "Can I tell her who's looking for her?"

Diana panicked. If Mary knew it was Nora Lindstrom's great-niece, would she refuse to see them?

Brooke stepped in front of Diana. "Brooke Sheldon on behalf of an old friend of Mary's."

"Okay. Thank you."

Brooke nudged Diana. "You have got to pull yourself together."

"I will. I was afraid if she heard the last name…"

"She wouldn't see us."

"Right."

"Oh, look." Brooke pointed to the right. "Here she comes."

"She's in great shape," Diana said.

The tiny woman accompanying the balding man carried a cane but didn't seem to need it.

"I'm Mary Trask." Her gold-brown eyes were keen and alert, and her beautifully flowing gray hair appeared as though she'd recently had it done.

"I'll leave you to it, then. Holler if you need me, Mary."

"I'll be fine, Will. Thank you." Mary turned her attention to Brooke and Diana.

"Will says you're here on behalf of a friend of mine?" Mary gazed from one of them to the other.

"Yes," Brooke answered. "My name is Brooke Sheldon. This," she touched Diana's arm, "is Dr. Diana Lindstrom."

Mary stumbled a step and Brooke caught her by the arm. "I'm sorry. Did you say your last name is Lindstrom?"

Diana nodded and swallowed hard. "Y-yes. I'm...I'm Nora Lindstrom's great-niece."

Brooke kept hold of Mary's arm, for which Diana was grateful. Mary's face had gone pale.

"My word. I haven't heard that name in a very, very long time."

"Why don't we sit down over there?" Brooke pointed to a grouping of comfortable-looking chairs to the left. She led Mary in that direction and helped her sit. "Can I get you some water?"

"No." Mary put her hand to her heart. "I'm fine, dear. I just need a minute."

Diana squatted in front of her. "Are you sure you're all right?"

Mary nodded.

"Maybe we should get her some water anyway?" Diana said to Brooke.

"That won't be necessary. Really. I'm fine. This is quite a shock, though."

Diana chose the seat next to Mary and Brooke flanked her on the other side.

"You're Nora's great-niece, you say?"

"Yes. Her brother, Bill, was my grandfather."

"I see." She stared at her so long Diana squirmed. "Now that I look at you, you certainly favor her. Those piercing eyes and blond hair. I..." She took a moment to collect herself. "Let's just say there are some things one never forgets."

"I can tell you Aunt Nora never forgot you."

Her eyes opened wide again. "Didn't she?"

"No," Brooke said softly. "She kept all the letters she wrote you after the war."

"She…"

Diana took her hand. "May I speak plainly? Will it offend you?"

"If you mean am I still in the closet, the answer is, heavens, no. I'm an old woman. If anybody minds that I'm a lesbian, they can tell it to someone who cares."

The answer surprised a laugh out of both Brooke and Diana.

"Okay, then," Diana said. "I'm glad we cleared that up. Mary, you were the great love of Aunt Nora's life." She felt the impact of the words in Mary's grip.

"I-I can't believe it. Is Nora…?"

"She passed away a few weeks ago. She lived to be one hundred, and she was mentally sharp all the way to the end."

Mary closed her eyes as a tear leaked out. "Oh, dear." Brooke handed her a tissue. "Was she alone at the end? Please tell me she wasn't all alone at the end."

"We were with her," Diana said. "She knew she was loved."

"How on earth did you find me?"

"Aunt Nora left us her papers, including a journal she kept during the war."

"Ugh. That damn journal!" She shook her head. "She was always writing in it before lights out."

"As I mentioned, she also left a stack of unopened letters addressed to you. They were all marked return to sender."

She sighed. "Yes, I know. I've regretted that for years."

"You have?"

Her smile was sad. "Oh, yes. Eventually I grew up, you know. And I understood. I understood that she was just following orders like the rest of us—that she was in an impossible position. I was very unfair to her, I'm afraid."

"Why didn't you tell her?" Diana asked softly.

"I tried, once. It was a few years after the war. I finally came to my senses and I wrote her a long letter of apology."

"You did?"

"Oh, yes. I sent it to the last address I had for her, but it came back to me. It was marked return to sender, but not in Nora's handwriting. It said Nora didn't live there anymore, and there was no forwarding address."

Diana nodded. "That must've been after she moved to Hiroshima."

Mary stiffened. "She did what? She moved to Hiroshima? The city we bombed?"

"Yes," Brooke said. "She went to work for the Atomic Bomb Casualty Commission. In fact, she devoted many years to studying the effects of the radiation exposure on the Japanese survivors and their descendants."

"After that," Diana chimed in, "she moved back to the states and worked to find a cure for childhood leukemia, which was one of the most prevalent maladies contracted by survivors of the bomb."

Mary dropped her head into her hands. "Oh, dear, sweet, Nora. You blamed yourself, didn't you?" When she gazed back at them, her face reflected pure anguish. "I did that to her. I was a young, naïve, foolish girl."

"I know Nora didn't think that," Brooke said. "She loved you until the day she died. She dreamed about you at the end."

"She did?"

"Yes," Diana agreed. "We think she meant for us to come find you."

"She did?" Mary cleared her throat. "You know, if I'm going to be honest, I never got over her either." She smiled wanly. "Oh, I moved on. I found a very lovely, understanding woman who didn't mind that my heart never fully belonged to her. She knew all about my Nora, and she loved me anyway. I was a very lucky girl. We were together for fifty-six years."

"What happened to her, if you don't mind my asking?"

"Eloise passed on a little over a decade ago. That's when I sold my parents' house to Eloise's youngest sister and moved into a retirement community. I figured I'd better prepare for the future."

"Good for you."

"Did Nora... Did she have a girl?"

Diana shrugged. "We don't know. Aunt Nora disappeared from my life when I was ten. I never heard from her again until she was dying."

Mary sat straight up. "That's horrible. Why would she do that?"

"It wasn't her choice. My grandfather found out she was a lesbian and blackmailed her into going away."

"That horse's ass. She never liked him, you know. The stories she used to tell."

"Unfortunately, I don't know much about Aunt Nora's personal life at all."

"I see. Well, I could tell you some things about her." Mary's eyes took on a far away, dreamy expression.

"I bet you could."

"She cut quite a figure, I'll say that. I was taken with her from the first moment I laid eyes on her."

Brooke laughed. "She said the same thing in her diary about you."

"She did? That sweet-talker."

"Mary? Are you okay?" The bald-headed man approached. "It's getting late. I don't want you to miss your trolley."

"I'm fine, Will. Don't worry about me."

"We're sorry. We didn't mean to take up all your time."

"You take the trolley home?" Brooke asked.

"Well, you certainly don't want me driving on the roads at my age."

"May we give you a ride home?"

"Oh, my. What a generous offer. Why, certainly. I think I'll be safe enough with you two girls."

Mary gave them directions to Atria Center City and they chatted companionably until they reached her apartment.

"Come in, girls. Please. I haven't had a chance to tidy up, so I'll apologize for that."

"Are you kidding? This place is immaculate," Diana said. She noted a framed picture on the wall of a much younger, smiling Mary, with a very handsome woman. "Is this your Eloise?"

"Yes. We were visiting the Grand Canyon. That was right before I told her I was terrified of heights."

"Before I forget, I have to go get something out of the car." Diana glanced at Brooke, who nodded at her in return.

When she came back, Diana handed Mary the stack of letters secured with the ribbon. "These are for you. Brooke and I couldn't bring ourselves to open them. These were between Aunt Nora and you."

"Oh." Mary gripped the chair arm for support.

"Here. Sit down." Brooke guided her into the seat.

"I can't believe she kept these all this time." She held the letters in her lap.

"She also kept this one." Diana produced the opened letter from Mary to Nora. "It's open because Aunt Nora opened it. We didn't read it."

"Golly, I wish I'd never written that letter." She sighed and added the letter to the pile.

"We don't want to tire you out," Brooke said.

"Yes, we should get going," Diana agreed.

"Wait. Where do you live?"

"We live outside of Boston. I'm a professor of neuroscience at Harvard. Well, technically not quite yet. I'm teaching at Columbia, but I'm about to transfer my research to Harvard."

"That's grand. I bet Nora was so proud of you." Mary set the letters on a nearby table. "You came all this way just to see me?"

"Actually, we're on our way to Oak Ridge. Nora asked that her ashes be buried at a place called The-Chapel-on-the-Hill."

"Oh." Mary clutched her chest again.

"She said her life began there. It was only fitting that it ends there."

"Oh, Nora." Mary shook her head. "You're going there now?"

"We have a flight to Knoxville tomorrow."

"Oh."

"Why?"

"Well, I'm sure I'm too late if you've already got plane reservations."

"Too late for what?"

"For me to come with you."

Diana looked at Brooke. "If we could arrange it, you'd come along?"

"If you wouldn't mind the company. I haven't been back to Oak Ridge since, but I feel like I owe it to Nora. It might bring us both closure."

"We'd be honored if you'd join us," Brooke said. "Could you leave tomorrow? We were only planning to stay for a day or so and fly back."

"It's not like I have anyone to answer to," Mary said. "I'll pack a few things. You tell me when I need to be ready."

❧❧

"Stop here," Mary said.

Diana did as she asked and stopped the car. "It looks so different, but that's where the Elza Gate stood. I came through there the first time I arrived at Clinton Engineer Works. There were armed guards and every person had to have a special ID pass."

"Do you still have yours?"

"Heavens, no. After I realized what we girls had been doing and I returned home to Philly, I threw everything away."

Diana resumed the drive into town.

"Turn."

Diana complied.

"It's still here." Mary put a hand to her mouth. "Jackson Square. That corner there was the Center Theatre, it's where Nora and I went on our first date."

Diana decided not to share with her that she and Brooke had read all about the date. "Apparently, we can't just drive to the Y-12 plant. That's where you worked, right?"

"Yes. That was home to the Calutron machines."

"There's a museum, though, called the American Museum of Science and Energy that has lots of the artifacts. Do you want to tour it?" Diana asked.

"This says they have a Calutron machine and one of the Flat Tops open for viewing. Isn't that where you and Nora lived?" Brooke asked.

"I suppose a once-through for old-times-sake wouldn't hurt."

Diana secured their visitor passes and they took the elevator to the second floor. When they reached the Calutron machine, Mary stopped short. "It's been a long time since I saw one of those. You know, all they told us girls was to keep this needle here…" She tapped the glass cover over the meter. "…between this setting and this setting. That was it. I got really good at it, I can tell you that."

Her hand trembled over the knob. "I didn't know that what I was doing was creating the enriched uranium for the atomic bomb. None of us knew."

"You believed Nora knew."

She nodded. "Yes. I figured she had to have known." She shook her head as if clearing the cobwebs. She moved forward, briefly glancing at the displays. "I'm sorry, girls. I could use some air."

Brooke led them to an area with a sign that indicated they were going outside. When she opened the door, there below them at the bottom of a stairway, was a flat-topped, square building, only slightly larger than a hut.

"That was where we lived."

"You lived in that?"

She nodded. "Or one just like it."

"It says we can go inside," Diana said. "Do you want to see it?"

She swayed. "I suppose I could show you girls how we lived."

"Will you be all right on the stairs?"

"If you'll support me."

Brooke moved to her side as she gripped the railing on the other side. They made their way slowly down until they reached the ground.

Mary stepped into the living room and stopped. For a long time she said nothing. "Well, Nora. It's just like no time has passed at all. There you are, over on the end of the sofa, teaching me how to read properly."

"You didn't know how to read?" Diana asked.

"I knew some. But I was dyslexic, although I didn't know it then. Nora was so patient with me. She taught me some tricks so that the words made sense. She really encouraged me to go back to school. She's the reason I ended up getting a degree in library sciences. Truly, I owe her so much."

The house was tiny, with a small kitchen with an electric stove, a double sink, and an icebox. There were two bedrooms, one slightly larger than the other. The bigger bedroom boasted a full-size bed.

"This was our room," Mary said. "Technically, it was Nora's room, but this is where we slept together every night. My clothes lived in the other room. I never thought I'd see this place again."

"Are you okay?" Brooke asked.

"You know, I am. Despite how it ended, I learned about life in this place. And I learned about love. Nora taught me that. She was seven years older than me and so much wiser and smarter. I'm a much better person for having known her."

Brooke caught Diana's attention behind Mary's back. "She looks tired," Brooke mouthed.

Diana nodded. "Maybe we should get going. We still have to bury Aunt Nora's ashes."

"Oh. Of course." Mary wiped away a tear. "I'm ready."

Diana retrieved the car and got it as close as she could so that Mary didn't have far to walk. They drove in silence except for Mary giving Diana directions.

"It's up there." She pointed and Diana followed the direction of her finger. "That's The-Chapel-on-the-Hill. I can't believe it's still standing."

Diana parked the car and they got out. Mary walked ahead of them. Diana whispered to Brooke, "Do you think she's okay?"

"I think it's a really emotional day for her, but she seems to be holding up well. I don't want to tax her too much more, though."

"This is where Nora plowed me over." Mary turned to them. Her face looked years younger. "I was minding my own business and she came flying down that hill, and bam! She ran right over me."

"That's what she meant by 'This is where it began,'" Diana said.

"Yes," Mary answered. "This is where it began for both of us."

"Do you know where she would want us to bury her ashes?"

"See that big tree to the left of the front doors?" Mary pointed to a grove of old-growth trees. "That was our spot. Whenever we had something special to celebrate, we would come here and picnic under that tree."

"Do you think that's where Aunt Nora meant for us to bury her?"

Mary smiled. "I'm certain of it."

Brooke ran back to the car and grabbed the small trowel they'd purchased at a local hardware store. "You know this is probably illegal, right?"

"This was what Aunt Nora wanted."

Mary nodded. "Trust me, we did worse things under the cover of these trees."

"Mary!"

"Well, we did."

Quickly, Diana selected a patch of dirt directly under the tree Mary indicated. She dug a shallow hole as Brooke kept watch. When she finished, she stood.

Brooke handed the container of ashes to Mary. "Do you want to do the honors?"

"Let's do it together," she said to Diana.

Diana stepped forward and helped her empty the bag into the hole, and then she replaced the dirt. She turned to Mary. "We should say—"

"My darling, Nora. I'm so, so sorry. I hope you can forgive me." Mary held back a sob. "I know I caused you so much pain. I think that's why I haven't come back until now. But I know, too, that in this place we were the happiest either of us has ever been. I loved you then, and I love you still. I know you are at peace, and I pray that when my time comes, I'll see you again, standing strong and proud, waiting for me to come home to you. I promise I will."

Brooke held Diana as she cried.

"Goodbye, Aunt Nora. I love you. You taught me so much. I hope I'm half the scientist, half the human being you were. Rest well, and thank you for the gifts. Thank you for teaching me how to open my heart to love again. Thank you for not-so-subtly pushing me into Brooke's arms. Thank you for letting us meet your Mary. Thank you for everything."

Diana turned into Brooke's embrace. Brooke extended her arms and pulled Mary in, as well. Together, the three of them bid a final farewell to Nora.

As they walked slowly back down the hill, the sun peeked out from the clouds and shone down on them. No doubt that was Aunt Nora, Diana decided, smiling down at the tableau.

THE END

Want to learn more about Nora's journey?

Coming in 2019:

Secrets Well Kept

The extraordinary love story of
Nora Lindstrom
&
Mary Trask

Acknowledgments

The impetus for *Chain Reactions* began with my wife, Cheryl, dropping a book on my desk along with a note that read, "I think there might be a story here." The book was the non-fiction *New York Times* bestseller, *The Girls of Atomic City*, by Denise Kiernan.

I read the synopsis, thumbed through the book, and was immediately hooked. Later the same day, I opened an e-mail from our favorite local bookstore to discover that Kiernan would be appearing at the bookstore that night. Talk about a sign!

Cheryl and I went to Kiernan's talk, met her, and I was even more determined than before that I wanted to write a fictional novel about the Atomic City girls.

I kept asking myself the same question: "How would I feel if I discovered, after the fact (as these girls did), that my work helped us win the war, but killed thousands of innocent people?" From that question was born the character, Nora Lindstrom, and the core concept for this novel.

As part of my research for the book, Cheryl and I drove to Oak Ridge, Tennessee, and toured the American Museum of Science and Energy. We took in all the exhibits, drove around the town, and I realized that I didn't want to write one book about the Atomic City girls—I envisioned two books. *Chain Reactions* is the first book. *Secrets Well Kept*, the prequel that chronicles Nora's World War II experience in full, will appear later this year.

I often explain that while writing a book is a solitary pursuit, producing a book is not. My gratitude, as always, to those individuals who so willingly give of their time and expertise to help me get it right.

To Dr. Michael Rosenblum, Director of the Rosenblum Lab at the MD Anderson Cancer Center, many thanks for timely and expert tips and leads. Thank you for reading through the pertinent sections of the manuscript. But most of all, thank you for your friendship.

To Professors Will Banks and Lia Uribe, thanks for answering my urgent questions about academia and grants. Your input helped me ensure accuracy and plausibility.

To my amazing nephew, Seth, who is busy becoming the world's best veterinarian, thank you for talking to me about your research on epilepsy. Your passion for finding a cure and your commitment to making this world a better place gives me hope for our future.

To Dr. Jenni Levy, one of my oldest friends, thank you for everything, but in this case, a special thank you for your compassionate and passionate care and advocacy for hospice patients and caregivers. I hope that together we've dispelled some myths and shibboleths in these pages.

To my dear friends, Anne Geary and Bev Prescott, thank you for your time and insights into your adopted cities. You helped me make Philadelphia and Cambridge come alive on the page.

It is true that a book is only as good as the collaboration between author and editor. To my editor, Ann Roberts, thank you for making me the best I can be. This is the beginning of a beautiful relationship.

To my wonderful first readers, thank you for reading. Your comments and questions provide me with invaluable feedback as I endeavor to make every book the very best book I've ever written.

To my little sister of choice, Ann "Thumper" McMan, thank you for another marvelous cover. When I sought you out six years ago and asked you to design my covers, I had no idea I'd be getting such a dear, dear friend in the bargain.

Finally, to you the readers, thank you for your continued love and support. No author can make a living at this without you. You rock!

Lynn Ames
2019

About the Author

Lynn Ames is the best-selling author of *The Price of Fame, The Cost of Commitment, The Value of Valor,* One ~ Love, *Heartsong, Eyes on the Stars, Beyond Instinct, Above Reproach, All That Lies Within, Bright Lights of Summer, Final Cut, Great Bones, Chain Reactions,* and one of five authors of the collection *Outsiders.* She also is the writer/director/producer of the history-making documentary, "Extra Innings: The Real Story Behind the Bright Lights of Summer." This historically important documentary chronicles, for the first time ever in her own words, the real-life story of Hall-of-Famer Dot Wilkinson and the heyday of women's softball.

Lynn's fiction has garnered her a multitude of awards and honors, including five Goldie awards, the coveted Ann Bannon Popular Fiction Award (for *All That Lies Within*), and the Arizona Book Award for Best Gay/Lesbian book. Lynn is a two-time Lambda Literary Award (Lammy) Finalist and winner of a Rainbow Award for Lesbian Romance. *All That Lies Within* was additionally honored as one of the top ten lesbian books overall of 2013.

Ms. Ames is the founder of Phoenix Rising Press. She is also a former press secretary to the New York state senate minority leader and spokesperson for the nation's third-largest prison system. For more than half a decade, she was an award-winning broadcast journalist. She has been editor of a critically acclaimed national magazine and a nationally recognized speaker and public relations professional with a particular expertise in image, crisis communications planning, and crisis management.

For additional information please visit her website at www.lynnames.com, or e-mail her at lynnames@lynnames.com. You can also friend Lynn on Facebook and follow her on Twitter.

Published by
Phoenix Rising Press
Phoenix, AZ

Lynn Ames books are available in multiple formats through
www.lynnames.com, from your favorite local bookstore, or
through other online venues.